LIBERATION DAY

A gripping romantic thriller full of suspense

PIPPA McCATHIE

First published by The Book Folks

London, 2020

Mass market paperback, 2024

ISBN 978-1-80462-299-5

www.thebookfolks.com

This book is dedicated to the beautiful island of Guernsey and its people.

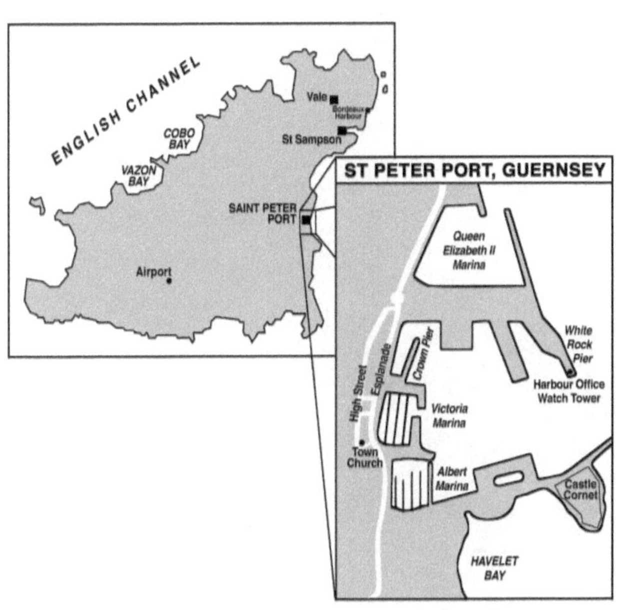

ENGLISH CHANNEL
Vale
Bordeaux Harbour
COBO BAY
St Sampson
VAZON BAY
SAINT PETER PORT
Airport
ST PETER PORT, GUERNSEY
Queen Elizabeth II Marina
White Rock Pier
Harbour Office Watch Tower
High Street
Esplanade
Crown Pier
Victoria Marina
Town Church
Albert Marina
Castle Cornet
HAVELET BAY

CHAPTER 1

"Come on! Come on!" Caro Bennett begged desperately as she turned the boat's ignition key again and again, but nothing happened. The engine stayed stubbornly quiet. "Oh shit! What the hell do I do?" she asked aloud. With a trembling hand she brushed tangled black hair back from her forehead and took a deep breath of the cold, salty air.

The silent boat rolled in the swell and the dark water slapped at the hull. She steadied herself as she slid off the helmsman's seat. The wind was getting up, veering north west, just as the forecast had predicted.

"Great, at this rate I'll be blown all the way to Guernsey," she muttered, desperately trying to block out thoughts of anything worse.

The waves stretched for miles all around with not a scrap of land in sight. In the far distance she could see what looked like a tanker, and high overhead a jet trailed its split white tail. It was hard to believe all those people, in the aeroplane and on the ship, had no idea of her predicament. And no other sign of life in all that expanse of sea and sky.

It was different out here on her own. With Craig it hadn't seemed nearly so daunting. She gave herself a shake.

This was one of the busiest waterways in the world. No way would she and the crippled cabin cruiser go unnoticed for long. But as she stood gripping the rail, gazing out to where the menacing grey sky met the dark, navy blue sea, an icy shiver of fear slid down her back. The waves seemed malevolent, as if they were watching her, waiting in cold anticipation to swallow her up.

She checked her mobile again. Still no signal. But of course, there was the radio. Why hadn't she thought of that? Craig had taught her to use it. "Even you can master this, Caro." His patronising smile had annoyed her.

She stumbled to the cockpit and picked up the handset.

There was little of the static that usually greeted you. Her fear increased. Something was wrong. What should she do next?

Craig's voice sounded in her mind again. "One of the cardinal rules of boating, my sweet, is never go out without telling the harbour office or some responsible person where you're going. That way if you get into trouble, they'll come looking for you."

And what had she done? Zoomed off in a rage, pinched his damn boat, and run out of fuel. For a moment the anger with herself blotted out the fear, but not for long. The water, so deep and increasingly choppy, was pushing the wallowing boat this way and that, making it impossible to keep her balance without holding on. Caro glanced at her watch. It was four o'clock and the sunny late April morning had turned into a cold afternoon. Not since her mother had died had she felt so helplessly alone. She shut this thought off. Get a grip, she told herself. Wrapping her blue Puffa jacket more firmly round her body, she turned back to the radio. Surely it was worth a try?

"Mayday! Mayday! Mayday! This is the cruiser *Sally Anne*, registration WH464. I've run out of fuel. Please, someone, help. Mayday! Mayday!" Was that the right thing to say? For goodness' sake, who cared! Swallowing hard she took a deep, steadying breath. "Mayday! Mayday! Please, someone out there, help me!"

She waited, gripping the handset until it dug into her palm, but there was only a faint crackling sound which seemed to accentuate her loneliness. She tried again, but still no voice through the distant static. And again. Nothing.

She'd almost given up hope when the longed-for voice sounded, very faintly. "Cruiser *Sally Anne*, this is *Pauillac*, registration GU786. Give your position. I repeat, please… your position. Over."

For a moment she didn't believe the voice was responding to her. Clutching the handset like a lifeline, she shouted, "Hallo? Can you hear me?" and then, as an afterthought, "Over."

"Yes," said the faint, disembodied voice, "… only just. Give your position. Over."

"How do I do that?" Caro asked desperately, praying he would answer.

"Have you got a GPS system?" The crackling took over, then she heard, "… satellite navigator?"

Now that was familiar. Craig had shown off all the equipment on the *Sally Anne* with great pride. "All state-of-the-art stuff, this."

"Yes," Caro shouted at the handset as she stared at the blank computer screen.

"Good. Can you find the latitude/longitude button?"

"Hold on… Ah! Got it!" she cried triumphantly.

"Right, now turn…" But the voice was swallowed up in static again. She felt a wave of sickening panic. He couldn't leave her now! A second later relief poured through her as she heard the voice once more. "Are you there? Turn on your lat/long button."

Quickly she flicked the switch and the screen sprang into life. "It's working! It says latitude 49.805000 North, longitude 2.274000 West. Is that it?"

"That's it. Right. You're just north of the Casquettes. I'm about fifteen minutes away. Let off a flare, that'll help…" the crackling blotted out the voice again, but only for a moment "… able to see me. Fishing boat, due west of you. Leave your radio on. I'll be there soon. Over."

Caro slumped back in the helmsman's seat and put her hands up to her face. She felt a dry sob rising in her throat but pushed it down. No way was this wonderful stranger going to find a snivelling heap when he arrived. Set off a flare, he'd said. Where were they? For a moment her mind was a blank, then she remembered.

Stumbling along the rolling deck to the wooden seat at the stern, she lifted the top. It didn't take long to find the cylindrical canister. Here was something else Craig had taught her. She held it high above her head and pulled hard at the tag on the bottom. The bright orange light lit up the sky and Caro shouted, "Wheee!" But the creeping hysteria was brought to an abrupt halt as a wave caught the boat broadside. Caro was thrown sprawling across the deck. With a sob she pushed herself upright and rubbed at her arm. Sit quietly until that lovely man arrives, she told herself. No, let off another flare, just to be on the safe side. Once again, the comforting orange light lit up the sky.

Under the seat she also found several life jackets. She felt much safer once she'd clipped one on. Then she remembered the crackling voice had said she might be able to see his boat – due west, wasn't it? She gripped the rail and gazed out into the greyness. At first, she could see nothing. Even the tanker had disappeared. But a moment later there it was, frighteningly far away, but unmistakably a fishing boat.

"Please, please let it be him," she muttered.

The boat crept nearer and nearer. It seemed like an eternity but soon it was close enough for her to see a tall, dark figure standing in the wheelhouse. Caro thought she'd never seen anything so beautiful in all her life. She stood waving an arm above her head, grinning from ear to ear.

The two boats were just a few feet apart now. Caro leaned on the rail as the man came out of the wheelhouse. All she could see was that he was very tall, but his yellow sou'wester and close-fitting woolly cap made it hard to distinguish anything else. He cupped his hands around his mouth and shouted over the chug of his engine and the noise of the wind and waves.

"Hallo, *Sally Anne.* I'll throw you a rope. Make it fast to the forward cleat."

"The what?"

"The T-shaped piece of metal on the deck right at the bow. Given the weather and your position, I'll have to tow you to Guernsey. Can't be helped."

Without waiting for her reply, he threw the rope, but it slithered down into the water before she could catch it. Caro swore. Silently he gathered it in, looped it round his hand and threw it again. This time it landed neatly at her feet. She grabbed it and went forward to tie it firmly as he'd instructed.

"You're sure that's made fast?"

"Yes!" she shouted back. "What next?"

"There's nothing else you can do now, except make sure the rope stays firm. We'll get going." He went back to the wheelhouse and Caro could see him standing with his back to her, swaying effortlessly with his boat as he turned the wheel. The fishing boat gathered momentum and the rope tautened, showering spray as they began to move. Caro slumped back into the helmsman's seat, feeling weak and exhausted, unable now to stop herself thinking back to the horrors of the last twenty-four hours.

* * *

When was it she'd started out for London? Yesterday morning? Strange how events distorted time. It felt more like a week ago.

The traffic had been awful, and the lashing rain hadn't helped, cutting visibility down to a matter of metres. Up round Bournemouth and onwards, the rain had persisted. It wasn't until she got to the M3 that it let up and she'd been able to make some headway. And as she'd driven, she'd gone over and over her resentment at having to make the journey at all.

Her heart had sunk when Craig had asked her to make the trip. She resented his assumption that his work came before hers, but more than that, she couldn't stand his business partner, Jason Logan. She'd only met him a few times, but her dislike had increased at each encounter. It was something to do with the way he looked you up and down, and the way he stood far too close. It gave Caro the creeps.

But when she'd mentioned her feelings to Craig, he'd told her not to be silly. "Jason's a first-class antique dealer so, do try to be nice to him," he'd said. "He's found some damn good pieces for me over the years. Anyway, all that's going to happen is that he'll hand you the package and then you can leave. What's so difficult about that?"

But on that boring slog to Jason's warehouse in Enfield her anger had grown. Craig seemed to feel she was at his beck and call. Damn it, she had a successful business of her own to run. Wasn't Caroline Designs just as important as his antiques business? Driving up to London had eaten into her time. Why on earth had she agreed to go? But it was always the way.

When she'd met Craig, just after her mother's death, he'd quickly taken charge of her life. She'd been too grief-stricken and shocked to put up any resistance. Now it seemed to have become a habit, and although she felt the occasional stirrings of rebellion, they never lasted long. He'd turn on the charm, gaze at her with those cool grey eyes of his, give her a sideways smile, and she'd give in.

Craig hadn't told her exactly what she was collecting from Jason. He'd just said that he'd rather not entrust it to the usual carriers. "I'd much rather send someone I trust, my darling. You will go won't you, sweetheart?"

And she'd agreed. Stupid woman, she moaned at herself. Look what he gets up to while I'm away.

Caro had arrived at the rendezvous about midday, parked the car in the warehouse yard and looked around for any signs of life. She'd wrapped her arms around herself, knowing the chill she felt wasn't entirely due to the weather. There'd been no-one in sight, but as she'd walked round the back of the building, she'd heard voices coming from inside. She'd recognised one as Jason's. The other was unfamiliar to her, a harsh voice with a London accent. Without consciously deciding to do so, she'd stopped to listen.

"Look, I've told you." Jason had sounded agitated. "It's entirely safe. You know Craig, he's safe as houses, you can be absolutely sure of that."

"If I was, would I be here?" The tone had been aggressive. "I'm not so sure, and nor's the boss. He don't trust those Frogs. Nor do I. Never have, never will."

"There's only one man involved, Jean Peron, and we've known him for years. Good chap. He applied for the job at the furniture place and got it quite openly."

"And does Craig know this Peron bloke?"

"Course he does. He's helped with getting the stuff across before."

"I still want you to get on to your mate and have a word."

"But I told you, I have already."

"Well, 'ave another, alright?" The aggression was more marked now. "Believe me, if the cops get on to this, the boss is not going to be pleased. You know what he's like when he's not pleased." He'd sounded like some B movie gangster, but no less threatening for that. "And he'll deny any knowledge of you and your little outfit, so – after 'e's finished with you, you and your poncey friend will be on your own, understand?"

"Okay, okay, I'll talk to him again." There'd been fear in Jason's voice.

With a cold feeling of foreboding, Caro had been certain she didn't want to be discovered eavesdropping. She'd crept back around the corner and, leaning against the wall for a moment, tried to steady her breathing. After a few minutes, with a cough and louder footsteps, she'd announced her arrival.

Jason had come out to greet her, all smiles and wafts of Armani aftershave. There had been no sign of his companion, but from the other side of the warehouse she'd heard a powerful car roar away.

On the long drive home, she'd gone over and over the conversation she'd heard. It had to be Jason working on his own. Surely Craig would have nothing to do with dubious deals? He probably has no idea what Jason's up to, she'd assured herself. She'd wondered sickeningly what was in the box on the back seat of her car. She could always undo it and have a look, but with all that parcel tape round it – no, Craig would know. The nagging doubts and unanswered questions had plagued her all the way back to Poole.

She'd gone straight home as she knew Craig was busy that evening, but after a restless night, she'd given up trying to sleep. At half past six she'd got up, thrown on jeans and a jumper, and made her way to Craig's flat, anxious to be rid of the package. Carrying it upstairs, she'd unlocked the front door and crept in, not wanting to wake him too suddenly. Placing the package on the hall table, she'd made her way to the kitchen, made coffee for them both, then carried the mugs through to his bedroom.

The door was ajar, so she'd pushed it open and made her away across the room to the bed, saying as she did so, "Craig, I've brought you some coffee."

The suddenness with which he'd sat up had made Caro jump and slop coffee all over the carpet. The second, much greater shock was the sight of the woman lying naked beside him. Caro knew her at once. It was Craig's assistant, Vanessa.

CHAPTER 2

With a jolt Caro came back to the present. To the swaying boat, the sea and the wind, and the comforting chug, chug of the fishing boat's engine. Dusk was falling. She turned up the collar of her jacket and stepped carefully along the deck to check that the rope was still firmly tied. It was. Glancing ahead at the fishing boat, she could just make out the dark shape of her rescuer at the wheel and wondered who he was. She didn't even know his name.

Craig had taken her to Guernsey a few times on the *Sally Anne*, but they'd met very few of the locals. Moored in the visitors' marina in St Peter Port, most of the people they'd encountered were fellow visitors, the sort of rich, prosperous companions Craig always cultivated. He insisted it was good for business. With a boat like that, Caro doubted this man would search out the same sort of people, she thought as she watched the small vessel rising and falling in the waves. It looked so sturdy and safe with its rounded body, built specifically for these dangerous waters and entirely at home in them.

Shivering, she realised how cold she was and made her way quickly back to the shelter of the cockpit. Ahead she could see the twinkling lights of Guernsey, and to the east the lights of the other islands, Sark in the distance and Herm and Jethou nearby. It was so comforting to be in sight of land. She hugged herself with relief.

They finally arrived in the sheltered waters of St Peter Port just after eight. As they glided slowly in through the harbour entrance, Caro felt overwhelming relief and utter exhaustion. But there was no let up yet. When they'd moored alongside a gently rocking pontoon in the Victoria Marina, several navy-blue clad men wearing life jackets arrived on board – harbour officials, border force officers. Caro, in her dazed state, was enormously grateful for her rescuer's presence as he helped her with the formalities.

She knew now that his name was Alex Devereaux. Without the woolly cap, his dark hair flopped over his forehead. His deep blue eyes were reassuring. The men from the port authority seemed to know him, and the border force officer greeted him like an old friend. Alex introduced him.

"This is Paul Le Page," he told Caro. "He'd like to have a quick word. Okay, Paul, I'll leave you to it."

Caro watched Alex's retreating back as he left the *Sally Anne's* cabin, feeling strangely bereft without him.

"Right, Miss Bennett," the officer said, sitting down across the table from her. "Just a few questions, purely routine. I gather you are not the owner of the *Sally Anne*."

"No. I thought I'd explained that to the man from the harbour office. My friend, Craig Paxton, owns her."

"And you say he doesn't know you… er… borrowed his boat?"

Caro could feel her cheeks burning. "No, he doesn't. I took it out this morning."

"Could you explain how that came about?"

"Well–" Caro bit her lip. Why should she tell him? The silence stretched out, then she shrugged. "We had this row."

"Tell me about it."

She was too tired to resist his cold enquiring gaze. "I found him in bed with another woman. It made me very angry. I suppose I took the boat out to, sort of, get my own back."

"I see."

He sat looking at her for a moment. Caro remained silent, anger making her stubborn. No, you don't understand at all, you stupid man, she wanted to yell at him.

At last he went on, "Is this a common occurrence?"

"Is what a common occurrence?"

"You, taking the boat out on your own?"

"No. I've never done it before. That's probably why I got into difficulties." At least she was being upfront about it, which was more than he was. What on earth was all this about? With another little spurt of anger, she added, "I really don't know why you need to ask all these questions. I was foolish and I was careless, I admit it, but that's all, surely?"

"It's just routine." His smile was bland and humourless, and he didn't answer her question. "Have you visited Guernsey before?"

"Yes. A few times. With Craig."

"When was this?"

"I can't remember actual dates." She leant her head back against the bulkhead, closed her eyes for a moment. When she opened them again, he was still sitting watching her with those cold eyes. "The last time was towards the end of the summer. September last year."

"And how long do you think you'll be staying this time?"

"I've no idea," she said with spirit and no little irritation. "Since I didn't know I'd be ending up here, it's difficult to tell. I suppose I'll be getting back tomorrow, if possible."

For the first time it dawned on her that Craig would insist on coming to fetch her. She had no doubt he'd make a real meal of it, manipulate the whole situation so that she'd end up the one who had to apologise and beg forgiveness. Maybe I'll just stay here and never go home, she thought irrationally, but what she said was: "I suppose I'll have to contact Craig, see what he wants me to do."

It was impossible to tell from Le Page's impassive face whether he believed her story. But by the end of the interview, polite though he was, she had a strong suspicion he didn't. She couldn't understand why. Okay, she'd been impulsive, and she'd admitted to being careless. Was it all so hard to believe?

"I might want to speak to you again tomorrow, Miss Bennett," he said as he rose and shrugged on his overcoat.

"But why?" Caro protested, thinking wearily that here was yet another man trying to order her around. She had enough of that with Craig.

"Just a few loose ends to clear up," he said. "Please don't leave the island without informing me. You'll be staying on the *Sally Anne*?"

"Yes? Where else?" she said, running out of fight.

"Good. I'll bid you goodnight."

Once he'd gone and she'd felt the dip of the boat as he jumped onto the pontoon, she slumped back on the divan. For a moment she closed her eyes, hardly thinking, until the boat gave another dip and she heard footsteps. Her heart began to beat faster. Oh no, what now? But a moment later Alex's tall silhouette appeared at the door of the cabin. Looking up at him, she felt a mixture of relief and guilt.

"Oh shit, are you still here?" she exclaimed. "I'm so sorry. You've done so much. I don't know how I would have managed without you." To her acute embarrassment her voice wavered, and her eyes filled with tears. She bit her lip hard, but it was no good, the tears began to slide down her cheeks. She gave a rather undignified sniff.

He stood for a moment looking down at her, his face unreadable, then he stepped into the cabin and picked up her jacket.

"Come on. Put this on." It was as if he was speaking to a difficult child. "You're coming with me."

"But–"

"No buts. You can't stay here on your own."

"There's a perfectly good bunk," she protested. "And I told that officer I'd be staying on the *Sally Anne*. If I leave, he'll start all over again. He already seems to think I'm some criminal or other."

"Never mind about Paul. I'll handle him. I'm not leaving you alone and that's final." He gave a sudden grin and she was taken aback. His rather severe expression disappeared, and she had a glimpse of a totally different personality.

"It's okay," he assured her. "All I'm going to do is take you to my grandmother. What could be more innocuous?" Once more he cut into her protests. "I've told her we're on our way. She'll be delighted to have you, she loves visitors. Come on, stop worrying."

With a wave of relief she was not about to admit to, Caro gave in. She hitched her bag onto her shoulder and followed him up the steps to the deck. He guided her along the pontoon and onto the pier, where the statue of Prince Albert looked down on them in apparent disapproval. As she followed in Alex's wake, she hardly noticed the brightly lit restaurants and shops, the little Town Church, carefully floodlit, and the people walking along the esplanade. He led her to a car, a sleek BMW. Vaguely it occurred to her this wasn't the sort of car she'd expect a fisherman to be driving, but then his accent hadn't seemed to fit either. Her mind niggled around these puzzles, coming to no conclusion.

Soon they came to a roundabout and turned inland up a tree-lined avenue. Caro leant her head back and closed her eyes. Sleep beckoned, but barely a minute or two later they turned off the main road between high railings and crunched to a stop on a gravel drive. Before them was an elegant Regency town house and, even in her exhausted state, she took in every detail. The small flight of steps led to a porch flanked by slim fluted columns. On the ground floor, tall sash windows reached almost to the drive, and each of the first-floor windows had a small wrought-iron balcony. There was an imposing panelled front door with a gleaming lion's head knocker set in the centre panel.

"Is this where you live?" The surprise must have sounded in her voice. Alex smiled ruefully as he glanced at her.

"Not anymore, but it used to be. My grandmother brought me up and she still lives here. Welcome to Villette House. Come and meet her."

The front door swung open as they got out of the car and Caro could see a tall woman standing in the doorway, silhouetted against the light from the hallway. When she got closer, Caro realised there was a familiarity about her – in the way she held herself, her head bent slightly to one side. It's as if I've met her before, she thought, it must be because she's like Alex. But her hair, swept back from her face, was silvery, and there was a warmth here that Caro had not found in Alex.

"Hallo. I'm Eleanor Devereaux." Her voice was deep and melodic. She held out both her hands and took Caro's, drawing her into the house. "Come in, my dear. Alex has told me all about your ordeal. You must be exhausted."

It was as if they'd known each other for years. And in her present state, her senses heightened and raw, she realised why. It wasn't the likeness to Alex. No. With a jolt she realised Eleanor Devereaux reminded her achingly of her mother.

* * *

Eleanor had been delighted when she got Alex's call. Life seemed very humdrum these days and the unexpected always pleased her. They may have been known as the Daring Devereaux in centuries past, but nowadays it was more like the Dull Devereaux as far as she was concerned. Maybe this unexpected visitor would add a bit of spice to life. Just because she was nearly eighty, didn't mean she couldn't look forward to some fun.

After Alex's call, she'd gone upstairs and prepared a bed in one of the spare bedrooms, then she'd gone back downstairs to await their arrival, impatient to meet this girl whom Alex had rescued. Eleanor wondered why she'd been out there, miles from anywhere and on her own. In the past, of course, smuggling would have come to mind. Guernsey's folklore was peppered with many a daring sea rescue, or wreck, and smugglers had often been involved. Eleanor had grinned and told herself not to be such a romantic.

As Alex ushered Caro into the hall, Eleanor took in every detail of her appearance. She was barely five feet tall, with creamy skin, now rather pale, and wildly curling dark hair. Her grey-green eyes, shadowed now, gazed up at her hostess. As Eleanor led her into the warmth of the kitchen, she couldn't help noticing how straight she stood, in spite of her exhaustion. Alex has certainly fallen on his feet this time, she thought. Let's hope he doesn't put her off.

"Sit down, my dear," she said to Caro, "and I'll get you something to eat. A glass of wine first, though, that's what you need most. There's nothing so reviving as a good red. Here, Alex, open this would you, darling?" She handed him a bottle.

Alex leant his long body against the work surface and did as she asked. Eleanor glanced at him occasionally while she put out bread, pâté and cheese. He too looked tired, but there was something else there. He looked alive, that was it, as if he'd thoroughly enjoyed himself.

"Tell me about your ordeal," she said to Caro as Alex poured the wine. "It sounds as if you've had an awful time."

"It was my own fault, I'm afraid. I should never have taken the boat out."

"It's your own boat, is it?"

"No, it's not. It belongs to— to a friend of mine."

Eleanor noticed the hesitation, and the slow flush that crept up Caro's cheeks. Her curiosity increased, but she was tactful enough not to probe. "And so, there you were, stuck in the middle of the channel, and along came my grandson."

"Yes, that's about it. I don't know what I would have done if Alex hadn't arrived."

It was obvious Caro was far too tired to talk for long, so she let her eat, talked to Alex about his side of the story, and when Caro's eyelids began to droop, she said, "Come on, my dear, time you were in bed. I've put a pair of my pyjamas out for you, and you'll find a toothbrush and toothpaste in the en suite. Alex, off you go, you must be tired too."

Stumbling over her words with exhaustion, once again Caro tried to tell Alex how grateful she was, but Eleanor cut her short.

"Never mind about that now. You can thank him properly tomorrow. Now it's time for bed."

Briskly she ushered him to the front door then led her guest upstairs, said a brief goodnight and left Caro alone. Curious though she was, she'd have to wait until the following day to find out more.

CHAPTER 3

Caro woke with a start and, for a moment, couldn't remember where she was. She looked around the room – white walls, green and pink striped curtains, furniture with a French feel to it. And who had painted those watercolours? she wondered. They're rather lovely.

Wide awake now, yesterday came flooding back to her. Lying curled up with eyes closed, she went over all that had happened, and what the day ahead was likely to bring. Apart from having to face Paul Le Page again, and that idea wasn't pleasant, the worst thing was the thought of speaking to Craig. She buried her face in the pillow and groaned. What an awful mess! But then the thought of Eleanor and Alex came into her mind. It wasn't all bad.

Caro looked at her watch. Her heart sank when she saw that it was nearly ten. Throwing back the duvet, she padded across the thick carpet to the bathroom. Here again there was evidence of understated luxury – in the softness of the towels, the bottles of bath oil, shampoo and shower gel neatly placed in one corner of the bath.

After she'd dressed – no choice but to put on the jumper and jeans she'd had on the day before – she made her way downstairs.

She could hear voices coming from the kitchen. Eleanor was saying, "But come on, my darling, you'll never sell it in its present state. What it needs is a major overhaul, and a professional decorator." She broke off as Caro came into the room. "Good morning, my dear, have you slept well?"

"Very well, thank you, but I'm sorry to be so late." She smiled uncertainly at Alex who, once again, was leaning against the work surface. He returned her smile and Caro's eyes widened, that smile could melt ice. He looked very different this morning in neat jeans and what she was sure was a cashmere jumper. There was nothing left of the rustic fisherman. Caro felt self-conscious, she'd felt rather more comfortable with last night's Alex.

"Nonsense, my dear, you're not late." Eleanor's voice broke into the awkward little silence as she glanced from one to the other. "It's probably done you good to have your sleep out. Come and sit down, have a cup of coffee and a croissant."

She filled a mug with coffee from a cafetiere on the table.

"I was wondering," Caro said tentatively, "if you have a charger for an iPhone? Mine is totally dead."

"I've got a tangle of them." Eleanor pulled out a drawer and rummaged around. "There you are. You're bound to find one that fits in that lot. Plug it in over there."

Having selected the appropriate adaptor, Caro did as she suggested then joined her at the table. "Alex and I were just talking about his house. He's thinking of selling, but it's in a frightful mess, needs a serious makeover." She twinkled at Caro, drawing her into their conversation and Caro began to feel less awkward.

"Really, Nella," Alex sounded embarrassed, "I'm sure Caro isn't interested in my problems."

"Don't be stuffy, Alex," said his grandmother breezily. She helped herself to a croissant, which she dipped into a mug of dark coffee. Catching Caro's eye, she grinned, looking all of a sudden much younger. "A habit I learned from my French mother. It's the best way to eat good croissant. For goodness' sake, Alex, sit down. You're making the place look untidy."

"She's an awful bully, my grandmother." He gave Caro that sideways smile. "Okay, I'll have some coffee." He poured himself a mug and pulled out a chair, but as he did so the telephone rang in the hall.

"Be a dear, Alex, and answer that for me," Eleanor said.

"It's bound to be for you." But it wasn't a serious protest.

"So, tell me about yourself, Caro." Eleanor's eyes were bright with curiosity. "Do you live in Poole?"

"Yes, I was brought up there, but I work all over Dorset, and sometimes further afield."

"Oh yes? What work do you do?"

"I've got my own interior design business. I run it from home."

Eleanor's eyes lit up and she clapped her hands together. "What a lovely coincidence. Would you consider–" But they were interrupted by Alex's return. The smile was gone and there was a frown between his eyes.

"It's for you, Caro," he said shortly, and held out the handset.

"Me? But no-one knows I'm here." Her stomach lurched. Surely Craig couldn't have found out where she was already?

"It's Paul Le Page, the border force chap you saw last night." Alex studied her face as he spoke. "He wants to have another word."

She frowned and took the handset then went out into the hall, feeling a need for privacy.

"Ah, Miss Bennett." The cold voice came down the line. "I'm afraid there are a few points I need to clarify with you. Would it be convenient for me to come round?" He didn't wait for her to say yes or no. "You've not arranged to leave the island, have you?"

"No, but I don't really see–"

"I'm sure you've nothing to worry about, Miss Bennett." It sounded like a challenge. "I'll be round in half an hour. And, one other thing, I'll need the keys to your boat, just to check it over. I hope you have no objection?"

Caro felt a spark of anger, feeling manipulated and out of control of the situation.

"Fine. If you must." She'd intended to sound cool, but it just came out as sullen. Angry with him, and with herself, she banged the receiver back on its rest and found that her hands were shaking.

"He's coming round," Caro said as she came back into the kitchen, trying her best to sound unconcerned. "Is that alright?"

"Of course it is," Eleanor said, then gave her grandson a sharp look. "What do you think Paul's up to?"

"I don't know." His voice was cool. "He seems to think there might be more to Caro's arrival than meets the eye."

"What?" Caro asked, rather offended by this, and wondering where the other Alex had gone.

Alex shrugged, gave her another unsmiling look, then turned away. "Probably just doing his job. He's thorough, is Paul, never gives up."

Caro couldn't get away from the idea there was an underlying message in what Alex was saying. Eleanor's voice, warm and slightly amused, was a welcome distraction.

"Well, I'd call it just plain stubborn myself." She smiled at Caro and patted her hand. "Don't you worry. Alex is probably right. Paul's just being overzealous. Such a pity he had to join the border force, it brings out the worst in him."

Caro wasn't reassured, but she told herself it was ridiculous to feel nervous. "I do feel I'm imposing on you an awful lot. I really ought to get back to the boat. He could come and see me there."

"Nonsense, my dear." Eleanor's tone left no room for argument. "We can't leave you all by yourself. And anyway, I love having company, I'm far too much on my own as a rule." Caro doubted this, but Eleanor held up a hand, forestalling any protest. "I don't want to hear any more about it. You must stay as long as it takes to sort things out, mustn't she, Alex?"

Alex's face was expressionless, and it was impossible to tell what he was thinking, but he followed his grandmother's lead. "Of course. I told Caro last night that you enjoyed a bit of adventure."

"And you were right." Eleanor smiled at him approvingly. "But if you're going to be with us for a few days you'll need some clothes. We'll have to go on a shopping spree. What a lovely thought! Shopping's so much more fun when you do it with someone else."

"And it's someone else spending the money," her grandson said drily. Eleanor ignored him, and Caro hardly took in the exchange.

"But there's something else," Caro said. "He says he wants the keys to the boat, to have a look round. He called it another formality, but why on earth would he want to search the *Sally Anne*?"

Eleanor glanced at Alex, caught his eye, then looked away again. "Oh, it's bound to be just a formality. As I said, Paul takes his job very seriously. We've known him a long time. He and Alex were at school together. I'm sure there's nothing to worry about, aren't you, Alex?"

Once more Caro saw her silent appeal to him, but there was a distinct pause before he said, "Paul's just doing his job, that's all."

Caro was sure he thought there was more to it. Stiffly she said, "I'll go and get the keys. They're in my bag." And she could feel the two of them watching her as she left the room.

As she returned down the stairs, she could hear their voices, low and urgent. They sounded as if they were arguing. But when she came back into the room, silence fell abruptly. Feeling uncomfortable she stood hesitating, jingling the keys in her hand. She put them on the work surface.

"Now," continued Eleanor cheerfully, apparently oblivious to the atmosphere, "you and I, Caro, are going on a tour of my lovely garden until Paul arrives. I'm very proud of it and I love to show it off." She rose from her chair. "We'll see you later, Alex," she said briskly, and swept Caro out through the hall, then stopped in her tracks.

"Hold on a moment, I must just ask that boy something." She turned back and called, "Alex darling?"

He came out of the kitchen, frowning. "Yes?"

"While I think of it, could you do me a favour? Take this down for me." She touched the ornate gold frame of a landscape in oils which hung at the end of the hall. "I must have it cleaned. If you'd put it in my car, in the boot please, I'd be awfully grateful."

Alex gave her a questioning look and Caro wondered what was going on. But then he nodded and said, "Okay, Nella, I'll do it now."

"Thank you, darling, before Paul arrives. You can put up that watercolour from the landing in its place."

"Will do."

"Thank you, my darling." She put her arm through Caro's. "Let's go then."

She led Caro across a comfortably furnished sitting room, full of an assorted collection of sofas, chairs and the same honey coloured furniture as Caro's bedroom. There were photographs everywhere, but Caro didn't have time to study them, and the walls were covered with an assortment of portraits and other paintings. Eleanor led her through French doors into the garden. It was a beautiful sight, the flower beds crowded with a riot of yellow, cream and white daffodils and narcissi, and beyond a path to the right was a large bed full of colourful shrubs. The path ended at a wrought-iron gate set into a hedge which spanned most of the far end of the lawn. Outside the kitchen door, to the left, was a well cultivated vegetable patch, newly dug over and waiting for the spring planting, and at the end of this stood a gnarled and ancient oak tree with a rope swing hanging from one of its branches.

"Alex's swing. My husband put it up for him when Alex was seven." Eleanor smiled at the memory, but Caro found it rather difficult to picture Alex as a grubby seven-year-old, playing on the swing and climbing the tree. His lean, cool elegance made a childhood Alex hard to imagine.

They walked slowly across the lawn to the gate and here was a swimming pool, glittering blue in the morning light. How lovely to have one's own pool, Caro thought, always there to relax in. They must lead such a different life to mine. She felt a pang of envy, but there was no point in hankering after what she couldn't possibly have.

They sat down on a wooden bench by the pool.

"This whole garden was an absolute wilderness when Alex's grandfather, Marcus, and I bought the house," Eleanor said. "It must be nearly fifty-six years ago now. During the war it was commandeered by the Nazis and they left it in a dreadful state. Did you know that Guernsey, Jersey and the other islands were occupied?"

"Yes. My mother used to talk about having friends who were evacuated to the village where she was brought up. I think they were from Jersey."

"A lot of islanders went to the mainland," Eleanor went on, "my family included."

"How long were the Germans here?"

"For the whole of the Second World War." Although her voice held very little emotion, Caro could tell the memories moved her. "My brothers and I were evacuated to Bolton, but I was too young to remember much." She brightened. "And after the liberation, which we'll be celebrating with a bank holiday in a couple of weeks' time, we came home as soon as we possibly could."

"It must have been incredible to be home again."

"I can't really remember much about it. I was too young." She smiled a little wistfully. "When we bought the house, it had been empty for years, so we managed to buy it for a song. This" – she swept a hand round in front of her, taking in the pool, its grassed edge and nearby flower beds – "was a tennis court, but it looked more like a field back then. We had the pool put in when Alex was twelve. He's a keen swimmer."

For a minute she was silent, then she turned to look at Caro. "I'm afraid Alex may seem a little prickly at times, but he isn't really. Poor boy, he's had a bad time one way and another."

Eleanor paused and Caro waited to hear more.

"My son and his wife died when Alex was five. They had a little cabin cruiser and they were on their way to Sark for their first holiday since Alex had been born. He stayed with Marcus and me. They hit some hidden rock, the waters between here and Sark are pretty dangerous, and the boat went down. By the time help got to them, it was too late."

"Oh, how awful." Caro's soft heart was touched.

"It was rather dreadful. It took us all a very long time to recover. You never forget, but you do become accustomed."

Caro knew just what she meant.

"And time does heal," Eleanor went on. "It's always surprised me, for instance, that Alex loves the sea. Every moment he has he's out on *Pauillac*. I've sometimes thought he has a feeling that he's taming the sea. Silly really."

"I don't think so," said Caro. "It sounds quite feasible to me."

"Maybe. So, I ended up grandmother and mother rolled into one." She smiled fondly. It was clear that she adored her grandson. "He's a dear boy, not that I'm biased of course, and he's kept me young. Even when Alex went off to university, he always came home for the holidays.

When he got his degree he decided, with a little persuasion, that he wanted to come home for good, go into the family firm; we're wine merchants, you know. I was delighted, couldn't wait to have him home, and the twins, my two younger sons, were all for it. All they wanted to do, the lazy pair, was hand over to Alex and retire early." She smiled again and put up a slim hand to tuck an escaping strand of hair behind her ear. "I, of course, had visions of his living here with me and everything going on as before. Silly really. Life never stands still, does it?"

"What happened?" Caro was keen to know more.

"When he arrived home, he brought a fiancée with him." Her voice took on an edge. "Oh, he'd told me about this girl, Naomi, one of his fellow students, but I had no idea how serious it was." Eleanor was staring out over the blue water of the pool. "She was a beautiful girl: tall, sort of cool looking, but I just couldn't take to her. There was something shallow about her. Do you know what I mean?"

Caro nodded. She found herself thinking of Craig and realised she understood completely.

"She couldn't bear it if Alex's attention was on anyone else. She didn't like him to see his old friends, or me that much, and yet she flirted with every male in sight. Poor Alex used to get so jealous. I could tell she didn't really love him, but he just couldn't see it, he was besotted. And then, two weeks before the wedding, she upped and left him. By then he'd bought his house and was renovating it, working night and day to have it ready for them, and she just walked out. Went off with some Swiss banker she'd met. I think they still live in Zurich."

"Oh, poor Alex. It must have been absolutely dreadful for him, and for you."

Eleanor sighed. "He was shattered. I was worried that he might, you know, jump off a cliff or something. There are quite a few suitable ones around our coasts." Her eyes were dark with remembered pain. "But, somehow, we pulled him through, the family, his friends, Paul, for instance. But it's left scars. Yes, it's certainly left scars."

For a while Eleanor was silent and Caro didn't interrupt, then Eleanor turned and smiled at her, straightened and said brightly, "But that was all of seven years ago. He's so much better now. One day I'm sure he'll find some nice girl and settle down."

Caro felt a pang of envy. Alex was lucky to have someone who cared so much about him. But then she told herself not to be a wimp, she had good friends who always looked out for her. Curiously Craig didn't enter her mind.

Eleanor turned to Caro, put a gentle hand on her arm. "But enough about us. Tell me about yourself."

"There's not that much to tell."

"I can't believe that."

Caro gave her a twisted little smile. "Well, I'm thirty years old, a little too round, a bit scatty, but quite efficient. I run my own business in my own untidy, artistic–"

"And your family?" Eleanor interrupted.

"My parents are dead." But it was obvious this bald statement wasn't going to satisfy Eleanor.

"Tell me about them," she said softly. "I'd really like to know."

Caro had no doubt of Eleanor's sincerity, but she wasn't sure she wanted to bare her soul, not just now. Rapidly editing as she went along, she gave Eleanor a précis of her life, leaving out anything that would take too much explaining.

"My father was an archaeologist, not really a worldly man at all. He and my mother lived for his work. She used to help him with all the cataloguing, the boring parts, I suppose. They both died quite close together, just over two years ago. I expect I get my artistic side from him, my interest in interiors, albeit modern ones."

"And you've been on your own ever since?"

"Yes, more or less." Caro tried to sound matter-of-fact. "I've very little other family. They were both only children. Of course, I've got a lot of friends."

"Like Craig Paxton?"

No, Caro thought, not like Craig, but she didn't say it aloud. "Yes, I suppose so. But it's not like family, is it?"

"No," said Eleanor, "family's different, for better or worse. However much you're stuck with your relatives, at least you know them, warts and all. If you're lucky you know they'll always be there."

"Yes."

"You must have been very lonely at times, my dear." Eleanor's words, and the light touch she gave to Caro's hand, were almost too much. Caro felt a tearful lump rise in her throat. It was hard not to give in and unburden herself to this woman with whom she felt so comfortable. It felt as if they'd known each other for ever. There was such a temptation to forget about everything else, stay here and not go back to all the hassle. Eleanor was right. Although Caro hadn't admitted it before, she realised now how lonely she'd been over the last few years. But she straightened up and gave Eleanor a bright smile.

"I suppose I have been a bit lonely at times. But then, I've had the luxury of independence, able to do as I please most of the time. I love my work, wouldn't give it up for anything. Life's pretty good, one way and another." But she knew she didn't believe what she was saying, any more than she thought the woman sitting beside her did.

"I'm sure it is," Eleanor said. "Now, tell me about Craig."

Caro decided the easiest thing was to give in and do so.

CHAPTER 4

Eleanor and Caro came in from the garden and as they entered the house, they could hear Alex's voice in the hall.

"What? Just for one house? It's an old Guernsey farmhouse, for goodness' sake, not a stately home!" He sounded thoroughly exasperated. "Never mind. I'll leave it for now. Thanks for your time."

A moment later he strode into the room and glared at the two women standing by the French windows. "By the way," he said to Caro, "Paul sends his apologies, something's come up and he can't get here until later this afternoon, about half two. I hope that's okay?"

"I haven't got much choice, have I?" Caro pointed out.

He scowled at her and Eleanor thought it best to intervene.

"Who was that on the phone?"

"Another of those bloody people. You wouldn't believe the prices they want for doing up La Cotte."

"What bloody people?" Eleanor asked him sweetly as she sat down on a chintz covered sofa, drawing Caro down beside her.

"Interior decorators, designers, whatever they call themselves." His tone would have been more appropriate if he'd said money lenders. He threw himself into an armchair. "I've contacted three different firms and they're all asking ridiculous money. Such a rip-off! I'll just do it myself and have done with it."

Eleanor glanced at Caro, amusement and apology mixed in her expression. "Caro is an interior designer," she said to Alex with sweet deliberation. "Why don't you ask her advice?"

It took a moment for her words to sink in, but a moment later they were both talking at once.

"But no, if Alex wants to manage on his–"

"Oh, is she? Well, I didn't mean…"

They fell silent, Caro very pink in the face, Alex still scowling. Eleanor intervened, seemingly unperturbed by their reactions.

"Now, listen," she said firmly. "Alex, this lovely girl and I have been talking and, for various reasons, Caro would be quite glad not to have to go back to Poole immediately, so why don't you let her have a look at La Cotte and see if she can help? Seems a good idea since she's staying with me anyway."

"But, Eleanor, I don't think–" Caro broke off, then retreated into practicalities. "What about the *Sally Anne*? Craig isn't going to want it stuck in Guernsey."

"But he can't have it back yet anyway," Alex put in bluntly, "given that Paul and his lot are… doing what they're doing."

"What do you mean?" Caro's hand flew to her mouth. "Oh Lord! I haven't even phoned Craig yet. I really must do that."

Eleanor was frowning across at Alex, then she turned to Caro. "Of course, you're right, you must give him a call and explain what's happening. But when you do, why don't you tell him you're researching a job. If you decide to take on Alex's house and stay a while, Craig can fly over and fetch the boat. Let's face it, after the way your boyfriend has behaved, maybe it'll teach him a lesson."

It was like being organised by a benevolent bulldozer. Whatever Caro came up with as a reason why she should go home, Eleanor had a calm alternative argument to offer. In the end Caro gave in. She smiled uncertainly at Alex, who looked back at her, frowning and tight-lipped.

"I'll come and have a look if you like," she told him, "give you a few ideas, no charge."

His answering smile didn't reach his eyes, but a moment later he was saying decisively, "Okay. Let's go now, why don't we?" He didn't quite add, get it over with.

For goodness' sake, Caro thought, it's me offering to do him the favour, not the other way around. But then she thought of last night. When it came to favours, the one she owed Alex would take some repaying. And she remembered what Eleanor had told her in the garden. Stop being so self-centred, she told herself severely. Maybe it has nothing to do with me directly. It could be just the way he is with women generally.

"That's a good idea, you've got time before Paul arrives," Eleanor was saying with enthusiasm, obviously pleased that her scheming had worked. "And when you've finished with Paul, we can go on that shopping trip, you and I."

Eleanor linked arms with both of them as they walked across the tiled hall, but as they did so there was a loud knock on the front door.

On the doorstep stood a tall and very beautiful young woman. Her blonde hair fell with carefully created untidiness to her shoulders, and she was wearing a dress that screamed designer. A conventional social smile parted her rather full lips, but the look in her eyes did not match. With a calculating glance, she took in the tableau created by the three of them as they stood in the doorway.

"Alex, darling." She leant forward and kissed him, full on the lips, and neatly detached him from Eleanor. Every gesture was possessive. "And Eleanor, I've not seen you for ages. I hope you don't mind my coming in search of this lovely man. I couldn't find him at La Cotte, so I thought he might be here. Alex, darling, why don't you ever answer your phone? It's about tonight, could you pick me up an hour earlier than planned, say at half six? Jacqueline has invited us for a drink before we go on to the dinner, and it'd be so much nicer for us all to arrive together."

Caro stood beside Eleanor feeling very much an intruder and, in comparison to this stunning looking woman, thoroughly outclassed. In normal circumstances she would have found it hard to compete – right now it was impossible. So far, the newcomer hadn't acknowledged her existence, although she had thrown her a hard, speculative glance. Caro had a strong feeling they'd met before. She studied the beautiful face, trying to work out why it seemed familiar.

Alex was muttering something about that being fine, half six it was, when Eleanor intervened.

"Ashley." Her voice was cool. "How are you? Not in the office today?"

"No, like Alex I'm skiving off." She gave Alex a dazzling smile. "We shouldn't be though, should we, darling? What with the spring wine tastings to organise, and the beginning of the tourist season, every hotel is wanting their order yesterday. It's been a positive nightmare, hasn't it, darling?"

But Alex seemed to have been struck dumb.

"Let me introduce you to a friend of mine." Eleanor slipped her arm back through Caro's.

At last Ashley turned to acknowledge Caro, and then her eyes widened. "Haven't we met before?" Her voice was sharply bright. "I'm sure we have. Oh yes, aren't you Craig Paxton's girlfriend?"

Caro took a deep breath. Now she remembered. It had been on the boat the last time they were in Guernsey. Ashley and Craig had hit it off far too well. Suddenly she found herself determined not to let this woman have it all her own way. "Not anymore," she said firmly, in answer to Ashley's question. "You came to the *Sally Anne*, with your husband, Karl, isn't it? How is Karl, by the way?"

She felt a twitch in Eleanor's arm and didn't dare look at her or Alex. She kept her eyes on Ashley, whose own had narrowed.

"Don't talk to me about that man!" she said, waving a dismissive hand. "Let's just say we're separated and leave it at that. Is Craig here?"

"No," said Caro, running out of steam. Luckily Alex seemed to have found his voice.

"Right. Well, we must be going." He placed a hand firmly in the small of Caro's back and almost pushed her down the steps towards his car. "I'm afraid we're in a bit of a rush. Caro is coming to have a look at La Cotte, she's an interior designer. I'll see you later, Ashley."

Glancing back Caro could see her gazing after them, a scowl of annoyance on her beautiful face, while Eleanor stood beside her unsuccessfully trying to suppress a mischievous grin.

* * *

They drove along in an uncomfortable silence. Caro, completely unable to think of appropriate small talk, gazed out of the windows, taking in the surroundings of St Peter Port and beyond.

They drove past a roundabout with a tall mast in the middle, flags flying from its top. Turning left, they followed along past office buildings one side and a packed marina the other, then past terraced houses looking out to the sea and the other islands. She'd never been this far out of St Peter Port before. As they passed what looked like a small castle high above the coast road, she opened her mouth to ask what it was called, but changed her mind, having glanced at the stony face beside her. But this is ridiculous, she told herself, and turned back to Alex. "Where are we going?" she asked.

"To my house."

"I know that," she snapped. "I mean where is your house?"

His mouth twitched and she thought he was going to smile, but he didn't. "We've just been past what's called The Bridge, where the shops were. It marks the boundary between two parishes, the Vale and St Sampson, and up until Georgian times they were only connected at low tide. This bay we're coming to now is called Bordeaux. Are you any the wiser?" he asked.

"No," she rallied, "but I'm still interested."

They fell silent once more and Caro gave up trying to make conversation. If he wants to be bad tempered, let him, she thought. But resentment boiled inside her. Look at how kind he'd been last night, and now this sullen silence. I wonder if he blows as hot and cold with his friend, Ashley.

Her mind went back to the encounter on Eleanor's doorstep. How strange, and how awkward, bumping into that awful woman again. She remembered their first meeting. It had been a sunny lunchtime in September last year; Craig had invited Ashley and her husband to the *Sally Anne* for a drink, there'd been some business he was doing with Karl Guilbert. Caro remembered feeling very much out of place as the other three got down to some serious drinking. After several whiskies, Karl was soon slumped back, gazing mindlessly ahead at nothing. Meanwhile Ashley had set out to charm Craig, and he'd been all too responsive. Caro had felt as if she was the one playing gooseberry. After they'd gone Caro had complained about his behaviour, but Craig had told her not to be naive, all he'd been doing was buttering up a potential client.

"Grow up, Caro," he'd said scornfully. "This is the real world."

"I thought it was her husband who was the client."

"So what?"

"Well, he didn't have much to say for himself, did he?"

"So? I'd be selling the antiques to them both, wouldn't I? Anyway, it's usually the wife who calls the shots."

It had been an argument she knew she couldn't win, but the resentment had festered for weeks afterwards.

Determinedly she pushed her unpleasant memories aside and looked out of the car window. They were winding their way through narrow lanes, bordered by fields on one side containing rich brown Guernsey cows, and another field dotted with brown and black sheep. She wanted to ask if this was unusual but didn't.

A little further on, the car slowed and turned through a gateway into a gravelled yard. It seemed they'd arrived, and Caro gazed, wide-eyed and enchanted by what she saw.

It was quite a large house, long and low and built of granite, like so many of the houses she'd noticed as they drove through the lanes. One end wall was flush with the road and the other three sides were surrounded by a garden, or perhaps a wilderness would be a better description. At the end she could just see an old timber and glass greenhouse, now collapsing unhappily in on itself. Caro longed to get her hands on the garden, let alone the house.

Alex led her to the back door, past a round tower set into the wall which she presumed contained a staircase. "That's a tourelle," he told her, noticing her studying it. "Very traditional. Quite a few old farmhouses have them. The stairs wind up to the first floor inside."

"I thought so." Her eyes glowed as her love for old buildings cancelled out her annoyance with him. "I've read a book about old Guernsey houses. It was fascinating. Have you got an arch over the front door?"

He looked surprised, and pleased. "Yes, with the date the house was built, 1748, carved into the granite at the top."

"Oh lovely! You must show me. I want to see everything, absolutely everything," she insisted as he opened the door and stood aside to let her in, stooping slightly himself to avoid hitting his head on the lintel.

Guernsey farmhouses weren't built for men as tall as Alex Devereaux.

"And have you got an old furze oven, and tiled floors?" He must have found her enthusiasm infectious, as he smiled with real amusement for the first time that morning. It made him seem much more like the person she'd met the evening before.

"Yes, that and more underneath all the mess, for which I apologise. Come and have a look."

As she followed him from room to room, Caro could feel excitement mounting inside her. So much of the original farmhouse had been preserved. There was an old granite fireplace in the living room with a solid wooden beam above, the marks of the axe with which it had been shaped clearly defined. Sure enough, the furze oven was let into the side of the fireplace in the dining room, and red tiles, polished smooth by many, many feet, covered the floor in the kitchen and the hall.

But Eleanor was right, the decor was in a dreadful state. Small windows and thick granite walls gave it a sombre atmosphere. Light and bright colours were needed. Alex had left some ugly Victorian wood panelling untouched and this too added to the gloom. There was a half-finished air about many of the rooms, as if he'd started work on them then lost heart.

Only one room on the ground floor showed any sign of warmth or life. A small study where books lined the walls and an ancient armchair was pulled up in front of the open fireplace. Caro bent to read the titles of some of the books. There were several tomes about wine with titles like 'The Wines of the Loire' and 'The History of Veuve Clicquot', but a little further along she came across several books on another subject. Here was the latest edition of 'Halliwell's Film Guide', a biographical dictionary of film and an enormous volume simply called 'The Movies'.

"You seem to be a bit of a film buff," Caro said.

He shrugged. "I suppose. Do you watch much?"

"My favourite recreation is to settle down to a good movie with a bottle of wine and a large bag of cashew nuts."

"Sounds good to me." He smiled, looking more relaxed. "We must try it some time."

Caro didn't quite know how to respond to this unexpected suggestion. Glancing at him she saw his face close, as if he'd spoken without thinking and was now taken aback by what he'd said. Caro said quickly, "Well, let's get on."

She turned to survey the rest of the room. A computer stood incongruously on an Edwardian partners desk, and an extremely expensive looking sound system was stacked to one side of it. Under this were two shelves containing hundreds of CDs. He obviously didn't believe in streaming his music. Caro guessed this was the room he used most, not least because of several used coffee mugs about the place.

As she followed Alex around, she began to forget about everything else and to plan what she would suggest. She couldn't wait to start talking about colour schemes and discuss what fabrics to order. They went up the curving stairs of the tourelle, holding on to the thick maroon rope, looped from strong brass rings, which did service as a bannister. First, he showed her two sparsely furnished spare bedrooms, both of which looked as if there'd been no changes made since the 1950s. A third small room was full of junk, tea chests, odd bits of discarded furniture and an ancient surfboard leaning up against the wall.

Alex grimaced. "A bit of a mess," he said.

"That's something of an understatement."

"Yes, well, I just sort of chuck things in here if I can't think where else to put them. I hate throwing anything away."

"What on earth is that?" she asked, pointing at what looked like part of an engine.

"Oh, that. It's from *Pauillac*, poor old girl. I had to replace part of her innards. That's the bit I took out. I thought it might come in useful some time." His grin was sheepish. "Or, of course, I might get something for the parts."

Caro found this glimpse of a softer side to him endearing, but she told herself to concentrate on the job and asked briskly, "Right. Where next?"

Alex closed the door on the mess and led her on to what looked like his own bedroom. Again, like the room downstairs, this was full of books. There was a distinct waft of the aftershave he used, but also shades of another scent, sweeter and more cloying. As Caro turned to leave, she noticed an almond green silk and lace negligee hanging on the back of the door. I wouldn't mind betting that belongs to Ashley, she thought. Somehow this took the edge off her enjoyment of touring the house. But when they were back in the kitchen her enthusiasm took over once again.

"This house is gorgeous, there's so much I– you could do with it. It could be made much lighter, and there are some great features. I wish you'd let me have a try." She hugged herself at the thought and her eyes glowed. "I could come back over from the mainland and do the job properly, once all this nonsense with the boat is over. I'll give you a quote once I've had a proper look round, get some material and catalogues for you to go through. My charges aren't that bad, at least I don't think they are." She realised she was letting her tongue run away with her and pulled herself up short. "Sorry. I didn't mean to go overboard. Maybe you like it as it is."

"No, I don't, that's the point, and I'll never get a good price for it in its present state." He gave her a hard look. "But what about your work back home? Can you leave it just like that, on such short notice?"

"Let me worry about my workload," Caro said, determined not to be put off.

"And you'd let me have a say in what you do?"

"Well of course, you'd be the client, wouldn't you?" She looked up at him challengingly, her cheeks slightly flushed, dark curls wild again. "I don't know how you can think of selling it. It's your home, for goodness' sake."

Alex, a head and shoulders taller than her, looked down into her. For a moment they stood in the cold kitchen, trying to communicate something too hard to put into words. He lifted a hand and she thought he was going to touch her face, but the next moment he took a sudden step backwards. The spell was broken.

"Do me a quote and I'll think about it." His voice was cool and business-like. "We'd better get back. Paul will be arriving soon."

Caro wished he hadn't reminded her. It was so confusing, the way he blew hot and cold, friendly and kind one minute, austere and suspicious the next. However attractive he was, his mood swings were a pain, they gave her a feeling of standing on shifting sand. Suddenly she felt very tired. Alex's moods, Paul Le Page's suspicions, Eleanor's benign bullying, and on top of all that, her own mixed feelings. It was like being on the deck of the *Sally Anne* yesterday, never quite sure of your footing.

As she followed him out to the car, she wondered what on earth she was getting herself into.

CHAPTER 5

Eleanor persuaded Alex to stay and have lunch with them and they were still sitting in the kitchen, drinking coffee, when Paul Le Page arrived. He was accompanied by one of his fellow officers which made it all seem more official.

Alex waited in the kitchen while Eleanor ushered the two men and Caro into the sitting room. He could hear her enquiring after Paul's wife and children, offering the men coffee and refusing to take no for an answer. It was a tour de force of social grace and, he suspected, a calculated attempt to undermine them.

When she came back into the kitchen Alex looked at her, his expression a mixture of amusement and disapproval. "You," he said severely, "are a wicked old woman. All that natter about Paul's kids. Really, Nella, you mustn't interfere."

"I don't know what you're talking about." She turned the kettle on then began to load the dishwasher. "It's such a long time since I've seen Paul. It's only natural I should ask after the family."

"Come on, Nella, you know what I mean." He sat looking at her, not certain how to say what was in his mind. "You realise Caro might be involved in something illegal, don't you?"

"It's always possible, Alex, but somehow I doubt it."

"No, listen to me." He got up and came to stand beside her. "Paul told me this morning that this Craig character has been under surveillance for some time. They're pretty sure he's involved in smuggling, and it could be that Caro's part of the set-up."

She turned to look at her grandson. "I've been around a long time, my darling, and one thing I know I'm good at is summing people up. I have a strong feeling that girl isn't knowingly involved. We had a long talk in the garden this morning and she's told me all about her *ex*-boyfriend and their relationship. There's a lot you don't know."

"Like what?"

"It's up to her to tell you, if she chooses to."

Alex tried to protest, but she ignored it. "Give her a chance, she might well confide in you," she told him. "You should relax a bit, try to get to know her, as I am going to do. Craig helped her out when she was feeling particularly vulnerable, just after her mother died."

"But, Nella, Paul says her father–"

She held up a hand. "Alex, just give it time." The kettle boiled and she prepared the coffee, then placed the mugs on a tray, but she didn't pick it up straight away. "I believe one of Caro's problems," she went on thoughtfully, "is that she's desperately loyal, even if that loyalty is misplaced. There's no doubt she still feels an obligation to this Craig person. She's reluctant to judge him without sufficient evidence, and I understand her feelings, although I don't agree with them. I think that's the kind of person she is."

"Nella! You only just met her last night. How can you know these things about someone who's practically a stranger?"

"I don't know, I just have a strong feeling. Instinct, intuition, call it what you will."

Alex felt resentment rising in him. "You speak as if you've known her for years."

"It's strange, but I feel as if I have." Eleanor turned from him and looked out through the kitchen window to the garden beyond. "I've rarely met someone I felt such a connection with so quickly. I think she feels the same. She told me I remind her of her mother." She turned back, put a gentle hand on Alex's arm and her face softened. "I know you find it hard to trust women, but believe me, my darling, I think I'm right about Caro. If it turns out I'm wrong, you can crow as much as you like."

Alex didn't reply and Eleanor picked up the tray and left the room. He realised there was a part of him desperately hoping she was right, and he was disturbed by the discovery. If his grandmother had known what Paul had told him earlier in the day, she probably wouldn't be half so sure of Caro. But she didn't know, and he couldn't tell her. Paul shouldn't even have told him.

* * *

Earlier that day Eleanor had been showing Caro round the garden when Paul himself had arrived to fetch the keys to the boat. Alex hadn't called them in, just handed the keys to his friend.

"What do you need to search the boat for?" he'd asked. "Bit excessive, isn't it?"

"Not really, not with what we know."

"And what's that?"

"Come on, Alex." Paul had shaken his head. "You know I can't tell you that."

Alex had looked at him, eyebrows raised, waiting, and thirty years of friendship had done the trick.

"Okay, but you have to keep this to yourself." Alex nodded and Paul went on, "The chap who owns the *Sally Anne* is on a list we get from the mainland. They think he's been doing a neat little trade in stolen artefacts, usually small stuff, jewellery and the like. The trouble is the UK force has never been able to catch him at it or work out how he's moving the stuff. What's more they think he might be involved with a much nastier set of villains, but they haven't got enough proof yet. If they're right, your new girlfriend could be way out of her depth."

Alex opened his mouth to protest that Caro was no girlfriend of his, then closed it again as Paul went on, "I just want to take the opportunity to have a look around while his boat's in the marina, and I also want to check on Miss Bennett. It's more than likely she's involved."

Alex had been surprised at how much he wanted to reject the idea. He'd turned away from Paul, saying casually, "On the other hand, she might have no idea what her boyfriend is up to."

"Yup. That's a possibility, but I doubt it. There's also some information about her father that needs checking. I don't know the full story, but I will very soon. Anyway, I should be able to find out more this afternoon when I question her." Paul had studied him, a sharp look on his face that Alex knew all too well. "What's your interest? Fancy her, do you?"

"No, of course not," Alex had assured him, a little too quickly, "but Nella's taken to her. I wouldn't want the old girl to feel let down."

"Oh, I see," Paul had said with a slight smile. "Well, there's always a chance she's clean." He hadn't sounded as if he thought it very likely. "I dare say we'll find out soon enough."

When Paul was gone, Alex had wandered restlessly around the house, unable to settle to anything. He couldn't get rid of the niggling suspicion that Caro was, in fact, an accomplished little crook. But another part of him rebelled against the thought. And what about Nella? It was obvious she'd taken to Caro, and her judgement was usually sound, at least it was when it came to people. Still, even Nella could get things wrong sometimes. And back he'd gone to the beginning, with no idea what to believe.

And now here was Nella trying to persuade him that all his suspicions, and Paul's for that matter, were unfounded. Once again, he wished he could believe her. But women were women, in his experience untrustworthy, excepting Nella of course. The fact that this one had enormous, candid grey-green eyes and a face glowing with openness and honesty, probably meant she was just a very good actress.

* * *

In the sitting room the object of his thoughts sat on the sofa, her hands clasped in her lap to stop them trembling, as she looked across at the two men sitting opposite her.

Paul handed her a bunch of keys. "Thank you for letting us have these. We won't need them anymore." He paused, studying her face, then, conjuror fashion, he produced some photographs from his breast pocket. "Do you recognise any of these?" he asked as he handed them to her.

Caro took them from him. They were photographs of various pieces of jewellery, most of them antiques she was sure. She leafed through them, keenly aware that both men were watching her every move. The first photograph was of a gold necklace, collar shaped with row upon row of interlinked chains. The second was of a pair of delicate pearl and diamond drop earrings resting on navy-blue velvet. Next was a brooch in the shape of a starburst, the heavy setting encrusted with emeralds, diamonds and seed pearls. Caro thought it rather ugly.

At first, she recognised nothing and was about to hand them back when the last photograph caught her eye. It was of an ornate gold buckle in the shape of two snakes, twined round each other to form the clasp, and set into the metal were countless tiny jewels, mostly rubies and sapphires. It was a distinctive piece and Caro knew with cold certainty that she'd seen it before. A sickening wave of apprehension gripped her as she remembered where.

It had been about two weeks ago. She'd arrived at Craig's shop and walked through into the office in search of him. He'd been sitting at his desk, and in front of him, resting on a piece of black velvet, had been this buckle. She remembered exclaiming, "Oh Craig, isn't that beautiful."

"Ah, my darling, hallo," he'd said, as he'd scooped up the brooch, and the velvet, and put them in a drawer. She remembered him kissing her, leading her back into the shop with his arm around her shoulders, and she'd forgotten all about the buckle, until now.

Aware that the silence was dragging on, she handed the photographs back to Paul. Apprehension had settled, like a stone, in her stomach. If she told them she'd seen it before, she'd have to tell them where. But if she did that, what on earth would happen to Craig? And what would he say? She knew she couldn't drop Craig in it, it would seem so disloyal, even after finding him with Vanessa – was that really only yesterday morning? No, not even after that.

Caro knew she'd hesitated too long and suddenly she found herself telling them, "I'm sorry. I don't recognise any of them. Why do you ask?"

Immediately she'd spoken she regretted what she'd said, but too late now, she couldn't take it back.

"You've never seen any of them before?" Paul's voice was cool.

"No – I'm sure not." There was no changing her mind now.

It was hard to tell whether he believed her. His face was completely expressionless as he took the photographs and placed them carefully back in his pocket. Caro could feel her heart thumping as she waited for what would come next.

But just at that moment Eleanor waltzed in with their coffee. "Here you are, sorry it took so long." She stood for a moment, her face bright with friendly curiosity, but even her determination couldn't break into the silence that dragged out after the polite murmurs of thanks.

"Well," she said, after a moment, "I'll leave you to it." With a bright, encouraging smile in Caro's direction, she glided out of the room.

With slow deliberation Paul helped himself to sugar, stirred his coffee, placed the spoon back on the tray, then turned back to Caro. Giving her a direct look, he asked, "How long have you known Craig Paxton?"

At least this was a question she could answer without hesitation. "Just over two years. He commissioned me to do the interior design for his antique shop."

"Oh yes, I gather you're a decorator."

"An interior designer," Caro said firmly, with a feeling of being back on familiar ground.

"And he's a close friend of yours?"

She hesitated, uncertain again. Hadn't she told them enough on the boat last night? "Well, not as close as before," she said, grudgingly.

"Oh?" Paul's eyebrows lifted in seemingly polite enquiry.

"I thought I'd told you this already?"

Paul smiled and leaned forward, his elbows resting on his knees. "Please, just run through it for me again."

"Alright," Caro shrugged, trying to seem unconcerned. "We had this row. I got to Craig's flat early on Friday morning and I found him with somebody else, his assistant, if you must know," she said wearily. "I was absolutely furious, and we had an enormous row. He's always objected if I so much as look at another man, so I thought he was being a hypocrite. I hate double standards. When I left, I was so furious that I wanted to get my own back. He's potty about his boat and I knew it would really annoy him if I took it out, so I did. But I forgot to check the fuel, and that's why I ended up having to be rescued by Alex." Neither of her listeners said anything so she went on, anxious to fill the silence, "I realise now how irresponsible I was, and I'm sure Craig's livid." She rallied. "But then I was pretty angry myself."

"Quite understandable, I'm sure." He leant back, smiling, as if this was some social occasion. "I gather you might be doing some work on Alex's house."

"How did you know that?"

His smile broadened. "Aha, the Guernsey grapevine, a very healthy plant. Won't you find it difficult to get the right materials and the like over here?"

"No, not really. Most of what I use I order from London, from France, or sometimes further afield. It depends on the job."

Caro had almost forgotten about the younger officer, but she happened to glance at him at this moment and surprised a quickly suppressed gleam of satisfaction in his eyes. What had she said to cause that reaction? She hated the feeling of not knowing what was in their minds. Paul's next question increased her resentment.

"And what kind of transport do you use?"

"I don't really understand why you need–"

"Humour me, Miss Bennett," he said and smiled at her once again, but it made her feel no better than the last time.

"Sometimes I fetch things myself," she spoke slowly and deliberately, as to a child, "in the van I use for my work, or I contact one of the carriers. There are two firms I use quite regularly. In fact, I'm expecting a consignment over from Calais in about a week's time, and I'm using the same French carrier I always use for that. I'll have to be back home when it arrives." She tried to sound firm about it.

"I'm sure you will be." Abruptly he rose and so did his colleague. "Well, that seems to be all for now. Thank you for your co-operation, Miss Bennett, we'll see ourselves out."

But as he got to the door, he turned. "Oh yes, one more thing. Will Mr Paxton be coming over to fetch the *Sally Anne*?"

"I don't know. I haven't spoken to him yet."

His eyebrows rose in a look of disbelief, but all he said was, "Well, when you have, could you let me know. Just another one of those formalities we're so fond of. All we want is a quick word with him."

Caro felt cold. Into her mind came a picture of the jewelled gold buckle sitting on Craig's desk. She dreaded the prospect of speaking to him but knew she would have to soon. She knew she should have done so already. She suddenly felt very tired and wished that the last few days had never happened.

CHAPTER 6

Paul Le Page and his colleague were just about to get into their car when Alex came striding down the steps. "Got what you wanted?" he asked casually.

Paul wasn't deceived. This was no casual enquiry.

"More or less, but not as much as I'd have liked." He looked hard at Alex, then drew him away from the car towards the lawn, leaving his colleague sitting tapping his fingers impatiently on the steering wheel.

"I gather Miss Bennett might be doing a job on your house?"

"How did you–? Ah, Eleanor."

"No, Ashley Guilbert, as a matter of fact. I bumped into her in the High Street. Ashley didn't seem awfully keen on the idea."

"It's not actually any of her business," Alex said coldly.

"No?" Paul's eyebrows rose in disbelief.

"No," Alex snapped, then went on quickly. "But yes, Caro might do it, we haven't come to an agreement yet. Eleanor's very keen for her to take the job. Why do you ask?"

"It'd be quite useful if she was in the island for a bit longer." Paul kept a close eye on Alex's face as he spoke. "Particularly if that lures her boyfriend over. I wouldn't mind succeeding where the mainland boys have failed."

"And you're hoping that I'll help you keep her here?" Alex was surprised at how distasteful this thought was. He felt that he would be colluding against Caro, but surely it would be better for Eleanor to find out the worst before she became too fond of the girl.

"Eleanor's taken to her," he said, not looking directly at Paul. "I don't want her upset."

"No, but I've got my job to do. And anyway, I'm not sure she's the sort of company your grandmother should be cultivating."

"Come off it, Paul."

"Alex, I mean it."

"And still you're wanting me to persuade her to stay."

Paul shrugged, acknowledging the criticism. "Just for a bit, until I've finished delving."

"Okay, I won't put her off. But I'm not going to push her into staying just for your sake."

"Fair enough." They began to walk back towards the car, but before they reached it Paul stopped and placed a friendly hand on Alex's shoulder. "And Alex, you watch out for yourself as well. It's not only Eleanor who could get hurt."

Alex scowled at him then, without a word, thrust his hands deep into his trouser pockets and stalked back into the house.

* * *

"I'm a terrible game show addict, and there's one I always watch on Saturdays. Do you mind?" Eleanor asked Caro as they sat in the sitting room that evening.

"No, of course not, you go ahead."

Directly the two officers had left that afternoon Eleanor had dragged Caro off on the promised shopping spree. They'd combed the shops up and down the cobbled High Street in St Peter Port, Eleanor encouraging her to spend as much money as she could afford. Slowly thoughts of the unpleasant interview had receded into the back of her mind, where they lay waiting to come to the surface again. Their progress through the town had been interrupted time and again by meetings with people Eleanor knew, all of whom had been introduced to Caro as if she was an old family friend.

When they'd got back to Villette House, Alex was gone. Caro had been relieved, the atmosphere he created was so unnerving, yet part of her had missed the vitality of his presence. She needed something to take her mind off him. Remembering that while they were shopping, she'd bought a book to read, she went upstairs to fetch it and, as she was coming back through the hall there was a knock at the front door. She hesitated, wondering if she should answer it. The television was quite loud, maybe Eleanor hadn't heard. Caro went and opened the door herself.

On the doorstep, a small overnight bag slung over his shoulder, stood Craig Paxton.

Caro stared at him in disbelief. She'd been putting off contacting him all day, knowing she should, but unable to bring herself to do so. And here he was, sleek blonde hair, pale yellow shirt, soft tweed jacket and all. He looked down at her and his cold expression made her heart sink, the cruel twist to his thin lips something she'd never really noticed before. It was obvious that he was very angry indeed.

"Well, my darling, are you going to let me in?" was the first thing he said.

Without thinking Caro moved aside and he stepped into the hall.

"How did you know I was here?"

"I had a phone call from a friend."

"Who?"

Caro thought immediately of Alex, and felt a wave of relief when he said, "Ashley Guilbert. Remember her? She was kind enough to let me know your whereabouts, which is more than you bloody did."

His cold, clipped voice bit out the words, and his eyes never left her face. Caro felt the sick churning of fear inside her stomach, followed swiftly by a wave of relief as Eleanor appeared in the door of the sitting room.

"A visitor, how nice," she said coolly, taking in the situation with one quick glance. She came across the hall, hand outstretched. "I'm Eleanor Devereaux. I don't think we've met."

Craig had no choice but to take the proffered hand. "Craig Paxton, I–"

He wasn't given the chance to say any more. "Ah yes. This is your friend from Poole, isn't it, Caro darling? Do come in. We were just about to have a drink. I'm sure you'd like one."

Linking her arm with Caro's she propelled her across the hall and Craig had no choice but to follow.

Eleanor was the perfect hostess, settling them in the sitting room. Even when she went to get a bottle of wine and glasses from the kitchen, she didn't give them enough time on their own for any real communication. Once the wine was poured, she chattered on brightly, making sure the conversation remained general and, after a while, eyes wide and innocent, she asked, "Where are you staying, Mr Paxton?"

"I… um… hadn't actually booked anywhere," Craig said.

Caro had never seen him so unsure of himself, but he soon rallied. "I came straight here from the airport, but I'll be fine on the *Sally Anne*. I presume it's in the visitors' marina, Caro darling?"

"Of course. I'll get the keys for you," she said.

Quickly she left the room, immensely relieved to have a breathing space. Taking the stairs two at a time, she went to her bedroom, then stopped. What am I hurrying for? Slow down, there's no rush. She stood quite still for a moment, took a deep, steadying breath, collected the keys, then went slowly downstairs again. There was no murmur of voices as she reached the sitting room door and when she stepped into the room the atmosphere was strained to breaking point. Craig was showing signs of being in a towering rage, but Eleanor was her usual serene self. She smiled and rose from her seat as Caro came in.

"I hope you two young things don't mind, but I think I'll leave you to talk. I find at my age early nights are usually a good idea." Caro didn't believe a word as Eleanor held out her hand to Craig. "So nice to have met you. Do pop in again some time. And Caro, I'll be just upstairs if you want me, dear." Her eyes spoke volumes as she bent, kissed Caro's cheek and, with a cheery 'goodnight', left the room.

Caro felt as if she'd been deprived of a lifeline. But this was ridiculous. She owed it to Craig to explain her behaviour, and she had to face the fact that a confrontation was inevitable, she might as well get it over with. It didn't take long. Craig waited until Eleanor was barely out of earshot, then exploded.

"What the fuck is going on here?" he spat out, towering over her. "And who is that old bat anyway? She had the gall to suggest I should 'be nice to you', said you'd had a bad time. *You've* had a bad time! What about me, eh?"

He started to pace up and down the room. "You pinch my bloody boat without so much as a by your leave, end up in the middle of the channel, and you don't even have the grace to let me know where you are. Do you have any idea how worried I've been? And the first news I get is from someone I barely know." He snorted derisively. "And I'm supposed to be nice to you. I don't think so!"

Caro stood quite still. She could feel anger growing inside her and was glad. Anger gave her courage. When he ran out of words she asked quietly, only the smallest of tremors in her voice, "How's Vanessa?"

He turned slowly to look at her. "Oh, Caro, is that why you ran away with my boat?" Chameleon-like, his whole attitude had changed. His voice became soft, he knew the power of it. He smiled down at her, turning on the charm full blast.

Caro cut in before he could say more, "Strangely enough, finding you with another woman in your bed made me a tad angry, particularly after all your protestations of faithfulness after your last little mistake, as you called it. You're the only one for me, Caro, I'll never let you down again, Caro," she mimicked. "Do you think I'm so grateful for your attention that I'll turn a blind eye to your affairs? And to anything else you choose to do?" And into her mind came the photographs Paul Le Page had shown her yesterday.

"Caro, Caro, darling." His head on one side, his smile soft and begging for her understanding, he spread his hands before her. "I'm just a weak man, and Vanessa is an extremely determined and attractive woman." He put up his hand to brush a curl back from her cheek, saying very softly, "And you, my darling, have to admit you've been rather cold towards me lately. Don't you know how much I love you?"

"Hah! And this is the way you show it."

"My darling girl, I'm a red-blooded male. I have needs."

"Oh, bugger off, Craig! Stop churning out ridiculous clichés."

"But Vanessa meant nothing, nothing," he insisted. "Can't you forgive and forget, just this once?"

He moved closer, but she stepped back quickly. "Just this once?" she snapped. "I took you at your word last time. Is it unreasonable to expect you to keep your promises?" She took a deep breath and plunged on, "If you can't, then we're finished."

"Darling, you can't mean that."

Caro was taken aback by his vehemence. There was desperation in his voice, almost as if he was afraid. She dismissed the idea. It was just that she wasn't caving in as she always had before. He managed to grab her wrist and, when she tried to pull away, he just gripped tighter.

"Let me go, Craig. It's no good. It won't work anymore."

"Ah, come on, love, you've had a bad time, you'll change your mind soon enough." It was obvious he was making a great effort to sound sweetly reasonable. "I know you're angry with me, but I promise I'll behave. Don't make a decision we'll both regret."

She managed to free herself and rubbed at her wrist. "My mind is made up," she said, trying to put as much conviction into her voice as she could.

Craig looked down at her and came closer. She couldn't escape. Behind her was the firm bulk of the sofa, and to duck and run would seem so cowardly. She stood waiting for his next move, her heart beating hard.

He put up a hand and gripped the curls at the nape of her neck, pulled her against his body. "Oh no, Caro, I don't think so." He pressed his mouth to hers and she could feel his tongue probing against her closed lips. She struggled against him, but it was pointless. When he lifted his head, he gave a twist of a smile. "You and I, we're a pair. I care about you so very much, more than I've ever cared about any woman, and I need you far too much to give you up so easily."

He kissed her again, more softly this time. "And what about my business, and yours for that matter? We're useful to each other. Look at that trip you made to fetch the stuff from Jason, I couldn't have trusted that to anyone else, could I? What if they'd opened the package? You see, you're as involved as me, little Caro, there's no getting away from it. Come back to the boat with me and then we can go home."

A trickle of cold fear slid down Caro's back. The threat in his words was clear. Now she was certain that Paul Le Page was right – Craig was involved in some illegal scheme. And she realised at last that he'd have no qualms about involving her in any deals he may have done. She must think quickly. He mustn't know how scared she was. Pushing down rising panic, she put her hands up to his chest and tried to smile.

"I'm sorry but I can't right now, Craig. You see, I might have a job to do here, and it's a really good one."

"And what job is that?"

"It's for Alex Devereaux, Eleanor's grandson. I– I'm going to be doing his house, and that will mean I'll have to stay for a bit." She watched his face carefully as she waited for his reaction. "It's an absolute plum of a job. I'd be a fool to pass it up."

"And when did you arrange all this?" His voice was hard.

"No, not yet," said Caro, and immediately regretted sounding hesitant.

"In that case you'll tell him you can't do it. You'll find other so-called plums to work on." His voice mocked her. "I want you to think carefully about what I've said. I'm sure you'll realise I'm right. You need me around to keep you out of trouble, and you know I can't do without you, my little darling."

At that moment Caro felt very little indeed. "Alright," she said, "I'll think about it." She closed her eyes for a moment, trying to control the churning mixture of anger and fear inside her, remembering other occasions when she'd tried to stand up to him. The words stuck in her throat, but she managed to say, "Perhaps I was a bit hasty."

He seemed to be satisfied, gave her an approving smile and bent to kiss her. She moved her head and the kiss landed on her cheek, but he didn't seem to mind, he thought he'd won. "That's my girl, I knew you'd see reason." He glanced his watch. "I'll get down to the boat now. And you should get some sleep, you look all in, not at all your usual self."

She followed him out to the hall, feeling exhausted. At the front door he turned. "If you insist on staying a while, then I stay too. I'm not leaving without you, do you understand?"

Caro nodded, too drained to say anything.

"Good. Say my goodbyes to the old dear."

Caro felt a spurt of anger at this but didn't comment.

"And Caro, no careless talk, understand? Remember what happened to your father."

He went striding down the steps and didn't glance back to see the shock and fear in her face. Her body trembling, she wrapped her arms around herself, tight, to stop the shaking.

CHAPTER 7

Caro closed the front door and turned, her eyes enormous in her pale frightened face. Eleanor was standing at the bottom of the stairs.

"My dear girl, what is wrong? What did he do to you?"

"I thought you'd gone to bed."

"How could I?" she asked as she put a gentle arm round Caro's shoulders, led her out to the kitchen. "I know what you need. A large brandy."

She reached down a glass from the cupboard in the corner, filled it with a swirl of golden liquid, and brought it back to press the glass firmly into Caro's shaking hands.

"Take a gulp then tell me what happened."

But Caro couldn't speak. There was an obstruction in her throat and the words wouldn't come, but the tears would and, totally unable to stop herself, she started to sob like a small child. Eleanor removed the glass gently from her hands, gathered Caro into warm arms and rocked her, murmuring quietly comforting nonsense until she was calmer. After a while a handful of tissues were thrust into her hand.

Caro blew her nose and scrubbed at her face. "I'm so sorry. I'm not usually such a wimp." She gave Eleanor a watery smile. "I don't know what's come over me."

"Don't apologise, it's good to have a howl occasionally. Now, would you like to tell me all about it? You don't have to, you know."

"Oh God, I have to tell someone! It's all so awful!"

"Go on then. It won't go any further."

Taking a deep breath, she began to talk. "Remember I told you, when we were in the garden, about Mum dying and how Craig helped me afterwards? Sort of taking over, just being there?" She stopped, gave a dry little sob. "I think I know now why he did it. I suppose he does care for me in a way. He gets incredibly angry if I so much as look at anyone else. But on another level, he's been using me. Oh, I've been so, so stupid!"

"We all like to think the best of people," Eleanor said, "and it's hard to accept that someone we're close to isn't what they seem."

"I suppose." Caro took a shuddering breath. "The thing is, I think Craig has been using me as some sort of courier. When Paul Le Page was here, he showed me some photographs of jewellery, asked me if I recognised any of the pieces. The trouble is, I did."

Eleanor made no comment, so Caro went on.

"One of the pieces was an ornate buckle. It was a really striking piece, otherwise I might not have remembered it." She turned to Eleanor, her eyes wide and bleak. "I'd seen it before, in Craig's office. I remember remarking on it, but he put it away quickly and I forgot about it. How stupid was that? At least, I did until this morning."

"And you think this buckle was stolen or something."

"Yes, otherwise why would Paul have a photo of it."

"Perhaps Craig didn't know." Eleanor didn't sound convinced.

"But there's something else. I sort of let Paul think I hadn't seen any of the jewellery before."

"That probably wasn't a very good idea," Eleanor said firmly.

"I know." Caro slapped her forehead. "What an idiot! I don't know what came over me. Yes, I do. I didn't want to get Craig into trouble, and now I've got myself into trouble instead."

"I'm sure Paul will understand if you tell him about it." Eleanor's voice was matter of fact. "I'll come with you. We can go down to his office tomorrow."

Caro didn't respond to this and Eleanor looked at her and asked, "There's something else, isn't there?"

"Yes. The day before yesterday I went up to London on an errand for Craig. He asked me to go because he said he couldn't trust anyone else. I've often collected things for his shop, and that's what I thought this trip was about, but when I got to Jason's warehouse–"

"Jason?" Eleanor interrupted.

"Sorry. He's an associate of Craig's. A horrid, smarmy little man. I can't stand him."

"And what happened when you got to this warehouse?" Eleanor asked, her eyes alight with interest.

Caro told her about the conversation she'd overheard. "And it sounded as if Craig was involved. Jason sounded scared. He said he'd talk to Craig. When I finally plucked up the courage to let them know I was there, the other man had gone." She thought back to that endless drive back to Poole. "All the way home I kept telling myself Craig wouldn't know anything about it, that it was Jason who was involved with these people, but after what Craig said this evening..."

Eleanor took Caro's hands in a steadying grasp. "Tell me, what did he say?"

"I can't remember exactly. I was in such a panic."

"Yes, you can," Eleanor spoke slowly and firmly. "This could be very important, Caro. Try to remember."

Caro closed her eyes, thought back to Craig's soft, menacing voice. Her eyes flew open.

"Yes, I remember," and she told Eleanor what Craig had said. "What have I got myself into, Eleanor? I've been such an idiot! What am I going to do?"

"There's only one thing you can do, Caro. Go and talk to Paul."

* * *

Alex was not enjoying himself. The band was too loud, the people too noisy, and he longed to be at home with his books and his music. Or sitting in Eleanor's kitchen drinking coffee. Into his mind came a picture of the homely room that was so familiar to him, but the woman his imagination saw there was not his grandmother but Caro. He was exasperated with himself. What was it about the girl? Barely twenty-four hours ago he'd never even met her. And she was trouble. He'd be much better off keeping well out of her way. But it was no good. Right now, he knew he'd much prefer Caro's company to Ashley's. Particularly as Ashley was being impossible this evening.

His relationship with her had been one of mutual physical attraction. He'd thought that neither of them wanted anything more serious, until now. But this evening she was being particularly clingy and had hardly let him out of her sight since they arrived. Each time he'd got up to dance with one of the other women at their table, he'd noticed her watching him, and if she danced with someone else, she kept giving him covert little smiles and waves. When they were sitting down, she kept touching him, giving him an occasional kiss, a touch to the cheek. He was beginning to feel trapped.

But there was no way he could escape. This do was in aid of the local branch of the RNLI and was being sponsored by Devereaux's Wine & Spirit Merchants, and most of the people at their table were valued clients. As their host, he had to stay.

"Good do, Alex," his immediate companion said, a rather large and florid financier with the unlikely name of

Vivian Crump. "Lucky man, you are, lucky man." His words were enunciated rather carefully as he'd put away a large amount of Alex's best wine. "Lovely woman, Ashley. She's certainly all woman, eh? Quite a handful, in more ways than one." He gave a coarse laugh and, nudging Alex in the ribs, then nearly fell off his chair.

"Viv, darling," protested his equally large and loud wife sitting on his other side. "Careful, you silly old fool." She leaned across her husband and grabbed Alex's wrist. "Always overdoes it, my husband, but he certainly knows how to enjoy himself! So, when's the happy day?"

"Which day's that?" Alex gave her a tight little smile and ran a finger under the collar of his dress shirt, wishing even more that he could escape.

"Come on, Alex, don't be coy. The wedding day, dear boy!"

"Ah, that one." He tried to smile again, but it didn't quite come off, and he was actually relieved when soft hands slid down his shoulders and there was a waft of Ashley's expensive perfume.

"Did you miss me?"

"Of course," Alex said, and felt a coward for doing so.

"Then come and dance. You don't mind if I steal this lovely man away, do you?" She gave the Crumps a dazzling smile. "Come on, darling, it's a nice slow one."

He followed her onto the dance floor, for once unaffected by the voluptuous sway of her hips, covered tonight in a thin layer of shimmering peacock blue silk. Her arms came up and she clasped her hands behind his neck, her lips very close to his and her soft hair brushing his cheek.

"Fed up with the Crumps?" she asked.

"Somewhat. They are rather overpowering."

"You're not really enjoying this much, are you, darling?"

"Oh, you know me." Alex tried to shrug it off. "I hate these dos, having to butter up people I hardly know, and usually don't want to be with, just because they're clients. Bores me stiff."

"And what about me?"

"What about you?"

"Do I bore you stiff?" she asked sweetly.

"Don't be silly." He knew he sounded irritated. That definitely wasn't the right response. Her eyes glittered in the half light of the hotel ballroom.

"I'm not being silly, Alex. You have been rather preoccupied tonight? You keep disappearing off into some daydream or other. What's on your mind?"

"Nothing in particular, maybe I'm just tired. I didn't get much sleep last night."

"Ah yes, your Sir Galahad bit." She was smiling sweetly but her tone of voice didn't match. "Could it be your mind is taken up with thoughts of your grandmother's little house guest?"

With a frown, and too quickly, Alex denied it. "Of course not. I hardly know the girl."

What Alex didn't account for was that, when it came to her own interests, Ashley was sharp as a tack. For a moment she was silent. He could feel her body was less relaxed against him, its swaying less pronounced. Her voice casual, she asked, "Have you met Craig Paxton?"

Alex frowned as he looked down at her, wondering what she was up to. "No, I haven't."

"I didn't think so, not really your type. Absolutely charming, but as crooked as they come."

"What makes you say that?" He tried to sound unconcerned.

"Partly intuition, partly rumours." Soft fingers stroked the back of his neck. "Surprising really that that rather scruffy girl should be going around with him. I'd have thought he was way out of her league."

"She was only scruffy because she didn't have a change of clothes," Alex said defensively. "She actually runs her own design business."

Ashley smiled inside. He'd walked straight into that one. "Maybe. Perhaps the wide-eyed innocent look is a facade. I wouldn't be surprised. Very useful to Craig if it is, of course."

Alex couldn't resist asking, "In what way?"

"We-ell." Her voice was deceptively bland. "He's a dealer with a pretty dubious reputation, but if he can push this innocent looking little madam up front, that could lull people into a false sense of security. They'd make a pretty unbeatable team, his charm and shrewdness and her wide-eyed plausibility."

Alex just stopped himself from jumping to Caro's defence again, but there was a sharp edge to his voice when he spoke. "You seem to have it all worked out. I didn't realise you knew him so well."

"I don't, but Karl does, that's how I met Craig and his girlfriend in the first place. He's just the sort that my ghastly husband would take to. Karl told me once that Craig's very good at – how did he put it? Oh yes, acquiring things from under the noses of the authorities." She gave her deep throated laugh. "Neat way to describe it, I thought."

* * *

For the rest of the evening Alex was even more preoccupied, which confirmed Ashley's worst suspicions. Her mind raced. She was honest enough to admit that she didn't actually love him, but love was a highly overrated commodity as far as she was concerned. She did, however, find him extremely attractive, and he was rich enough to make her very comfortable. She'd do anything that needed to be done in order to keep him.

After the dance, when they were in the car, she slipped her hand across and softly stroked his thigh.

"Why don't I come back to La Cotte, darling?" she asked softly. "Cheer you up after your boring evening."

Past experience told her that Alex would find this invitation hard to resist, but this time, it didn't work. To her dismay, he said, "Not tonight. I'm shattered, and I've got to be up at crack of dawn tomorrow."

"I wouldn't mind that." She wasn't going to give up that easily. "I could help with whatever you've got to do." Still the fingers travelled softly up and down.

Alex laughed with real amusement. "I don't think stripping down *Pauillac's* engine is quite your scene, is it?"

"Maybe not, but I could bring you coffee, or beer and sandwiches. You know my crab baguettes are to die for."

"It's a lovely idea, but no." His voice was firm. "Not tonight. I wouldn't be any use to you. It's not your fault, I'm just too tired."

Ashley gave up her attempts to arouse him and placed her hand, clenched tight, in her lap. "My name might as well be Josephine," she said sulkily, turning to gaze out at the dark countryside beyond the car window.

Alex reached across and gave her leg a pat, which did nothing to mollify her. "Another time, love," he said, apparently unaware of the seething resentment his rejection had caused.

"Too preoccupied with thoughts of Eleanor's prissy little guest, I suppose," she snapped.

"Don't be ridiculous." Alex's voice was far too sharp for comfort.

"Well, it sticks out a mile that you fancy her." She spat out, allowing her jealousy to get the better of good judgement. "Rescuing her from her own stupidity and taking her to your precious grandmother. Then arriving on Eleanor's doorstep first thing this morning to check up on her and toddling off to show her your precious house. Eleanor approves of her, doesn't she? That was pretty obvious, which is more than she does of me. I hope she doesn't feel too let down when she realises she's got a cuckoo in the nest."

"Ashley, this is a pointless conversation," Alex said wearily. "Shall we drop the subject?"

"By all means." She realised she'd gone too far and could have kicked herself. Sitting in silence for the rest of the drive, she desperately tried to think of some way to regain lost ground. When Alex drew up in front of her house and switched off the engine, she turned to him, her head on one side and a wide-eyed look of contrition on her face.

"I know I'm being silly. It's just that I do rather care about you, darling, and that makes me a bit jealous sometimes. Am I forgiven?" Once again, she ran her fingers softly up and down his thigh.

He was looking at her but in the half-light she couldn't see the expression in his eyes. "You're forgiven." Neither was it any easier to tell what he was thinking from his voice.

Ashley seethed with anger and frustration. Angry with herself for not being more careful, but mostly with Caro for causing the problems in the first place. She leant forward and pressed her body against Alex's, began kissing his neck, nuzzling his ear. In the darkness he turned to her and they kissed. Ashley's hands began a progress up his thigh, but he caught hold of her fingers.

"I can't, love, not tonight. Another time."

She gave up. She knew when she was beaten. "Maybe," she said, "maybe not." And opened the car door.

"Thank you for this evening," said Alex quickly. "It would have been very boring without you. I'll see you at the office on Monday."

It was a dismissal. Ashley was so angry she could hardly contain herself. But showing her anger had already backfired. She had little choice but to get out of the car and stand watching as he drove away.

She stamped into the house and slammed the front door behind her, went into the kitchen and threw her wrap and bag onto the kitchen table. They flew across it and fell down the other side, and her mobile phone spilled out onto the tiled floor. "Bugger," she said, and went around to pick it up and realised she had a text.

> *Thanks for the phone call. I did as you suggested and got the first flight over. Can we talk? I need some local info. I'm on the Sally Anne. Could we meet up tomorrow? I'd be most grateful, Craig.*

With a little smile of satisfaction, she slipped the phone back into her bag and was just about to go upstairs when she changed her mind. Quickly she took out her mobile and tapped in a text in response.

CHAPTER 8

Eleanor had insisted they should have a quiet day on Sunday. "I usually go to the ten o'clock service at the town church. Do you want to come?"

Caro had shaken her head apologetically, but Eleanor waved an airy hand. "No problem. It's a habit with me, and I do love the singing. You have a lie-in. I'll see you when I get back."

But Caro woke with the birds and couldn't get back to sleep. She got up and decided to spend some time making notes of what she needed to do to reorganise the various jobs she had on the go, and phoning her long-suffering PA at home to give her instructions.

Apart from being her assistant, Alison Woodfield was a close friend and she wanted to know every detail of the events leading up to Caro's sudden departure. How had she ended up in Guernsey? Where was she staying? Why hadn't she come straight back? But Caro wasn't ready to talk quite yet. She played down Alex's rescue and the events of the day before, made no mention of border force men and requests not to leave the island, and managed to avoid too many searching questions. Once Alison's curiosity had been partially satisfied, and she'd said enough 'I told you sos' about Craig – she'd never been a great fan of his – she asked again, "But why are you staying in Guernsey?"

"Because there's this chap who wants me to do a job on his house," Caro said in an unguarded fashion, and something in her voice must have given her away.

"Aha." Alison pounced. "And I suppose he's young, good-looking, well off!"

"Course he is, a positive Ross Poldark," Caro said, trying to joke her way out of a corner. "He's actually the man who came to my rescue when the *Sally Anne* ran out of fuel."

"Caro! Romantic or what? Tell me, tell me!"

"No, not now. Anyway, he may be fanciable–"

"So, you admit it–"

"–but he's also bloody moody, and he has a very attractive girlfriend. He's made it pretty obvious he doesn't like me, probably thinks I'm an impulsive idiot with no sense of responsibility. It's Eleanor's idea that I should do the job, she's his grandmother. She's such a dear, and anyway his house is an absolute gem. I can't wait to get my hands on it. I don't think I'm going to be able to resist if he decides he wants me to do the job."

"Eleanor's the one you're staying with?" Alison asked casually.

Caro wasn't deceived.

"Aren't you the clever one! Yes, but enough of that. Listen, I've jotted down some notes about the Parker's job, and that new one for Wilkes & Co, have you got a pad?"

Quickly she gave her instructions. "Have you got all that?"

"Yup. Anything else?"

"Well, yes, I want you to do me a favour."

"Another one?" Alison protested.

Caro laughed. "Go on. Pretty please. I promise I'll tell you the whole story soon, with all the gory details, and I'll bring you some duty frees when I come home, booze, perfume, you name it."

"Okay, okay, but it's going to have to be a mega bottle of my favourite perfume at the very least."

"It's a deal," Caro told her.

"Right, so what do you want me to do?"

"Could you go to the flat and pack up some clothes for me? Just a few."

There was a snort from the other end of the line. "Is that all? Why didn't you say? Do you want the black lace underwear, and which sexy nightie should I include?"

"Don't be an idiot, I've got nothing to wear except some stuff I bought today," Caro said. "Just bung in a few pairs of jeans, jumpers, you'll know what to put in. And the other thing, more important really, is I need as many of the fabric books and furniture catalogues as you can fit in, and my laptop, that's by my bed I think."

"I could pack a case and bung it on the ferry for you."

"I hadn't thought of that, but won't that make too much work for you?"

"I'll get it couriered."

"You are an absolute gem. Thank you so much."

"You're a pest and a pain, but I'll do it." Alison's tone of voice changed suddenly. "And Caro, watch out for yourself."

"What do you mean?"

"Vis-à-vis Craig, I mean."

"Of course, I will," Caro said, with far more confidence than she felt. "Don't worry. And you're a dear."

"An idiot more like."

Caro laughed. "Never that. I'll phone in a couple of days. Let me know if there are any problems before I do. Bye now."

Caro settled down to some serious thought about Alex's house. She needed the distraction. Gradually she became engrossed in the notes and sketches she was making and didn't come back down to earth until she heard a knock at the front door. Thoughts of work receded immediately and, as she went down the stairs, her mind was taken over by worries about who it might be. It could be Paul Le Page, it being a Sunday wouldn't deter him, or maybe it was Craig, which would be worse.

It was Craig, and he was in a towering rage.

"Is she in?" he asked as he pushed into the house and slammed the door behind him.

"Who?"

"The old bat."

"If you mean Eleanor," Caro said, trying hard to keep calm, "no, she's at church." Then she called herself all kinds of a fool. How stupid to let him know she was alone.

He gave a derisive snort. "Might have known. Just as well. We have to talk, and I don't want her waltzing in and interfering."

Fear churned in Caro's stomach. She glanced at the grandfather clock which stood in the corner of the hall. Nearly eleven, surely Eleanor wouldn't be long now?

"She'll be back any minute," Caro said quickly.

"In that case I'll be brief," Craig snapped, glaring at her. "Thanks to you, my dear, I've just had an extremely unpleasant interview with a bloody officious little border force operative."

"Oh."

"Is that all you have to say? Oh? Do you realise what this could mean?"

"But they have to do their job, Craig," Caro said weakly, unable to think of anything else to say.

"They have to do their job, Craig," he mimicked. "For fuck's sake, woman, have you no idea how–?" He grabbed her by the arm and pulled her towards him. "No, I don't suppose you have, naive idiot that you are. What have you told them?"

"What do you mean? What could I have told them?"

"God knows! That's what worries me."

He stood glaring down at her and Caro waited. Afraid that he'd be able to read her mind. She tried not to think about her interview with Paul Le Page, and frantically pushed thoughts of those photographs out of her head.

"I've been asked," Craig spat out, "very politely, mark you, not to leave the island for a couple of days. You know, one of those requests that's couched in social terms, but you know refusing would be a bad idea? He made it abundantly clear that things would be taken further if I argued. Of course, I had to agree to stay."

Caro rallied a little. "You said you were going to anyway, until I promised to go back with you."

Craig didn't comment but, to Caro's relief, let go of her arm and started to pace up and down the hall. His first flush of anger seemed to be subsiding. "But I'm not hanging around long," he told her. "And you, my dear Caro, are going to give me–"

But Caro never found out what she was going to give him. At that moment the front door opened, and Eleanor stepped across the threshold. Caro felt a wave of relief.

"Ah, Mr Paxton, good morning to you." Eleanor's smile was a masterpiece of cool contempt. "Lovely morning, isn't it?"

"Lovely," said Craig, through tight lips. "I'm sorry to dash off just as you return," he went on. "But needs must."

He turned to Caro and muttered under his breath, "Keep quiet, do you understand?" And all she could do was nod.

Directly he had left, Eleanor closed the door firmly behind him, glanced at Caro and said, quite unexpectedly, "What we need is a good Sunday lunch, cooked and served by someone else. Come on. I feel like a party, even if it is just the two of us."

Doing her best to push Craig to the back of her mind, to be jostled around with all the other unresolved problems, Caro smiled and agreed.

"There's a lovely place up on the cliffs, in St Martins," Eleanor went on. "You can see the harbour and part of the town from their terrace, and there's a glorious view of the other islands as well." She looked at her watch. "Half past eleven. I'll give them a ring and book a table. Okay?"

Caro smiled at her. "Thank you so much." And it wasn't the lunch she was talking about.

"Nonsense, my dear," said Eleanor with complete understanding. "Now, I must go and take off these churchy clothes." Caro watched Eleanor's retreating back as she went upstairs and wondered how she'd ever managed without her.

* * *

They thoroughly enjoyed their lunch. Eleanor was right, the view was truly magnificent, and after lunch they drove across the island, parked the car at a beach called Vazon and went for a long walk beside the sea. Marching down across the smooth sand were the remains of tall wooden groynes, like sentinels. Eleanor said they were there to protect the beach from erosion.

"Alex climbed one of them when he was about eight years old," she said with a fond smile, "then slithered down and broke his arm, silly boy."

The breeze had stiffened and was whipping up white caps on the waves now. Wind surfers sped across the water, bright triangles of colour against the background of blue-green water, and nearer at hand were some wet-suited surfers. Caro even noticed a couple of swimmers brave enough to go in without suits.

"That must be pretty chilly," she remarked to Eleanor, as she wrapped her arms around herself to keep out the cold wind.

"They're probably used to it. Some people swim all year round, would you believe."

Caro gave an involuntary shiver. "I need at least seventeen degrees before I venture in."

"Me too. That's not the kind of excitement I relish one little bit."

"What is?"

"My kind of excitement?" Eleanor smiled, staring out to sea with her eyes narrowed. "Other sorts of risks. Alex says I'm not really happy unless I'm breaking the rules."

"Your rules or other people's?"

"I have to admit, mainly other people's laws I have no time for. At my age life's too short to be bound by decrees and dictates laid down by bureaucrats with no imagination."

Caro laughed. "You're a very unusual person," she said.

"Why thank you, my dear, that is a very nice compliment." Eleanor glanced at her and abruptly changed the subject. "Are you going to do Alex's house?"

Caro had been dreading this question and didn't answer immediately. Alex and La Cotte had not been far from her thoughts all day, but she'd tried to push them to the back of her mind. Now Eleanor was waiting for an answer.

"I'd like to."

"You don't sound too sure."

"It's– well, it's Alex," Caro said, embarrassed and apologetic. "I know you explained about his problems, but I do get the impression he doesn't like me much. It always makes a job more difficult if you don't get on with the client. But– I'm sorry, I shouldn't be talking to you like this, not about Alex anyway."

"Oh, don't worry about that. I know my grandson, warts and all." She smiled at Caro, touched her arm gently. "I'd be most grateful if you would take the job. I think it would be good for him, to see how lovely that house could look, and then maybe he won't want to sell it after all."

Caro hadn't thought of it like that. "If he really wants me to, I'll do it. I've asked the friend who works for me to send over some fabric books and other stuff. She's going to put it all on the ferry."

"Oh good," Eleanor said, with great satisfaction. "Can I tell him so? He'll be phoning later. He usually does on Sunday evening."

"Please, do. It'll be easier for him to tell you rather than me if he thinks the idea stinks."

"True enough," said Eleanor, in her forthright way, "but if he says anything of the kind, I shall do my best to persuade him otherwise!"

But as it happened Alex didn't phone that evening and the question of the job on La Cotte remained unresolved.

CHAPTER 9

Even before Caro was fully awake on Monday morning, she was aware of a feeling of sickening apprehension. This morning she had an appointment with Paul Le Page. Ten o'clock, he'd said. What she wouldn't give to be able to get out of it. But Eleanor was right, she really had no choice. With a leaden feeling of impending disaster, she got up and dressed. She decided on new jeans and a smart jacket. The more business-like I look the better, she told herself as she brushed her hair, trying to force the dark curls to behave. But they never did.

At Eleanor's suggestion, Caro had phoned Paul Le Page the day before to make the appointment. "Once that's done you can forget about it for a bit," she'd said, but of course Caro had done no such thing.

She'd managed to persuade Eleanor she'd be fine on her own and, having been given precise instructions on how to find Paul's office, head held high, she set off to walk the short distance down the hill into the centre of St Peter Port, and then on to what she'd been told was the White Rock Pier.

Caro had tried to rehearse what she would say, but nothing sounded quite right. 'I lied to you' sounded disastrous. 'I think my boyfriend's a crook' made her sound like the worse kind of tattle tale. 'I had no idea what Craig was doing' – well, that just made her sound stupid. By the time she was ushered into his office by his middle-aged, grey-haired secretary, she was no nearer deciding how to approach him, and her determination to keep up a confident front had evaporated.

"Good morning, Miss Bennett, do sit down." Paul indicated a chair opposite his desk. "I'm very glad you've decided to come and see me." There was little of the sharpness of Saturday. He smiled at her, asked if she'd like a coffee. In spite of herself she relaxed a little and accepted his offer.

"Black, no sugar please." At least her voice sounded more or less normal.

He went to the door and opened it, said, "Muriel? Could you bring us coffee please, both black, no sugar. Thanks." He came back to his desk and sat down again, looked across at Caro. "Do you mind if I record our conversation? At the moment this is informal, which is why it's just me, but I would like a record of what you say."

"I suppose – okay." What else could she say?

He fiddled around with the recording equipment, said who was present and what day and time it was, then turned back to Caro. "Now, what have you to tell me? You said you'd remembered something else."

Caro took a deep breath. This was it. There was no point in putting things off. "You know those photographs you showed me, of the jewellery? Well, it's not that I've remembered something, it's that I wasn't entirely honest with you in the first place. I did recognise one of the pieces."

One eyebrow crept up, but all he said was, "Which one?"

"The buckle." Its description was imprinted on her mind. "The one shaped like two interlinked snakes. I remembered seeing it before."

"Ah yes. Persian, fourteenth century, our experts tell us. And where did you see it?" His voice was quiet, casual.

In spite of everything, Caro felt like a traitor. She took a deep breath. "It was one evening in Craig's office, Craig Paxton. I walked in and it was on his desk, he was looking at it." She lifted her hands in a gesture, half of surrender, half of apology. "I'm sorry, I never should have let you think I didn't recognise it, but…" She hesitated. "Craig's been very good to me in his own way and I really was reluctant to get him into trouble. But I've given it a lot of thought since Saturday, and I've talked to Eleanor, and she said, what with one thing and another – I won't bore you with the details – she didn't think I owed him anything really. So, we decided I should come and see you. I'm sorry, I'm waffling."

"Not at all." At that moment they were interrupted by his secretary with the coffee. She gave Caro a sharp look as she placed the cup in front of her, her eyes behind her thick glasses speculative. Caro hardly noticed.

Once the woman had gone, she went on to tell Paul about her relationship with Craig and their respective jobs. After a while she came to a halt and Paul sat forward in his chair. "Now let me get this straight." He took her through her story several times, picking through every detail and going back over what she'd told him. At last he said, "Good. That's very useful." He put his hands on the arms of his chair as if ready to rise but sank back into his seat when Caro spoke again.

"There's something else. I don't know whether it's relevant, but I think you ought to know." Quickly she explained about her trip to London on Thursday and the conversation she'd overheard at Jason's warehouse. Paul's eyes widened as she spoke, but he showed no other sign of increased interest.

"Of course," Caro said, trying to be as fair as possible, "there's always a possibility that Craig doesn't know about Jason's activities. Maybe they're just using him, Jason and this other man. Oh well, I suppose not," she added, responding to the sceptical look on Paul's face.

"Eleanor was right, you really had no choice but to come to me with this information." He turned to the computer on his desk. "The Frenchman they mentioned, you say his name was Jean Peron?"

"Yes, I'm sure that was it."

He tapped away at the keyboard for a moment, then nodded in satisfaction, but said nothing as he turned back to Caro. "And did they mention any other names?"

"No – yes, wait a minute, they did."

He waited patiently while Caro, a deep frown between her eyes, tried to remember. But in the end, she shook her head. "No, it's no good. I'm sure they mentioned the name of this boss person, but I'm sorry, it's gone."

"Never mind. It might come back to you." If he was disappointed, he didn't show it. "Now, Miss Bennett, I hope you don't mind me giving you a little friendly advice."

"It depends on what it is."

"It might not be very easy, but it is very important, and it might be safer for you."

She wondered what on earth he was going to say.

"I think it would be a very good idea if Craig Paxton believes your relationship is unchanged, at least that you'll be willing, in due course, to go back with him to Poole. It'd be much better for you if he believes he's been forgiven for his little lapse."

Caro's heart sank. "Little lapse?" she said, and screwed up her face in distaste, making her sentiments all too obvious.

Paul leant forward and clasped his hands on the desk. His eyes didn't waver from her face. "I realise it'll be difficult for you but, believe me, it will be safer. The thing is, if Mr Paxton is involved in illegal trafficking of goods, the people he's involved with could be very dangerous. Believe me, they're not the kind of crowd you'd want to have anything to do with if you could avoid it. And if they have so much as a whisper of a suspicion that someone's informed on them–" He snapped his fingers in all too expressive a gesture.

Caro felt coldly sick. "Surely they wouldn't–" She couldn't bring herself to put her thoughts into words.

"Last week," Paul said, "the French coastguard fished a body out of the sea off St Malo. It was identified as the owner of a small antique shop in Dinan. He was honest enough, but the French authorities knew he'd had dealings with a local syndicate, one they'd been watching. They persuaded him to talk. He told them about some eighteenth-century porcelain someone had bought from him. It'd been taken to the police by the new owners who'd become suspicious, thought it might have been stolen. He was, in the end, very generous with information about the man he'd bought it from, and two days later he was dead. I'm sorry to sound so melodramatic, but these are the people we could be dealing with. You can understand why I want you to be careful."

"Yes," said Caro through a dry throat.

"I'm very sorry to sound so personal, but does Mr Paxton think he still has a chance with you?"

"I did tell him I wanted nothing more to do with him," Caro told him. "But he said that I was just as involved as him and that we were useful to each other. I've been trying to work out exactly what he meant. Maybe it was just that I'm not someone who's questioning him all the time. But he implied that if he went down, he'd take me with him. Oh God! I feel such a gullible fool."

"You're far from unique in preferring to believe the best of people."

"I suppose so," said Caro miserably. "Eleanor said something similar."

"A wise woman, Eleanor Devereaux." Paul looked at her, not entirely without sympathy. "But doesn't it make you angry that he might have involved you in illegal activities without your being aware? Surely that's a good enough reason to help us, isn't it?"

She looked up, not knowing whether she was being manipulated or whether he was sincere. "I suppose it is." She ran her fingers through her curls, then came to a decision. "I'll do my best," she said, hugging her arms round her body.

"Thank you, Caro." She hardly noticed his use of her first name. "As I say, I think it would be best to keep Paxton on side for now, and your help would be invaluable, and perhaps it would be best if we kept this arrangement just between you and me for now?"

"You mean say nothing to Eleanor?"

"Well, if that's possible, nor to Alex." He smiled suddenly. "I do realise keeping things from them might be difficult. I remember how Eleanor used to winkle confessions out of Alex and me when we were boys."

But Caro was too perturbed by what she'd heard to react to this attempt to lighten the atmosphere.

His smile faded and he became formal once more. "Thank you very much for coming to see me. Eleanor was right. You have a very good friend there."

"I know," said Caro, "she is such a dear. I feel as if I've known her forever."

He walked with her to the door. "And I gather you might be doing some work on Alex's house. Some undertaking, that. I seem to remember it's in a bit of a mess."

This did take her mind from her worries, just a little. "It is, but it's got such potential, and I've known worse. I can't wait to get started." She paused, her enthusiasm dying. "That's providing he agrees to let me do it."

"It's not definite then?"

"Not yet. Eleanor was hoping he'd phone last night, but he didn't."

"Don't you worry. He'll agree."

Caro wondered how he could be so sure.

She was halfway across the outer office when it came to her. Turning sharply, she said to Paul's secretary, "I've remembered something else I need to tell Mr Le Page. Can I go straight in?"

The woman's bright eyes shone with ill-concealed curiosity, but all she said was, "I'm sure that will be fine." She opened the door for Caro.

"Mr Le Page, Paul, I've remembered that name," she said as she stood by the door. "It was Jones. He was the one the other man called 'the boss'."

Paul had looked up sharply as she came in but now his face closed, hiding his thoughts. "Right. Thanks for telling me."

But just for a moment, before the shutters had come down, she was sure she'd detected a gleam of satisfaction in his eyes.

Caro walked back up the pier, breathing in the harbour and sea smells she loved, but finding very little comfort in them. One of the regular ferries from the mainland had just arrived, disgorging cars, trucks and foot passengers, and nearer to town she passed a much smaller craft, the one to Herm, slowly filling up with people. She walked on past the tall granite obelisk of the Liberation Monument, built to commemorate the fiftieth anniversary of the liberation of Guernsey from occupation, and crossed the road, oblivious to all the activity, completely taken up by the turmoil in her mind. It was as she began to walk on towards the High Street that she felt her arm firmly grasped and jumped out of her skin at the touch.

"Sorry," said Alex. "I didn't mean to make you jump. What are you doing in town?"

"I've just been to see..." She remembered Paul's request that she should keep their meeting to herself, and added hastily, "I was just walking, having a look around, that's all."

He frowned. She could tell he didn't believe her, but there was little she could do about that.

"Visiting Craig Paxton, no doubt?" Alex said, his voice tinged with scorn.

"No, as a matter of fact I wasn't, but would it be any of your business if I was?"

"No, of course not. Feel free to see whoever you want. Just make sure Eleanor doesn't get involved, that's all."

Caro had had a difficult morning. The guilt she had felt from the first had now been joined by fear, and a feeling that she was completely out of her depth. And now, on top of everything else, here was this arrogant pain in the neck suggesting she'd be careless of Eleanor's feelings. It was the last straw.

"You really are bloody impossible! Why don't you just leave me alone?" She turned sharply and began to walk away, but to her annoyance he fell in beside her. For a while they walked in silence, the atmosphere encircling them thick with resentment, each one unwilling to give an inch. They were halfway back to Villette House when Alex relented.

"Look, I'm sorry," he said.

Caro had to admit he did sound apologetic.

"Let's stop sparring, shall we?"

"That's okay by me." Her tone didn't match the words, but what he said next had her stopping in her tracks.

"I meant to phone you last night and ask you to take on the job at La Cotte?"

Caro frowned up at him. "Are you sure?"

"Yes," he said, not meeting her eyes. "I want you to do it, and so does Eleanor."

"But I haven't even given you a quote yet."

"Never mind, I'm sure it'll be reasonable."

She shrugged, trying to control her excitement at the thought. She was determined not to sound too enthusiastic. "If you're absolutely sure, of course I will. When do you want me to start? We'll have to go through the details, work out exactly what you want and whether it's possible. And I'll have to provide you with that quote." She couldn't resist adding, "Just in case you think my prices are as extortionate as those others you were given."

His lips twitched and he almost smiled. "Fine, but I'm sure we can come to some amicable agreement."

Caro nearly asked what gave him that idea, but she managed to bite her tongue. They walked on in silence until she prepared to turn off up the hill to Eleanor's.

"So," she said, not quite sure how to go on, "are you coming to your grandmother's?"

"No, I must get back to the office." Alex, changeable as ever, was back to his brusque and frowning self. "I'll pick you up this evening to go to the house. Be ready at eight. See you later." And he strode off, leaving Caro seething, once again, at his assumption that she was at his beck and call.

* * *

A few hundred yards away from where Alex and Caro parted, just the other side of the shops and across the esplanade, Craig had a visitor on the *Sally Anne*.

"Hallo-o?" called a husky voice. "Anyone at ho-ome?"

Craig, who'd started on an early gin and tonic, put his glass down and frowned as he went up on deck. Ashley was leaning down to look at him, her hair falling forward in a glossy wave and her shirt falling open to reveal a generous cleavage.

"Hi! Can I come on board?"

"By all means." Craig's frown dissolved and a broad smile took its place as he put out a hand to help her jump onto the deck. "I wasn't expecting you so early. Can I offer you one of these?" He held up his glass.

"If that's gin and tonic, you certainly can. Not too heavy on the tonic, please. I feel in need of a pick-me-up." She followed him down to the cabin.

Craig poured her a stiff double. "Sit down, do. Let's get comfortable."

He watched as she manoeuvred herself gracefully onto the bench seat. She leant back on the cushions and, allowing his eyes to roam appreciatively over her, Craig sat down opposite. "What a pleasure it is to see you again," he said. "How long has it been?"

"About six months, I think. It was just after we met that I got rid of my pain of a husband."

"No connection I hope – or do I?"

Her full lips opened in a smile, but she made no comment.

"Now," said Craig, after a slight pause, "you said that you wanted to talk, so fire away."

His attitude now was challenging. Warily they studied each other like sleek cats circling, not entirely sure whether they'd be allies. Craig was fully aware this woman could be useful to him, and a more intimate relationship was always worth exploring. Ashley's eyes were slightly narrowed, the corners of her lips still lifted in a smile. She leant forward and clasped her hands under her chin. She's come to a decision, he thought.

"I need your help," she said.

"Oh?" was his only comment.

"And I gather, from the message you left for me, that you need mine, so perhaps we can do each other a bit of good." She took a sip of her drink then slowly licked her lips with the tip of her tongue. Craig's eyes widened. The message coming across was clear.

"How can I put this?" Ashley went on. "Your little girlfriend is causing me a few problems at the moment."

He waited silently for her to go on.

"You know she's staying with Eleanor Devereaux?"

Craig nodded.

"Well, Eleanor's grandson and I have been seeing each other for a while now, but since he rescued Caro in that dramatic fashion, Alex has been a shade preoccupied. I'm sure it's some misguided knight errantry, but I'd be very grateful if you could persuade her to go home."

"And you think I'll be able to do that?"

"I do, unless of course there are things going on between you two that I don't know about?" She raised one delicately drawn eyebrow. "Obviously I wouldn't expect something for nothing. I'd make it worth your while."

"And how would you do that?" He let his hand rest briefly on hers, but she leant back, sliding her fingers away.

"You told me you wanted some local information. What sort of information?"

"Yes, I did, didn't I?" Craig wondered how much to reveal. "You may remember I'm in the antiques business, and I also deal in fine arts. Guernsey, and Jersey for that matter, have quite a large population, per capita, of the kind of wealthy collectors I like to cultivate, those that appreciate the occasional rare and interesting find. I was wondering if you could help me search out the right kind of customer. With your local knowledge, and that of your ex-husband." He paused. "You are on speaking terms, the two of you, I suppose?"

"When it comes to money, yes."

"Well, perhaps you could mention that we've spoken?"

"Of course."

"You could both be very useful to me." He was watching her carefully. "And, naturally, I'd make it worth your while."

By the time Ashley left they were much closer friends, delighted with each other and their arrangements. Craig stood on the deck of the *Sally Anne* as she swayed elegantly along the pontoon and up onto the pier. He lifted a hand in farewell as she turned to wave to him.

* * *

Ashley's arrival on the *Sally Anne* had not gone unobserved. Four floors up, in the crowded stockroom of a building overlooking the marina, stood a young man in jeans and a navy guernsey. He was gazing out of a window through extremely strong binoculars. His companion heard him grunt in satisfaction.

"Developments, I think. Come and have a look."

The other man approached the window, moved a camera on its tripod so that it was better positioned and trained it on the same spot as the binoculars.

"Interesting," he muttered as he took one photo, then another, then another.

"Do you recognise her?" the man in the guernsey asked.

"Yup. That's Ashley Guilbert. Remember we were watching her old man for a while, but it never came to anything."

"Should we tell the boss?"

"I think so. He said anything, however ordinary."

"Okay." He picked up a mobile and dialled. "Paul, I think we've got something. Do you want to come and have a look?"

CHAPTER 10

By mid-afternoon on Monday Craig was feeling deeply frustrated. He'd tried phoning Caro's mobile several times, but she hadn't picked up. He'd texted her and got no response. Then he'd resorted to phoning the landline at Villette House and, on each occasion, Eleanor had answered.

Her response to his first call had been, "I'm so sorry, Mr Paxton, Caro's just popped out. I'll tell her you called." And next it had been, "I'm afraid she's not back yet. You are having bad luck. Can I give her a message?" But there'd been no call from Caro.

In spite of what Caro had said on Sunday, he didn't really believe it was over between them. She'd come around, she always did. He shouldn't have been so careless about Vanessa. She wasn't the first, but maybe it was because Caro knew her that she was so angry. He was sure he could persuade her to forgive and forget. He'd be the one to finish with her, not the other way around, that was for sure.

In the end he decided to drop in unannounced. If I just turn up on the doorstep, he thought, like I did yesterday. She can wheel out the old bat to put me off, but I'm sure I can deal with that. This time she'll find it won't be so easy to get rid of me, and she's far too dangerous to be left to her own devices. Fifteen minutes later he was lifting the brass lion's head knocker on Eleanor's front door.

When she opened it, he gave her his most charming smile. "Good afternoon, Mrs Devereaux. I've come to see Caro. Does she happen to be in now?"

Before Eleanor had the chance to say anything, Caro herself came down the stairs. Eleanor stood aside reluctantly as Craig, smiling and triumphant, strode into the hall.

* * *

Caro knew it was inevitable that Craig would turn up at some time on Monday, and now he was here a small part of her was relieved because the unpleasant anticipation was over.

"I wonder if I could be awfully rude," Craig was saying silkily to Eleanor, "and ask for a private word with Caro? Do you mind?"

"That's entirely up to her," Eleanor said smoothly. "Caro?"

"I suppose so, can we go in the sitting room?"

"Please do," Eleanor said and, smiling at Caro, she added, "I'll be in the kitchen if you need me." Her meaning was clear, she made no effort to hide it.

Craig marched into the sitting room and Caro followed him. Directly the door was closed he turned on her. "Where the hell were you this morning?" he snapped.

Caro felt a cold wave of panic. Surely he couldn't know she'd been to see Paul Le Page? She sat down slowly on the arm of the sofa, playing for time.

"What do you mean?" she asked. "When this morning?"

"You didn't pick up when I phoned, and you didn't return my texts. I even phoned the landline here, but your hostess" – he made the word sound like an insult – "just made excuses. Did she tell you? Were you here? Was she just stalling me?"

A wave of relief replaced the panic. "I was out for a bit, and then I was working." At least it was partially true, just the wrong day. "Perhaps she thought I didn't want to be disturbed."

"Working? Come off it, Caro."

"No, I mean it. I was making notes about current work to pass on to Alison." She warmed to her theme. "And doing some rough plans for Alex's house. I–"

But he let her get no further. Grabbing her arm, he pulled her up to face him. "What do you mean, Alex's house? I thought we'd agreed that you weren't going to do that job."

"No, Craig, we didn't agree," Caro tried to sound as calm as she could. "You said I wouldn't be doing it. I didn't say anything of the sort."

"What are you playing at?" His fingers bit into her arm.

With an effort she spoke quietly and looked him straight in the eye. "I'm not playing at anything, and please let go of my arm, you're hurting me."

For a moment he gazed back, scowling, then suddenly let her go, pushing her from him so that she stumbled a little. Caro went to stand behind a large, protective armchair. It was easier to cope with her fear if there was some distance, however small, between them.

"I don't see why I shouldn't take that job," she said urgently. "It's an absolute gem, and if people hear about it, I may get more jobs here. Eleanor says there are quite a few people she can think of who'd be interested. This is a wealthy community, Craig, and there are bound to be plenty of potential clients." She knew this would appeal to him. Money always did.

But all he said was, "And what about his girlfriend?"

"Whose?"

"Don't be obtuse, Caro. Alex Devereaux's. I shouldn't imagine Ashley will be all that pleased to have you in cahoots with her man, pouring over fabrics and colour charts, discussing all the intimate little details."

"I can't refuse a job just because my client's male and got a girlfriend," Caro snapped. She was finding Paul's request for her to be nice to Craig, and her own need to keep up a show of compliance, difficult to maintain. She took a deep breath, telling herself she must make more effort. "Come on, Craig, let's not quarrel. I'll be back in Poole soon enough. Let's face it, I can't afford to stay away too long."

The seconds ticked by while Craig stood silently studying her face. His eyes narrowed as his fingers tapped a tattoo on the mantelpiece. At last he spoke. "Okay, but I'm going to hang around for a few days just to make sure everything's alright."

Caro didn't point out that, the day before, he'd told her he had no choice but to do so. No point in antagonising him further.

He walked across the room until he was standing beside her, put a hand up and grasped her chin in hard fingers. His voice was quiet, but all the more menacing for that. "And, Caro, don't try and get the better of me. You won't succeed. I'm watching you, my sweet, and if I suspect that you might be considering dropping me in it, I shall have no qualms at all about taking you down with me. Is that understood?"

"Yes," her voice came out in a whisper.

"Remember your father?"

She froze, hardly able to breathe.

"Well," Craig went on, his voice still quietly menacing, "the same could happen to you, couldn't it?"

The words hung in the air like a physical presence. Caro felt sick. If at that moment Eleanor hadn't come in, she dreaded to think what might have happened. But suddenly the door swung back, smacking into the wall with a crack, and Eleanor swept into the room carrying a tray of drinks.

Giving the two of them a dazzling smile, she said, "Here we are, who's for a drink? I usually make myself wait until six o'clock, but it's nearly that now, so what can I get you?"

Craig stepped back abruptly, releasing Caro, who stood silent, unable to collect her wits enough to answer. He recovered more quickly.

"It's very kind of you, Mrs Devereaux, but I must dash. A dinner appointment with a business associate who happens to be in Guernsey. William Courtney, Caro, do you remember him?"

She managed to nod.

"I'll see you tomorrow, my darling, and remember what I said." Deliberately he bent and kissed her on the lips, then nodded and smiled at Eleanor, the picture of politeness. "Don't let me disturb you, I'll see myself out."

When he'd gone Eleanor glanced at Caro and, without a word, poured her a large glass of wine and handed it over. Caro drank half of it in one gulp, then looked up at her new friend across the glass and gave her a shaky smile.

"You seem to spend a lot of your time pressing restorative drinks into my hand."

But Eleanor didn't reply directly. Her smile had faded and been replaced by an expression of tight-lipped anger. "That is one of the most unpleasant young men I've ever had the misfortune to meet!" Every word was delivered like a bullet. "I do hope you don't mind my saying so, I know he's meant a lot to you in the past, but I can safely say I don't think I'll be able to maintain this polite facade if he comes here again. I really don't. I think I'll just thump him!"

Caro gave a spurt of slightly hysterical laughter. "Eleanor! You were eavesdropping!"

"I was indeed. I heard almost everything. I may need to wear reading glasses, my dear, but there's nothing wrong with my hearing. What an arrogant, self-centred, self-satisfied shit. Ooh! I'm so angry!"

"I can see you are," Caro said shakily, "and it's absolutely lovely. Oh Eleanor, what a mess. I'm so sorry to lumber you with all this. This time last week you didn't even know I existed, and now – well, I've dumped all my problems in your lap."

"And I haven't enjoyed myself so much in years." Without warning Eleanor came over and gave her a hug. "I may be angry with your nasty friend, but I can sincerely say I'm having a whale of a time. I had no idea how humdrum my life had become, so don't you go feeling guilty. If the truth were known, you've done me more good in the last few days than anyone else in years."

Caro found this hard to believe but she didn't argue. She slumped down, exhausted, into the deep softness of the settee. Eleanor's enthusiasm had cheered her a little, but the effects of Craig's visit were not so easily dismissed. Eleanor watched her for a moment then came to sit beside her.

"Do you want to tell me about it?"

Caro didn't misunderstand. "Where to start, that's the problem."

"Well, begin with explaining why you're being so nice to that shit of a man."

"Oh, that's the easy bit. Partly because I'm terrified of what he'd do if I wasn't, and partly because Paul Le Page asked me to."

"But why?"

"From Paul's point of view," Caro said wearily, "so that Craig won't leave Guernsey for a bit. I suppose because they've got him under investigation, surveillance, whatever they call it. Paul didn't go into detail."

"And what's the difficult bit?" Eleanor asked, then she added softly, "Is it something to do with your father?"

Caro leant her head back and gazed up at the pattern of Tudor roses and grape vines that curled around the central light in the ceiling, but she wasn't seeing them. In her mind's eye she saw a courtroom, her father's gaunt body standing in the dock, an expression of hopeless resignation on his thin face. Then she saw her mother sitting by her father's bed, her fingers stroking, stroking at his hand, the tears pouring silently down her face.

The silence dragged on. She knew she must respond to Eleanor's question, but forming the words and getting them past her lips felt so very difficult. Eleanor's warm fingers clasped her hand.

"I'm sorry, my dear," she said, her voice full of contrition. "I'm a tactless old woman. I should never have asked."

"No, no. It's not your fault."

"Would you like to talk about it?"

"Yes, but not now." Her eyes were wide and dark. "I'd like you to know what happened. But I just feel too drained to talk about it at the moment. I'm sorry."

"Don't apologise, my dear. Just remember I'm here to listen when you're ready."

"Thank you," said Caro, her voice cracking a little. "Thank you."

* * *

When Alex arrived that evening, he found Eleanor and Caro sitting at the table in the kitchen drinking coffee after their meal. Caro looked even more strained than she had earlier on. He found himself wanting to ask what was wrong, but he didn't.

Eleanor smiled up at him as he dropped an absent-minded kiss on the top of her head. "Have you eaten, darling?" she asked.

"Yes, thanks, I had something with Ashley after work."

"Ah." The one syllable spoke volumes.

Alex frowned but didn't say anything and, without even greeting her, asked Caro, "Are you ready then?"

It was Eleanor's turn to frown. "Caro, why don't you go and get a jacket?" she said. "It's a bit chilly out."

Alarm bells sounded. He could read his grandmother like a book, and that look she'd given him was in capital letters. He was about to be told off. Sure enough, when Caro had left the room Eleanor turned to him, her expression severe. "I realise you have a problem with that poor girl, Alex, but do try to be a little more polite. You behave as if she's personally offended you."

"What do you mean?" he said, knowing it was the wrong reaction.

"You know perfectly well what I mean," she snapped. "What's come over you these last couple of days? When you brought her to me on Friday evening you were fine, in fact I thought you rather fancied her, but ever since Saturday morning you've been barely civil." Her voice softened a little. "There's an awful lot you don't know about her, Alex. I'd suggest you go carefully. And remember, sitting in judgement on other people is not an attractive trait."

He stood looking at his grandmother, trying to control the wave of anger her words had generated. For a moment he considered pointing out that she probably knew as little as he did about Caro, but he rejected the idea. In this mood she wouldn't listen. And anyway, knowing her, she'd probably found out a lot more than him. His anger subsided, replaced by a feeling of uncertainty. Eleanor had always been such a good judge of character. Surely, she couldn't be entirely wrong about Caro?

"You really think she's done nothing wrong, don't you?"

"Yes. I'm pretty sure that's the case."

"I wish I had your faith in people."

"I don't live life behind rose-coloured spectacles, Alex, but I am quite a good judge of character."

"I know, but—"

"Come on, darling." She gave him a quizzical look. "Tell me the last time I was wrong about someone."

He looked down at her, tried to think of some suitable response, and could come up with none. She was right. Her ability to suss people out was second to none. And yet, there was always a first time, he told himself. He sighed and said, somewhat grudgingly, "Okay. Sorry. I'll make an effort."

She patted his arm. "I think you'll find I'm right, you know."

Alex wished he could believe her.

CHAPTER 11

The drive to La Cotte was accomplished in silence, and Caro began to regret ever suggesting she'd like to work on Alex's house, but once there her enthusiasm took over.

They went from room to room on the ground floor, Caro making suggestions as to what could be done, what colours and fabrics to use, and bemoaning the absence of her iPad so that she could show him what she meant. Alex followed her, listening to every word, vetoing some ideas and agreeing to others.

When they got to the room he called his study, with its books, CDs and computer, Caro paused. "This is the room you use most, isn't it?"

"Yes, I suppose so."

"Would you want to change any of it?"

He put up a hand and pushed his fingers slowly through his dark hair, a slight frown in his eyes. "I don't know. I must say I rather like it like this, even if it is a bit of a mess. It's comfortable."

"Then leave it."

A look of surprise crossed his face as he turned to her. "You really know, don't you, about houses, the effect they have on people I mean."

Caro smiled, blushing a little. "That's my job."

"Yes, I suppose it is." He looked round the room again. "Perhaps we could just decorate it, you know, paint the walls, and that."

"Alright, but a paler colour. As I said the other day, with these small windows you need all the light you can get. And maybe lighter coloured curtains, that'd work."

"Okay. That's settled. Shall we go upstairs now?"

They made their way up the winding stairs and Caro got the impression Alex was beginning to enjoy himself. By the time they got to the last room, his bedroom, they were both quite relaxed.

The first thing she noticed was the absence of the negligee on the back of the door. She just stopped herself from commenting on it. Alex sat down on the edge of the bed and watched her as she paced about the room, her eyes half closed, silently concentrating for a moment.

"Yes, that's a good idea," she murmured at last.

"What is?"

"That bed's all wrong," Caro said, frowning. "It's too heavy. Sorry, I hope you're not deeply attached to it."

"Not that much, although it does have its uses." He grinned, taking her completely by surprise. She tried to ignore the effect this had.

"This is such a lovely room," she went on quickly, "with its low ceiling, and that view out over the fields, but it needs something more continental. There's this lovely man, Alphonse de Gersigny, he's an old family friend, lives just outside Dinan in Brittany. He makes the most beautiful timber furniture, beds, armoires, chairs, the lot. They'd look a treat in here. Ah." Caro waved a pointed finger in the air. "I've just thought of something."

"What's that?"

"I've got some stuff coming over from Alphonse for another job." Her face fell. "Oh no, of course, it'll be going straight to the UK from France."

"But we have a freight company that does the route between France, the Channel Islands and the mainland."

"So you do. We could divert the consignment, couldn't we?"

"I don't know." Alex was smiling now.

"What're you grinning at?"

"You, your enthusiasm. Takes you over, doesn't it?"

Caro felt slightly embarrassed. "Sorry. Am I assuming too much?"

"No, not at all." There was a slightly awkward little pause then Alex asked, "So, what else do you think could be done in here?"

Caro, relieved to get back to practicalities, plunged on. "Well, the walls would be best painted plain white, and I can see darker curtains in here, the light's not so important in a bedroom, maybe one of those Mexican prints. Obviously strip the paint off the door, let it go back to the original wood. Then strip the floor and sand it down, have a couple of kelim rugs. What do you think?"

He was smiling again. "Sounds good, although a kelim rug's a complete mystery to me."

"You'd like them. They're heavy fabric, ochre colours. If I had my iPad I could show you."

"We can have a look on my computer. But the way you describe it sounds good to me. I don't think I'll have a quarrel with any of that."

"That's good to hear," Caro said, then unable to resist the temptation, she added, "I was beginning to think I could do nothing to please you."

"But I've agreed to most of your ideas so far, haven't I?"

Caro flushed a little, wishing she hadn't said it. "Oh yes, about the house, you have. I meant other things – forget it."

"No." Alex got up and came towards her. "I think I owe you an apology."

"Oh?" Caro wasn't sure what was coming next. Feeling slightly breathless, she waited for him to go on.

"Nella told me off while you were getting your jacket, she said I'd been rude to you. She's right, and I'm sorry." He took one of her hands, looked down at it and began to trace a pattern on the back of it with one long finger. Caro stood absolutely still as he went on, completely taken aback by her body's reaction to his touch.

"One way and another," Alex went on softly, "with so many conflicting things going on, I just haven't known what to believe."

He was very close to her now, so close that she could feel the warmth of his body. For a second, she closed her eyes, amazed at the sensations his tracing finger was creating. Almost in a whisper she asked, "Do you mean you think–"

But she got no further. At that moment, and without any warning at all, the door swung open. Ashley stood there. Her eyes swept over them, taking in every detail. Caro and Alex jumped apart.

"Well, well, what a pretty picture!" Ashley said, head on one side. "Am I interrupting anything?"

Alex let go of Caro's hand as if it had suddenly become red hot. "We didn't hear you come in," he said.

"That much, my darling, is obvious."

Caro rushed into speech, her face aflame, "I've been giving Alex ideas–"

"That too is obvious."

"We've been discussing ideas about the house, so that I can put together a proper quote."

"And you've been making sure the decor will be to your taste, have you?" Ashley said, her tone stinging.

"Don't be ridiculous, Ashley," Alex snapped. "Caro is a professional interior designer and I've asked her to take on this job. She can't very well do it without having a good look round, can she?"

"If I were you, Alex," Ashley said sweetly, "I'd be careful."

"What are you going on about?"

Something in his tone of voice must have penetrated. Ashley's eyes widened for a moment, then, with deliberation, she smiled. "Never mind," she said and walked up to Alex, put her arm through his. "And have you two finished your tour?"

"Just about."

Caro could understand the sudden change of tactics. A pity, she thought, if only she'd persisted, Alex might have chucked her out. But no, probably not.

"Come on, let's go downstairs and get a drink," Alex was saying. "I certainly need one."

Caro thought she probably needed several drinks. She followed them down to the kitchen where Alex collected three long stemmed glasses and a bottle of wine and preceded them back to the sitting room. Caro was pleased they didn't go into Alex's study to check ideas on the computer, she didn't want Ashley chipping in with ideas and comments.

For the next half hour Ashley ruled the conversation. She sat close to Alex, her warm thigh pressing against his, her voice delicately patronising every time she addressed Caro. Several times she mentioned mutual friends of hers and Alex's, effectively excluding Caro. It was a crude tactic, but it worked, making Caro feel the outsider. She sat and seethed, her discomfort and embarrassment slowly replaced by anger, until at last she'd had enough. She got up, not caring if she seemed rude, and completely forgetting she was dependant on Alex for a lift.

"It's getting late," she announced. "I'd better be getting back to Eleanor's. I don't want to keep her up."

Alex rose too, looking profoundly relieved at the interruption. "Fine, I'll drop you back." He reached for his jacket.

"No, no, no." Ashley was all smiles. "Let me take you. It'd be really silly to drag Alex out when he's home already."

Praying that Alex would argue, Caro watched him, waiting with bated breath.

Ashley laid a hand on his arm. "Come on, Alex darling," she said, "no point in you going when my journey takes me past Eleanor's door. I'm sure Caro's far too kind to drag you out unnecessarily."

Alex turned to Caro, gave the smallest shrug, a look of rueful apology in his eyes. There was no avoiding it, so Caro agreed to the plan as graciously as she could manage. They said goodnight to Alex, Ashley lingering over a kiss that obviously embarrassed him, and made their way to the sleek sports car parked next to Alex's BMW. As Caro settled in the low seat and did up her belt, she took herself in hand. Perhaps it was her turn to go on the attack.

But that was not the way it worked out.

Once they were on their way Ashley began to talk, quickly and quietly. "You can keep your thieving little hands off Alex. Understood?" Her eyes glinted as she glanced across at Caro in the darkness. "I warn you, I'm quite capable of losing you this job. I had a long talk with your friend, Craig, this morning and I found what he told me about you very interesting. I won't think twice about using that information. Alex might not be quite so happy to employ you if he knew what I know. Do I make myself clear?"

Caro felt sick. There was no knowing exactly what Craig had told her, but she had a shrewd idea. The last thing she wanted was the past raked up yet again. It went against the grain to give in to this kind of blackmail, but she wasn't given the chance to respond.

"Like father, like daughter is what they'll say," Ashley went on venomously, "and once the mud is thrown it'll stick. I'll make sure of that. I'd be more than delighted to put Alex in the picture, and I can just guess his reaction. He's such an upright person, my Alex, so very honest, and he sets as high a standard for everyone else as he sets for himself. Imagine what he'd think if I told him the full story, just as Craig told it to me. I don't think he'd be quite so pleased to have you staying with his precious grandmother then, and even Eleanor might have second thoughts, don't you think?"

Caro's throat was so constricted with anger and disgust that she couldn't have spoken even if she'd tried. Ashley talked on, quietly and with great clarity all the way back to Villette House. By the time Caro fumbled her way out of the car in Eleanor's driveway, she was feeling completely demoralised and all the fight had gone out of her.

* * *

Alex couldn't settle to anything. He couldn't stop himself going over and over the events of the evening. He felt completely confused, not knowing what to think. On the one hand there was Paul, warning him to be wary. And Ashley, they'd been together for some time now, surely he owed her something? On the other hand, there was Nella, entirely on Caro's side, her attitude to Ashley unchanged. And then there was Caro – damn it, four days ago he hadn't even known she existed.

He put on a CD, tried to lose himself in the music, but it didn't work. He switched it off and flicked through the channels on the TV, but found himself staring across the room taking nothing in. In the end he decided to go to bed. No point in hanging around down here doing nothing. But he was only halfway across the hall when he heard the back door open, and a moment later Ashley walked through from the kitchen.

"Hallo, darling." Her voice was silky. "I hope you don't mind me coming back. There was no chance to talk, or anything else, with your grandmother's little friend here, and it's ages since we've had some time alone together."

She took off her coat and let it drop onto the back of a chair, then wrapped her arms around his neck. "I've missed you," she whispered. He could feel her body fitting itself to the curve of his, and her lips were very close. Few men could resist this much encouragement. Alex found his hands moving slowly down her back to her waist. But no, it was no good.

With gentle firmness he detached himself and stepped back. "Ashley, I really don't think…"

"Darling, what's wrong?" her voice was still soft.

97

He came to a sudden decision. This was as good, or bad, a time as any. If the truth were known, he'd been thinking about it on and off for weeks. Just as well to get it over with.

"Ashley, come and sit down." He took her hand, led her into the sitting room. Settling her in an armchair, he contrived to sit a little way from her. "There's no easy way of putting this," he began slowly, "and I've been meaning to talk to you for a while. It's only fair. Look, we've had great fun, you and I, but I don't think it's going to work any longer."

"What do you mean?" Her voice was no longer soft.

"It's not so much that my feelings have changed, it's just that they haven't… haven't developed. It wouldn't be fair to let you think anything's going to come of this relationship when I know it isn't. And working together makes it even more awkward."

Her face was blank. She didn't seem to be taking in what he was saying. He tried again. "I'm sorry. It's not your fault, it's mine. I'm just hopeless at relationships. I hope we can stay friends."

Slowly her expression changed. Her eyes narrowed, her full lips tightened, and the colour drained from her face. Alex stumbled on, trying desperately to be as kind as possible, but she jumped up and cut straight across his words.

"Are you ditching me, Alex?"

"That's not really how I'd put it–" He got no further.

"Oh, isn't it?" Her voice rose angrily. "Funny, that. I'd say it was a damn good way of putting it. And I suppose next thing I hear you'll be shacked up with precious little Caro."

"Nothing of the sort! It's got nothing to do with her."

"Come off it, Alex." She began to pace up and down like a caged animal. "I saw the way you looked at her. You can't wait to get your hands on her. And it's pretty obvious she's got the hots for you, and not averse to the money, either, I'd imagine. Well, I can tell you a thing or two about your new friend. She's not as dewy-eyed as she looks."

Alex should have refused to listen, told her to leave right then, but he didn't.

"Your Caro's father was a crook, did you know that? He started off as a professor of archaeology, very fancy, but he gave in to temptation, stole some artefacts from a site he was working on and sold them to a dealer. Trouble is the stupid man got caught."

Alex felt cold. He wanted to slap his hand across her mouth, stop the venomous flow, but he just stood there as Ashley laughed in his face.

"Oh, my darling, I wish you could see your poor, shocked face. Don't you remember the case? It made headline news at the time. The tabloids loved it. The site was a newly excavated Roman villa, just outside Dorchester, a really important find. That's probably why they threw the book at him. Your precious Caro's dad ended up in prison. It finished him, he died soon after he came out."

Alex had recovered himself a little. "For God's sake, Ashley, you can hardly blame Caro for what her father did."

"Come on, Alex, you know how it is. Like father, like daughter. And she's not beyond making the occasional dodgy deal herself, I'm told."

"Who by?" he snapped out, his voice stinging her into silence. "Go on, tell me who told you?"

"That's my business."

"I suppose it was that ex-boyfriend of hers, Craig Paxton?" Alex's mouth twisted in disdain. "Nice sort of friend he seems to be."

Ashley ignored this. "Well, I'm told she finds her business connections in France rather useful. A neat way of acquiring an interesting piece or two for her favoured customers."

And into Alex's mind came the sound of Caro's voice saying, barely two hours ago, 'I've got some stuff coming over from Alphonse for another job.'

"Her little interior design business," Ashley was saying, "is obviously a very good cover for her other activities."

At last she was silent. She stood in the middle of the room looking triumphant, breathing deeply as if she'd run a race. Not for a moment did she take her eyes off Alex's face, but he could hardly bear to look at her. He walked to the door and opened it.

"I think, Ashley," he said, his voice full of contempt, "that you'd better leave."

"Don't worry, I'm going."

"And don't bother to come in to work tomorrow."

"What do you mean?"

"I don't want you there." He made a dismissive gesture with one hand, as if brushing her aside. "I'll put together some kind of redundancy package, but until then think of it as paid leave."

It was obvious that in her haste to revenge herself she'd not thought of this possibility. Her eyes opened wide in angry disbelief. "You're sacking me?"

"If you want to put it that way. I'll consider what to do when I'm no longer as angry and disgusted as I am at the moment. Now, please go."

"You've not heard the last of this, Alex Devereaux, believe you me."

"Oh, for goodness' sake, stop being so bloody melodramatic." He took her firmly by the arm and began to guide her towards the door, but she shook him off and stalked out of the house without a backward glance.

Once she'd gone Alex leant his hands flat on the kitchen table, bent his head and took a few deep breaths, trying to calm down. He told himself that, in the circumstances, he shouldn't rely on what Ashley said. All that about Caro could be pure invention. But what about what Paul had said? There was no denying he seemed to think Caro was involved in some kind of dodgy business. But then, what about Eleanor, she was convinced there was nothing Caro need be ashamed of. For some time, he see-sawed backwards and forwards, one minute defending her, the next condemning. He tried to hang on to what Eleanor had said, but it wasn't any good, the damage was done.

CHAPTER 12

"Alphonse? Hallo? Alphonse?" The line wasn't good, and Caro wondered if he could hear her.

"*'Allo, ma petite* Caro! What a pleasure!"

"How did you know it was me?"

"A silly question. Your voice, it's so like your dear mother's. How could I mistake? Anyway, your name is clear on my mobile."

It was Tuesday afternoon and Caro had phoned Alphonse de Gersigny on impulse, wanting to hear a familiar voice. She stood looking out at Eleanor's garden and pictured his vast workshop, smelling of warm wood, varnish, bees wax polish, and honeysuckle from the riotous climber that covered the front wall of the granite building. He would be standing in the doorway of his office, supervising his workers with an eagle eye even when he was on the phone, and she could imagine the loving grin above his untidy white beard. "So, you are coming to see your lonely old Alphonse at last?"

"Lonely? Don't tell me you're without a *chère amie* at the moment? That's not like you."

"*Po, po, po.*" It was a sound she associated particularly with him and it made her smile. "I'm past all that kind of thing now."

"You old liar!" Caro laughed. "When the seas run dry you will be."

"Maybe."

She could hear that he was pleased.

"To what do I owe the honour of this call?" he said.

"I've got a new job and I may need some of your furniture."

"*Bon, bon,* and where is this job, what kind of house?"

"It's in Guernsey and it's an old farmhouse, just right for one of your gorgeous beds."

"*Guernesais?*" He pronounced it the French way. "The land of Victor Hugo. I know it well. You go a little further afield, *ma chère*. Soon you will be working in France, *n'est ce pas*? And who is this client of yours?"

"His name's Alex Devereaux and–"

"The wine merchants?"

"Yes. Why? Have you heard of them?"

"This is very strange. What a small world. You know my father was a vintner? He used to have a close friend, a William Devereaux, who came from *Guernesais*, younger than him but they had much in common. This William was a wine merchant, bought much from my father each year. Ah yes, and I remember, their love of art they also had in common. William was obsessed with collecting paintings. He'd search them out *avec une passion*, with great passion. My father found many a piece for him."

"There are some lovely paintings in Eleanor's house."

"Eleanor?" Alphonse asked.

"Alex's grandmother."

"Surely it must be the same family."

"Probably. Alex is in charge of the company now. He took over from his father, but he died some years ago."

"In a boating accident? Where he and his wife drowned?" asked Alphonse.

"Yes. They were. Did you know them too?" Caro was delighted with this unexpected connection.

"I did indeed. William's nephew and his wife. It was a great loss." There was a significant pause, Caro could almost hear the cogs turning. "So, this is the young man you do a job for. Is he married?"

"No," she said shortly, not wanting to travel down that path.

"Aha," said Alphonse. "He is handsome, this young man?"

"Not bad."

"And rich?"

"Enough, I suppose."

"You suppose? You should find out about these things, *ma p'tite*, they are important. Of course, the money, it comes second to the looks, and the romance, but–"

"Alphonse! Stop being a pain."

Something in her voice must have warned him. There was a significant little pause and then he said, "*Bon*, I will stop being the pain, as you put it. You have my latest catalogue?"

"Yes, or rather I will have tomorrow morning. Alison's put some stuff on the ferry for me. I want to know what your stock situation is and, if you haven't got what I want, how long's your waiting list?"

"But it's difficult to tell you this if I don't know what exactly you need."

"Just tell me what you have on the go."

They spent some time discussing the different designs. Caro gave Alphonse a graphic description of La Cotte, and he went into detail about some new designs he was working on.

"I've done some research and I can always divert a consignment via Guernsey," Caro told him, "if you have stuff ready now, like that *armoire* you just mentioned."

"But diverting the consignment, would it not be a little expensive?" he asked.

"I don't think that matters all that much to Alex."

"That is good," he said with deep satisfaction. "We will certainly be able to make the satisfactory arrangements, *ma p'tite*."

Then he turned to more personal matters. "So, how is this Craig of yours?" he asked. As usual he made his feelings all too clear.

"No longer an item."

"*Hein?* What does this mean, an item?"

"I've finished with him."

There was a gusty sigh of relief from the other end of the line, but he made no further comment as Caro went on.

"He decided he fancied more than one girlfriend at a time, and I didn't want to be part of a threesome, so that's that. At least, it nearly is."

"*Comment?*"

"It's a long story."

"I'm listening."

"I'll tell you another time, Alphonse." But he wasn't going to be satisfied with that. Caro knew she'd have to tell him something or he'd give her no peace at all. She gave him a brief account of Craig's supposed activities. As usual, Alphonse was quick to pick up the implications of what she had and hadn't said.

"They think you are in some way involved in these deals?"

"Yes— no, well they did, but I don't think they do any more."

"Not at all pleasant for you, my Caro."

"No, but I'll survive," she said with more confidence than she felt. "And Eleanor's been marvellous. I'm staying at her house. She's been an absolute treasure."

"I am glad you have so good a friend." There was a loaded little silence, but when she didn't fill it, he went on, "As you know I was never very happy with this Craig. And now he proves me right, *le salaud*. But this doesn't please me, because it means trouble for you. Be careful, Caro. Watch and listen."

Once again, she felt the cold lurch of fear in her stomach. Another warning. That's all anyone did, give her dark warnings. Be careful, Caro, watch out, Caro. But then maybe they were right. It seemed everyone else had seen through Craig's charming exterior. Why had she been so blind for so long? And what else had she misjudged? But there was no point in dwelling on it, that wouldn't get her anywhere.

"Oh, don't worry about me," she said, making a great effort to sound cheerful and unconcerned. "I can look after myself." She ignored the muttering from Alphonse. "So, I'll phone you in a couple of days about this order, okay?"

At last Alphonse seemed to have accepted her assurances, or probably just accepted there was nothing more he could say. But when he spoke again his voice was very firm. "You phone me all the same, whether there is an order, whether there is not. I want to know how it goes on with you, *compris*?"

"Understood. I'll be good and do as I'm told," she said, trying to smile. "It's been lovely speaking to you."

"*Au revoir, ma p'tite*, and look after yourself."

Caro cut off the call, no longer smiling. However hard she tried to fill her thoughts with the prospect of working on La Cotte, Craig and his activities always lurked in the background. Her feelings were in such turmoil. Fear at what Craig might do, anger with herself for being so gullible, and even deeper anger at having been used. There was guilt too, at dragging Eleanor, and Alex, into her affairs, and that awful journey back to Villette House in Ashley's car.

But underlying all this now were thoughts of her father, and her mother. God forbid that all that should be raked up again, just as she thought she'd begun to deal with the past. She wrapped her arms around herself as she stood there, feeling cold with an inner chill, then she gave herself a little shake and decided to go in search of Eleanor.

Caro found her in the kitchen making tea. They sat down at the scrubbed pine table and, pushing her fears and unhappy memories to the back of her mind, Caro told her about the conversation with Alphonse.

"It's such a small world," Caro said. "It's amazing that Alphonse's father should be a close friend of your brother-in-law, isn't it?"

"Yes. Dear old William. I don't remember meeting Alphonse de Gersigny myself, but I thought the name was vaguely familiar. The Devereaux family have very close connections in France, with a name like that it's hardly surprising, I suppose, and in the wine trade it's inevitable. We used to go on these marvellous trips to meet the vineyard owners, and the shippers. Such hospitable people. Harry and I actually spent our honeymoon in a château on the Loire which belonged to one of his father's wine friends. It was glorious."

"It sounds like it," Caro said.

"Such a long time ago," Eleanor said, deep in thought for a moment then, taking Caro by surprise, she came abruptly back to the present. "Is it tomorrow's ferry that's bringing the stuff your friend is sending?"

"Yes, and that reminds me," Caro made her voice very firm, "can you tell me where I can hire a car?"

"But my dear, that's not necessary."

"Yes, it is," she said firmly. "It's really not fair for me to call on you or Alex to chauffeur me all the time, and I don't want to have to wake you up at such an ungodly hour. The ferry arrives at six thirty."

"Well, you can borrow my old Skoda," Eleanor said briskly. "It's fully insured."

"Are you sure?"

"Of course, no problem."

* * *

Caro crept downstairs at six o'clock on Wednesday morning, found the car keys on the hall table where Eleanor had told her they would be, and got into the bright red car that was parked on the gravel. She drove down through the deserted town as the sun was coming up, relishing the quietness and the cold, clear air, but once she arrived at the ferry terminal there was more activity. The passengers, in cars and on foot, were just beginning to disembark. They all had a similar dishevelled look to them, common to most people who had endured a night crossing.

Caro stood and watched the activity for a moment, but soon she reminded herself she had work to do and went in search of the suitcase Alison had packed. She finally tracked it down and signed the appropriate papers to clear it through customs, expecting to be told to open it at any moment, but nobody stopped her. Not quite knowing why, she felt incredibly relieved.

When she got back to the house, Eleanor was waiting for her. "Why don't you take your work stuff out and leave it all down here? I just can't wait to have a look through the catalogues and samples."

Caro smiled, touched by her enthusiasm, and did as she suggested.

When Alex turned up at lunchtime, the two of them were crouched on the floor of the sitting room pouring over swatches of fabric, pages stuck with squares of carpet and other types of flooring, and glossy catalogues. Caro had her laptop open beside her and had been making copious notes. It was obvious they were thoroughly enjoying themselves.

It was Eleanor that noticed him first. "Hallo, my darling, you were very quiet." She smiled up at him. "I haven't seen you since Monday. Where have you been?"

"I've been busy." His tone was terse, and Caro frowned. What the hell was the matter with him now? The shutters were definitely down. Bloody man, she thought, her heart sinking.

Eleanor frowned at him then turned to Caro. "You must be ravenous."

Sitting back on her heels, Caro had been watching Alex, and for a moment she didn't register what Eleanor had said. She felt a soft touch on her arm. "Hungry, dear?"

"Oh, sorry, yes," she said, feeling her cheeks warm a little. "Maybe after lunch we could go through it all," she said to Alex, then to Eleanor. "Let me give you a hand getting things ready."

Alex followed them into the kitchen. While Eleanor put soup to heat and took cold meat from the fridge, Caro prepared a salad. Her every nerve was aware of Alex standing watching them. When she stole a glance at him out of the corner of her eye, she could see him watching his grandmother as she talked, telling him about the discussion they'd been having about La Cotte, but she could tell he wasn't really listening.

They sat down to eat, but for Caro each mouthful went down in a hard lump. Eleanor made valiant efforts to lighten the atmosphere, but halfway through the meal they all lapsed into silence, until Alex carefully put down his knife and fork. He straightened them once, then again. Without looking directly at either of them he said, "I really ought to tell you, I'm not sure I want the house done after all."

Eleanor looked up at her grandson, a piece of bread poised halfway to her mouth. "Why on earth not?" Her tone was thoroughly exasperated. "You can certainly afford it."

Caro said nothing, just concentrated on the last of her salad.

"I just don't think it's the right time," he went on defensively. "Not right now."

Eleanor slapped her hands down on the table and glared across at him. "Really, Alex, this is too much. I can't keep up with you and your moods. I thought you'd made a decision. It's a bit much to go back on it now. Caro's gone to all this trouble, got all that stuff couriered over, telephoned Alphonse de Gersigny in France about furniture, been through La Cotte and made copious notes, and now you change your mind!"

"Obviously I'll reimburse her for the work she's done so far."

"That's not the point. This isn't just a matter of money, Alex." Eleanor's voice was sharp, but she also sounded confused. "It's to do with good manners and keeping your word."

Caro intervened, deeply embarrassed. "No, Eleanor. Please, don't worry. After all, I haven't even given Alex a quote yet. If he wants to change his mind, that's up to him. I'd much rather we just dropped the subject."

But Eleanor obviously wasn't going to leave it at that. "Nonsense, my dear. I think he owes you an explanation." She turned back to Alex and the expression on her face was enough to reduce a person's age by half. "Well, Alex?" she said.

For a dragging few moments he sat frowning into his wine glass and Caro sat there desperately wishing she could just get up and leave the room. In the end she could bear it no longer. She turned to look directly at Alex, forcing him to meet her eyes. "You've been talking to Craig, haven't you?"

"No," Alex grimaced, "not exactly."

That gave her a jolt, then light dawned. "Ah, perhaps someone else, someone Craig has been talking to."

Alex made no immediate reply, but she saw his jaw tighten. She gave a sharp little nod and the accusation in her eyes was joined by contempt. A wave of anger rose up inside her and swamped all other feelings. "Enough of this," she spat out at him. "I'm not having it anymore." Caro turned to Eleanor. "I'm so, so sorry for lumbering you with my problems yet again, but I can't put up with this any longer."

"No apology needed." Eleanor patted her hand. "You go ahead, my dear."

Caro turned back to Alex. "I was pretty comprehensively warned off the other night by your friend, Ashley, and if it's her you've been talking to, heaven knows what you've been told. I don't take kindly to threats or to hidden, or not so hidden, agendas. Let's have everything out in the open once and for all." She took a deep, shuddering breath. "Have you been told that – how should I put it? Oh, sod it, that my father was in prison and that I'm heading that way?" She read the answer in his face and ploughed on. "I thought as much. God! It's so unfair, and it makes me so angry!"

Once again, the silence felt heavy around them, then Caro began to talk, slowly, but more quietly now.

CHAPTER 13

"Let me explain, and please don't interrupt." She was speaking to Alex, but it was Eleanor who nodded in assent.

"My father was an archaeologist. The only things of any importance in his life were his work and my mother. Don't get me wrong, I know they loved me, but they were totally bound up in each other, like two halves of a whole." She laced her fingers together tightly to emphasise her words. "I think ancient ruins and their history were more real to him than everyday life. He wasn't a worldly man at all, had no understanding of... of things like greed, love of possessions, anything like that. And he was completely hopeless with money or anything practical. Mum used to say that if she didn't put his clothes out for him or put food slap in front of him, he'd probably have forgotten to dress or eat."

For a moment there was the shadow of a smile in her eyes as she spoke, but it soon faded. "Seven years ago, the site of a Roman villa was discovered just outside Dorchester, Dad was beside himself with excitement. They dug up some remarkably well-preserved artefacts, even a few pieces that were unique, nothing like them had been found in England before. But there was a problem. There'd been plans for a luxury development on the site. Planning permission was about to be given and the developer was ready to go, but thanks to some enlightened civil servants in the borough council, at the last moment permission was refused. Of course, the developers were livid, it went to appeal, they did everything they could to revoke the decision, and it was pretty unpleasant for a bit, but my father and his colleagues won in the end. My mother told me that Dad got some awful letters, e-mails, threatening phone calls, the lot, but he just ignored them. That was typical of my father."

Caro stopped speaking. This was so difficult. But she knew she had to finish. "For weeks on end Mum and I hardly saw him, he was totally absorbed. Then, one night, he came home in a dreadful state. He was so worried, and angry too. He told us that some of the artefacts they'd found had been stolen, that the site was swarming with police and they'd had to stop the work. For days we had no idea what was going on, the police kept interviewing Dad, over and over, he was completely confused. Then on this awful, awful day, it was a Tuesday, I've never forgotten that."

There was silence for a moment, then Eleanor asked, "What happened on this Tuesday?"

"They came and arrested him."

She heard Eleanor's quick indrawn breath. "Oh my dear, how dreadful for you."

"They said they had evidence that he was behind the thefts, possibly actually carried them out." Caro swallowed hard. "He denied it, of course, but they told him they'd already arrested one of the workers on the site, a student from Exeter university called Darren Durward. It was because of what he told the police that Dad was arrested. It seemed this little bastard managed to convince them that he'd had nothing to do with it. They just let him go."

She put up her hands and rubbed wearily at her face. "Oh, I won't go into all the details. It was awful, awful. And when Dad was found guilty, we just could not believe it. It was like all our worst nightmares, but it was real. Mum and I knew he wasn't guilty. He just wasn't capable of anything of the sort, he couldn't have organised it for a start." Her mouth twisted in a bitter little smile. "But the evidence was so damning. He was sent to prison and while he was there, he became ill. It was his heart, but I've always been convinced it was because of what happened."

Her voice had begun to shake. She felt the warmth of Eleanor's hand on hers. "Caro, you don't have to go on if you don't want to."

"No, I want to finish. I want to explain it all so that Alex understands, and you." She took a deep breath, steadied herself. "Dad's solicitor was marvellous, so was the barrister, but it had been obvious from the start that the inspector in charge of the case was determined to get Dad convicted. He just seemed to have it in for him. And that bastard stood there in the witness box and told lie after lie. He sounded so, so plausible, put on a marvellous performance. We knew he was lying, but what did that matter? The police and the jury believed him. There was nothing we could do."

"What happened then?" Eleanor asked quietly. "Surely that wasn't the end of it?"

"No, thank God. There was a woman in the police team who came up with some new evidence. It was only then we could see any glimmer of hope. Apparently, she'd had doubts right from the start, but her superiors wouldn't listen. She dug up some information off her own bat. She got into awful trouble for it, but once it all came out, they had to take notice, and everything started up all over again."

Caro took another deep breath, as if she was refuelling for the next stage. "From then on things moved fast. The lying little parasite was interviewed again and started changing his story. Faced with the new evidence, he finally broke down and admitted that he'd lied. We never found out exactly why, he insisted it was all his own idea and they couldn't budge him on that. I'm sure she shouldn't have, but the policewoman hinted to Mum and me that there'd been some kind of cover up. We got the impression it might have been something to do with the property company who'd wanted to build on the site, but Mum and I didn't really care. All we wanted was to have Dad home."

"I'm sure you did," said Eleanor. "You must have been overjoyed."

"We were, in a way, but the thing is, it was too late. He was let out of prison even before the appeal came through, but he went straight into hospital, he was dying." Her voice was flat and emotionless now. "He died two weeks after the appeal was heard, and three months later my mother took an overdose, she just couldn't go on living without him."

Eleanor gave a little gasp of shock and said, "Oh my dear!" But Alex said nothing.

"When Craig was here the other night," Caro said, "I told him I didn't want anything more to do with him." She looked up at Alex, her eyes full of the hurt she felt, and of accusation. "Paul said not to tell you this, but I'm going to. Craig's been implicated in a smuggling racket. I was able to provide some information and Paul has asked me not to be too off-putting, towards Craig, that is. He says it would be quite useful to them if he stayed around for a bit. I don't believe he thinks I'm involved any more but, like you, he may have doubts."

Alex didn't even try to respond to this.

"The trouble is," Caro went on, "from my point of view, that makes things very difficult. Craig more or less told me the other night that if he's caught, he'll find some way of dragging me into it, in spite of the fact I've had nothing whatever to do with his activities. And people will remember about Dad, no smoke without fire and all that crap. Mud sticks. Your friend, Ashley, made a point of reminding me of that on the way home last night. Of course, she's right, isn't she, Alex? My parents and I certainly found that to be the case. And if you still don't believe me you can Google the whole thing. It's all there, go check it up."

At last she stopped talking. What else was there to say? She'd thought she had it all under control. It was in the past, she'd faced up to the ghosts and laid them to rest, rebuilt her life. And this man had come along and turned it all on its head. An overwhelming desire to escape flowed through her, she had to be on her own.

"I'm sorry, do you mind…" She didn't finish the sentence, just pushed her chair back and quickly left the room.

* * *

Alex could hear her footsteps crossing the tiles in the hall, heard the sitting room door open and shut. He looked across the table at his grandmother, shrugged and shook his head.

"Well, Nella, I've really screwed up this time, haven't I? Bells ringing, flags flying, a complete and utter balls-up."

"Yes, you have," she said. She'd never been one to beat about the bush. "Now you can go out there and put it right."

"What?" He gave a humourless little laugh. "She's hardly likely to listen to me now, is she?"

"That doesn't mean you shouldn't try."

He sat brooding for a moment. "Okay, but if she doesn't want to listen, I'm not going to push it."

"But you must still try." Eleanor looked at him, not entirely unsympathetic. "It really is about time you stopped dwelling on whether or not you're going to be let down. Think of Caro first, Alex, and yourself second. You might find it works."

She came around the table, put her hands on his sagging shoulders and kissed the top of his head. "My darling boy, you've got a very good heart. Let it tell you what to do and stop listening to that all-too-cynical head of yours."

"But what's the point, Nella. It's ridiculous. I haven't even known her a week yet. She probably couldn't care that" – he snapped his fingers – "for me or my opinion."

"Oh, Alex." She sounded truly exasperated. "Sometimes I wonder if there's a brain in that head of yours. What on earth does it matter how long you've known her? I knew within hours that your grandfather was the one for me."

He gave her a sceptical look.

"Now don't you look at me like that. I did." She sat down beside him, took both his hands in hers. "I know you think I'm impulsive, but I've got a feeling about this, here." She patted at her waist. "Look, love, I've said this before, but I'll say it again, I'm nearly eighty years old, that's a lot of years, and in that time, I've learnt a great deal about people. Believe me, this is the girl for you."

"Nella!"

"I'm right. Go on. Go and make your peace with her."

"Okay, I'll try." But as he left the room, he didn't notice her cross her fingers tight.

* * *

Caro sat on one of the stone benches by the swimming pool. Leaning forward, she wrapped her arms across her body protectively, and gazed unseeing at the tiles under her feet. There was a stiff breeze rustling the hedge surrounding the pool and fidgeting with the surface of the water, but she hardly noticed it. She was miles away, deep in her own oppressive thoughts, and she didn't hear Alex approaching until he was right next to her. When he sat down beside her, she didn't look at him.

For a moment he was as silent as she was, then he started to speak. "I realise saying I'm sorry isn't going to make much difference, but I'm going to say it anyway. I really am very sorry to have misjudged you. I'm sorry for being rude, blowing hot and cold over the house, everything."

She made no comment.

After a small pause he went on, "You're right. I did hear about your father from Ashley, when I told her last night that we were finished. She really enjoyed telling me all about it. And yes, you were right, she got the story from Craig. Trouble is, he seems to have told her his own version."

Caro slowly looked round at him. "You mean you actually believed what I just told you and your grandmother?" Her tone was acid and he flinched.

"I suppose I deserve that."

"You're dead right you do!"

"Come on, Caro, give me a chance," he protested. "But Nella's right, I was sitting in judgement. I've been trying to work it out in my mind. Apart from my usual cynical attitude, which I'm afraid is a bit of a habit, it was so important to me that you should be– be what you said you were. Not just for her sake, for mine too."

"Then why couldn't you simply believe me?"

"For goodness' sake, I've only just met you. It's been five days, Caro, only five days. How was I to know what to believe?" He looked at her, his mouth twisted in a bitter little smile. "Okay, so I should have listened to Nella. I'll try to in future, but for various reasons I don't find it easy to trust people."

"Women."

"Alright, women."

"I know. Eleanor told me," she said quietly, relenting a little.

"Ah, did she? Well, you've been a good deal more understanding of me than I have of you." He took her hand, softly stroked the back of it with his thumb. "Am I forgiven?"

Their eyes met as they sat there, and Alex put up his hand and gently tucked an escaping curl back behind her ear.

"Am I?" he persisted.

She didn't answer his question directly. "Did you say you and Ashley are finished?"

"Yes."

"I'm glad. She's a bitch."

He gave a little snort of laughter. "Yup."

"Are you sure it's all over?"

"Yes, absolutely."

Her heart was beating so hard she felt stifled. She wanted to say so many things, but she wasn't sure where to start. The silence dragged on as his hand slid slowly, softly down her cheek and round into the curls at the nape of her neck. She could feel the pressure of his fingers, pulling her towards him. Somewhere, in the back of her mind, a little voice warned that there'd be no going back if she let this go on.

It was at this moment they heard Eleanor's voice calling from the house.

"Alex? Your mobile is ringing. Do you want me to answer it?"

Saved by the bell, Caro thought. Quickly she sat back, putting some distance between herself and temptation.

"Alex, I've answered it," came Eleanor's voice again. "It's Sally. She says it's urgent."

"Oh bugger," Alex said. "That's my PA. It's probably to tell me I'm late. I should have been at a meeting twenty minutes ago."

"You must go then." But neither of them moved, not until Eleanor's voice called again, closer at hand. They jumped up, the spell finally broken, but Alex clasped Caro's hands.

"Please, can I see you this evening? Will you come out to dinner with me?"

"Yes." A gurgle of laughter bubbled up inside her. "I'll be here, I think."

"I want you to do La Cotte, and that's final, I want you…" His eyes widened as he looked down at her. "Oh yes, I definitely want you." He grinned. "I'll tell you later, half seven, alright?"

Caro, deciding she couldn't trust her voice, nodded. He lifted a hand to her cheek, and she held her breath, then he turned and strode off across the garden.

CHAPTER 14

The rising note of panic in Jason's voice could be heard clearly, even through the bad reception on Craig's mobile phone.

"He's serious, Craig. He's heard that you're stuck on that bloody island and he wants to know what the hell's going on. Says you should get rid of the girl once and for all, and I don't think he means ditch her either. Keeps on about how her father screwed things for him and he's not about to let her do the same."

"Tough. I'm not having him dictate how I should run my private life," said Craig with as much conviction as he could muster. "He tried that once before and I let him. As it happens it turned out quite useful, but this time I make the bloody decisions, and you can pass that message on if you want."

"Come on, Craig, don't be ridiculous. It's not as if she's even your type, for fuck's sake. There're plenty of better looking bits of totty out there. Look," Jason urged, "he's talking about coming to Guernsey himself. Says he's got business associates there, and he told me to tell you to expect him. Didn't say when, just said to expect him."

Craig swore as he stood on the deck of the *Sally Anne*, staring unseeingly at the few late shoppers, visitors and locals, passing by on the quay. At high tide it was almost level with the deck of the boat. But he wasn't thinking about them, or about the state of the tide.

"So? Let him come. You may be shit scared of the bastard. I'm not," he said, with far more confidence than he felt. "He's got to learn he can't threaten me. And how the hell did he find out I was here?"

There was a pause, then Jason said more quietly, and there was a whining tone in his voice, "Well, I happened to tell him you'd gone to fetch your girlfriend back. I had to tell him something, for Chrissake! Anyway, he obviously knows all about the routes we've been using, so it follows he'd know about your precious Caro."

"You're a great help," Craig said bitterly.

"Bloody hell, Craig, what else could I do? Anyway, he's got this thing about her. Hates her, seems to me. No idea why, but he seems to be obsessed with knowing all about her."

"Don't be ridiculous!" Craig said scornfully. He couldn't have Jason thinking like that. "He's hardly the type Caro would have anything to do with."

"If you say so. But, Craig, there's something else—"

"What now?" Craig snapped.

"He's going to send a couple of his heavies over, said they'd be there to give you a hand, said it with this bloody grin on his face. He might even come with them, except he's got to go and visit his boy."

"He'll never miss that."

"No, but the lad's been ill so they might tell him not to go this time. And then he might come and pay you that visit."

"Well, stop him," Craig spat down the phone. "It doesn't matter how, just stop him. I can't have him poking his long nose in."

"Oh yea? And how do you think I'm going to do that. Sorry sir, please sir, but Craig says you can't go to Guernsey today, sir. Come off it, Craig. If I try to persuade him not to, he'll just blow his stack. It'll make him even more determined. Anyway, I acted all innocent, said you'd be glad of the help, made out everything was going fine. At least that took the wind out of his sails."

Craig considered this and conceded that Jason might be right. "I suppose so. When do they arrive, these jokers, and how many of them?"

"Two, but I don't know when they'll get to Guernsey any more than I know when he will. You'd better be on your guard, that's all I can say, and bloody get control of that female of yours. She could screw the whole thing if you don't."

"Alright, alright. Leave it with me. I've got an idea of what I'll do."

"What?" Jason sounded suspicious rather than relieved.

"Never you mind. The less you know the better, in case you start blabbing to our friend again. Pretty obvious you can't be trusted to keep your mouth shut." He took no notice of Jason's muttered protests from the other end of the line. "I'll let you know what's happening when I can."

"Come on, man, I need to know." But Craig took no notice, just ended the call.

* * *

Back in the cabin of the *Sally Anne* he slumped down onto the cushioned seat. His lips were compressed into a hard line and his eyes narrowed in concentration as he sat there, his mind racing. He picked up his mobile again, scrolled down to the number he wanted and waited as the ringing tone went on and on. He was just about to give up when the call was picked up. "*'Allo. Qui parle?*"

"Jean? It's me, Craig," he said in French, "can you speak? Are you alone?"

"No, but I can talk." He switched to English. "Stupid woman doesn't speak the language, so there's no problem."

"Are you sure?"

Jean Peron sounded aggressive. "Have I not said so?"

"Alright, alright. Now, I need to know exactly when the consignment is due to leave St Malo. Have you got a date yet?"

"No, not exactly," Jean was scornful. "Your Mademoiselle Bennett, she cannot make up her mind. I thought it would be Friday this week, but I heard the boss speaking on the telephone earlier today. Apparently, they want to hold the lorry until after the weekend. They wish to add to the load. I think more furniture."

"What?" Craig swore comprehensively. "You've got to find out what's going on. And quickly."

Normally Jean would have argued, but something in Craig's voice must have persuaded him not to. "Okay, if you insist. What I can do, I will do."

"I'll make it worth your while."

"This, it makes a difference." He sounded altogether more willing now. "Tomorrow I contact you. Is that all?"

"Yes, for now," said Craig curtly. He cut off the call and went to the fridge to get a can of beer, sat for a while as he drank it, methodically going over everything that had happened. Not until his thoughts were interrupted by his phone, did he move once again. It was Ashley, at her most sultry and seductive.

"Hallo, Craig darling, how're things with you?"

His tone changed completely. This was very different from the last two calls. "All the better for hearing your voice, my sweet."

"Ah, bless you." Ashley paused for a moment before she said, "I've got a bit of news for you. Interested?"

"Depends what it is." He didn't want to sound too eager.

"It's about your girlfriend."

His curiosity was aroused, but the next moment she was saying, "But I'm not telling you over the phone. I have my price."

"Oh?"

"Yup. A drink, or two. How about the bistro up by the courthouse? Do you know it?"

"Lawrence's?"

"That's the one."

"I could buy you dinner," Craig suggested, smiling.

"How sweet of you. It's a date."

Fetching himself another beer, Craig hoped that the news Ashley had for him was better than Jason's or Jean's. But the way things were going, he had his doubts. On the other hand, at least with Ashley there might be something on offer after dinner.

* * *

Eleanor was consumed with curiosity, a not unusual state for her. When Caro had come back inside earlier that afternoon she'd gone straight up to her room, murmuring something about having work to do, and Alex had left a moment later. Neither of them had told her anything about their conversation in the garden. She didn't want to interfere – no, that wasn't true, she did, but she told herself she mustn't.

When Caro finally came downstairs, Eleanor was even more convinced something had happened out there by the pool. The look in Caro's eyes and the smile just hovering on the edge of her lips said it all. They sat at the kitchen table, hands round mugs of tea, while Eleanor tried to think of some way to ask what had happened. She was no nearer deciding how to broach the subject when Caro came out of her daydream, and the smile that had hovered broke out in full.

"Alex has asked me to go out for a meal tonight." She looked directly at Eleanor for the first time. "Is that okay?"

"Of course, my dear." She went on hesitantly, "So you've sorted out your differences, the two of you."

"He doesn't seem to think I'm a criminal anymore."

"Did he ever?"

"I don't think he was sure. But now it's okay, he apologised for being the way he was."

"Good, so he should. And I hope he apologised properly."

Caro smiled. "Very properly."

Eleanor sat there, hoping for more, but Caro had slipped back into her daydream. Finally, they were interrupted by a knock on the front door.

Eleanor got up to answer it and, when she returned, Paul Le Page was with her. The sight of him succeeded in wiping the smile from Caro's face. Craig and his activities jumped to the front of her mind once more, blotting out thoughts of anything else.

"Here's Paul to see you," Eleanor said brightly, as usual treating him as a friend rather than an official. "Why don't you go into the sitting room, Caro. You'll be more comfortable in there."

Once they were settled, Paul said, "We've got some new information and I thought it was only fair to come and put you in the picture. It's to do with the consignments of cloth and other merchandise you bring in from the continent."

Caro sighed wearily but said, "Fire away."

"You know you told us on Saturday about the methods you use for getting supplies from France?"

"Yes."

His pale blue eyes never left her face. "We've had some information from our colleagues over there, and it's been confirmed by the mainland border force, that Craig Paxton and his associates have been using your consignments to conceal smuggled or stolen goods."

Caro felt sick. She could hardly think, let alone respond. And he was watching her so closely, his face devoid of expression. When she didn't react, he asked, "Were you aware of this?"

"No!" Caro exclaimed. "Of course, I wasn't!"

"You had no suspicion at all?"

"None whatever. Do you think I'd have let it go on if I had?"

"Probably not, if there'd been any way for you to stop it." His voice was calm and business-like. "But I find it hard to understand how you had not even the smallest suspicion they might be using you?"

Anger rising, she took a deep breath, ready to protest, then closed her mouth again. This was a different question altogether. Her anger subsided under a wave of self-doubt. She bit unconsciously at a fingernail as she gazed across the room, looking at, but not seeing, the imposing gold framed seascape above Eleanor's mantelpiece. Yes, in the last few days the thought that Craig might have been using her had insinuated itself into her mind.

Paul was still waiting for an answer.

"Yes, okay," she said wearily. "I had become suspicious. I thought he might have used my consignments, but I couldn't work out how. And anyway, I hadn't even the slightest suspicion until these last few days."

"What exactly was it that made you suspicious?"

This question was much easier to answer. "The other day, when Craig was here, he warned me that I was as involved as him. Said I should keep quiet or he'd take me down with him. That scared me. I knew then I'd got a problem." She gave a mirthless little laugh. "And that's putting it mildly. This must have been what he was talking about." Her voice shook with anger and humiliation. "God! What a bastard. It makes me so angry with myself for being taken in, and with him too. How could he?"

"Pretty easily, I'm afraid," Paul said calmly. "He's a very smooth operator. You're probably not the first woman– person to have been taken in by him."

"But why haven't you stopped them, searched the stuff?"

"We're treading water at the moment. We'll act when the time is right, don't you worry." He smiled, but it didn't reach his eyes.

He's not yet written me off as a suspect, Caro thought, however much he wants me to think he has. Although the thought was disturbing it was accompanied by a degree of resignation. Par for the course, she told herself.

"If we keep a watching brief for a while," Paul was saying, "we stand a better chance of nabbing the whole gang rather than just the small fry."

"And that's what you think Craig is?"

"We're not sure yet."

In Paul Le Page's mind was she one of the small fry too?

"There is one other thing," he said.

"Yes?" Instinctively she pressed herself back into her chair. What now, for God's sake?

"This Jones chap you mentioned when you came to my office. Do you know anything else about him?"

"No." She was puzzled. "What sort of thing?"

"Well, has he any connections in the Channel Islands, for instance?"

"I've no idea. I think that time at the warehouse was the first time I'd heard his name, although it did ring a bell. Maybe Craig's mentioned him at some point and I just didn't take it in. No, I don't know anything else about him."

If Paul was disappointed, he didn't show it, nor did he show whether he believed her. "Never mind. You've been very helpful already. But if you do remember anything else, however trivial it may seem, please let me know."

"Of course."

He rose to go but stopped and looked down at her for a moment. "You know I asked you not to be too off-putting with Craig Paxton?"

Caro nodded.

"Well," he said, sounding a little embarrassed, "watch out for yourself."

For the first time since they'd met there was a touch of kindness in his pale eyes. "We'll be keeping an eye on him, and on you, so don't worry too much. Just don't take any unnecessary risks. If he contacts you let us know immediately, okay? And it'd probably be just as well if you try not to be alone with him."

Once again Caro could feel that trickle of cold fear down her back, tinged this time with angry resentment. First, he tells me to be nice to Craig, she thought, now he's warning me against him. He can't have it both ways, damn it.

CHAPTER 15

When Alex arrived that evening, he suggested they go to a restaurant at the other side of the island. "It's by one of our best beaches and the sunset should be spectacular. It'll only take fifteen minutes to get there."

The evening started well. At sight of Alex, tall and elegant in a dark green open necked shirt and pale Chinos, his waving hair swept back from his forehead, Caro had felt a tingle of anticipation. Eleanor, sharp eyes missing nothing, was obviously delighted with what she saw and ushered them off with assurances that they weren't to hurry back.

By the time they arrived at the restaurant, Caro had almost managed to convince herself all there was to think about was what the evening might bring. But a tiny part of her mind kept returning to Craig and what Paul had said that afternoon.

A waiter appeared at their table to clear the plates from their first course and, when he'd gone, Alex looked across at her. He frowned slightly.

"Something else has happened, hasn't it?"

"How did you know?"

"Maybe I'm becoming sensitive to your moods."

"Surely not," she teased him, playing for time.

"You keep drifting off somewhere, preoccupied. What's on your mind? Tell me," he said.

She took a deep breath. "I had another visit from Paul Le Page this afternoon."

"Oh? What did he have to say for himself?"

There was no way to wrap it up. "He came to tell me that Craig has been using my consignments of cloth and furniture to smuggle stuff over from the Continent."

Alex's brows snapped together, and she saw the muscles round his mouth tighten. "And you had no idea?"

It was Caro's turn to frown.

"Of course, I didn't. Do you think I would have kept quiet if I had?"

"No, sorry. I meant…" He tried to take her hand, but she wouldn't let him. "Caro, please. I just meant you might have had a suspicion."

"Well I didn't," she snapped, then relented. "No. That's not entirely true. Perhaps I did have a niggling suspicion he was using me in some way, but I hadn't thought of that. And I can't work out how on earth he could do it."

"So, what are you going to do about it?" he asked.

"What can I do? I'll have to leave it to your friend Paul and the rest of them to sort out. It makes me so angry, to have been used like that. How could he?"

She knew the question was unanswerable, but she still found his silence unnerving and studied his face anxiously, trying to work out what he was thinking.

He told her. "I have a strong desire to march down to the marina and throw your ex into the harbour. The way he's used you is unforgivable. As for how he could do it, I don't know, Caro. Paid off someone in the French customs, perhaps. He's a shit, that's what it comes down to, an absolute shit."

"So how didn't I realise that before?" She began to tear a bread roll apart, as if it was personally responsible for all her troubles.

"Eleanor says you're inclined to believe the best of everybody."

"Doesn't say much for my judgement though, does it?"

Alex didn't reply and they were both a little relieved to be interrupted by the waiter again. He asked them what they were each having for their second course and placed the appropriate cutlery. They both sat in brooding silence while he did so. But once they were alone again, Caro went on.

"It makes it so difficult for me to do as Paul asks and be nice to Craig. All I feel like doing is kicking him in the bollocks."

Alex grinned. He liked the sound of that. "And I'll join in. But seriously, you'll just have to keep out of his way. I don't want you putting yourself at risk."

"I can look after myself, Alex," Caro said firmly.

His whole expression changed as he reached out to take her hand, rubbing at the palm, sending a tingling sensation right through her body. "But I'd much prefer it if you'd let me help, starting tonight," Alex said softly.

Her heart began to beat fast, but she gently wriggled her fingers out of his clasp. She didn't pretend to misunderstand him, but she couldn't get rid of a sense of panic. Only five days, only five days, kept up a mantra in her mind. She felt pressured and out of control. Part of her wanted to plunge in with no holds barred and damn the consequences, but part of her held back, wary and uncertain. She'd trusted Craig and look what had happened. Would Alex let her down too? And how soon would it be before all his doubts about her swept back in again? The deeper she became involved, the more it would hurt if everything collapsed around her.

She tried to hang on to some vestige of common sense. "Let's not go too fast, Alex. Let's get this business over first."

For a moment Alex said nothing. He looked across at her, his eyes dark, but then he relented. "Okay. I'll behave. But please don't make me wait too long."

Caro's lips lifted in a provocative smile. "I'll think about it."

But she wouldn't let him take her hand again. She could think more clearly when they weren't touching, and she still had a problem she needed to talk about.

"The thing is, Alex, I spoke to Alphonse today and he says he's got one of those chests of drawers in stock, the one for your bedroom. It would be perfectly possible to divert the present consignment to come via Guernsey. And the material for the sitting room, you know that striped blue and white linen? That's one of Bellefontaine's fabrics, the factory I told you about near Renne. I know them well and I'm a good customer. I'm sure we could persuade them to process it quickly, in time to put in with the rest. But, and it's a big but, if Craig and his pals are using it to smuggle stuff, well that complicates matters, doesn't it?"

Alex frowned. "I suppose. Is it definite that they've stashed stuff in this particular load?"

"I don't know. Paul says they aren't going to do a search yet. Something about giving them a bit more rope."

"Why?"

"He says they want to get the whole gang, not just the small fry."

"Isn't that a bit risky, for you apart from anything else?" He sounded annoyed and protective.

"Paul says they'll keep an eye on me."

"Well, so they bloody should! And so will Eleanor and I. When's this consignment due to arrive?"

"It'll leave France on Monday and arrive here early Tuesday morning. The stuff I've ordered for you will be offloaded, then the rest will go on to Portsmouth two days later." An unpleasant thought insinuated itself into her mind. "Unless of course something happens, and Paul decides it has to be searched. Do you think he will?"

Alex opened his mouth to reply then shut it again as they were interrupted once again as the waiter placed their food in front of them, lobster linguine for Caro, lemon sole for Alex. When he'd left them to it, Alex leant forward. He was frowning again.

"I've no idea whether Paul would or not," he said. "You know, something's puzzling me. Paul's being awfully free with all this information. Why, do you think?"

"Perhaps he's decided he trusts me."

"Ooh, I don't know so much," he joked, but it didn't quite come off. "In my experience Paul doesn't even trust his own mother. Perhaps he thinks you'll pass it all on to Craig and bounce him and his pals into doing something stupid."

"Thanks a bunch!" She didn't know whether to laugh or be angry.

"No. I'm overreacting. That wouldn't be it."

But it sounded to Caro as if he said it a little too quickly. "What makes you so sure?" she asked.

Alex didn't give her a direct answer. "It must be because he's decided to believe you."

Before she could stop herself, Caro asked, "And you trust me too now, do you?"

There was the tiniest of pauses before he answered, "Of course." Ignoring his food for a moment, he took her hand again. "Now can we please talk about other things, like you and me?"

"Yes, but no pressure, please, Alex."

"Okay, okay." To her his smile seemed a little over bright. "I'll settle for your life story. Start at day one and go on until now."

"You don't want to hear all that," Caro said, shaking her head, still feeling slightly put out.

"I do," Alex assured her. "I want to know everything there is to know about you. Where you went to school, what size shoe you wear, what your favourite colour is, everything."

"Alright. Be it on your head." Caro told herself she was imagining the undercurrents and smiled at him. "But if you get bored don't you dare show it."

* * *

In a corner of a wine bar on the other side of the island Craig and Ashley had just arrived. They ordered drinks and studied the menu, but Craig soon put his down. He wasn't willing to wait any longer.

"Right," he said, a sharp edge to his voice in contrast to the smile on his face. "What's this news you have for me?"

He hoped Ashley wasn't going to play games, he wasn't in the mood. Luckily, she seemed to sense this and, leaning back in her chair, studying him as she spoke, she began to tell him what he wanted to know.

"I have a cousin who happens to work for the border force, in Guernsey, I mean. She's a secretary to a man called Paul Le Page. Have you heard of him?"

Craig nodded grimly. "Oh yes, I know him alright. He's paid me several visits on the *Sally Anne* in the last couple of days. Bloody nuisance, in fact." His eyes narrowed. "So, this cousin of yours is his secretary."

"Yes. Typical of Guernsey that. Everyone knows everyone else. The thing is my cousin, Muriel, is also an inveterate gossip. She's only worked there for a few weeks. I don't think they realise what she's like. I'm pretty sure she'd lose her job if they knew what a wagging tongue she's got. And, what's more, she's a dreadful one for listening at doors, you wouldn't believe—"

Craig interrupted, "And what did this cousin of yours have to say that's so interesting?"

Ashley sat forward, leant her elbows on the table and clasped her hands under her chin. She looked very beautiful, and she knew it, but Craig was unmoved. He wanted to hear the information she had, anything else could come later.

"On Monday she overheard parts of a conversation between Paul Le Page and your girlfriend, Caro," Ashley said with a rabbit out of the hat flourish.

"How can you be sure it was Caro?"

"Because my cousin described her, small, large eyes, dark curly hair, and her name was Bennett. Satisfied?" Ashley said, eyebrows raised.

"So?"

"It's no good looking at me like that. Do you want this information or don't you?"

He had to acknowledge that, for the moment, she had the upper hand. He gave her his most charming smile. "I'm sorry," he said. "This business must be getting to me. I really mustn't take it out on you just because I've got problems, must I?"

Ashley relented. With a little prompting she told him all about the conversation Muriel had overheard. "They were talking about some piece of jewellery or other, a buckle shaped like two snakes." Her eyes narrowed as Craig drew an involuntary breath. "Does it sound familiar?"

He forced himself to relax. He must be careful. No point in giving anything away if he didn't have to. "Possibly," he said casually.

"Anyway, Muriel is a great one for romantic adventure stories and the mention of exotic jewels really got her attention. So did Paul asking Caro to be nice to someone called Craig. I made her repeat that bit and she was absolutely adamant that was the name she heard."

Craig had himself in hand this time and managed not to react beyond a questioning look.

Ashley went on, "It all smacked of conspiracy, and there's nothing she likes better. She really enjoyed telling me all about it. It's possible she embroidered a little, but the bones were there, and I found it all extremely interesting."

"Was there anything else?"

"Something about a trip up to London and Caro overhearing a conversation which worried her. Seems an awful lot of eavesdropping goes on these days. Again, there was mention of you. Apparently, your naive little girlfriend couldn't believe you were involved."

His lips lifted in an unpleasant smile. "I've worked very hard to make sure she'd think that way."

"I'm sure you have."

"And what else did she hear, this very useful cousin of yours?"

"That's about it. Someone came in and she had to beat a quick retreat. Oh no, there was just one other thing. At the last minute, Caro asked to go back into Paul's office. She told him she'd remembered a name, and that it was Jones. Does that mean anything to you?"

"No, not really," Craig lied smoothly.

"Is any of this useful to you?" Ashley asked.

"Could be. I owe you one. I won't forget."

They looked across the table at each other with mutual understanding. They were two of a kind.

"So, how're you going to deal with your girlfriend then?"

"I've known Caro a long time. I know all her weak spots. Believe me, if I set my mind to it I could have her believing anything I want. Just leave it to me."

"No. I want to know what you're planning."

Craig looked at her, his eyes narrowed. Best to keep her on side at the moment.

"Okay." He outlined what he had in mind.

"Do you think that's wise?"

"What do you mean?"

"Well, wouldn't it be a bit risky?" Ashley said. "It could backfire."

"I don't think so. Anyway, a little risk makes life more exciting. And once it's done, your way will be clear to reclaim your boyfriend, if of course that's what you want?"

"Maybe it is, maybe it isn't." Ashley's smile became more explicit. "Depends what else there is on the horizon. I'm no one man woman. I get bored too easily. But I do take exception to being dumped for an unsophisticated little madam like that."

"He dumped you?"

"I'm afraid so, not a good move on his part." Then she added quickly, "I hope you don't mind my describing her like that."

"Doesn't worry me. My relationship with Caro was useful to me, nothing more." Deep down, he knew he was lying. "She would have liked it to be more than that, but," he shrugged, "I live in the real world."

"Indeed, you do, just like me. That doesn't mean, of course, that I can't appreciate how she felt."

Craig took this compliment in his stride. After all, he'd never had trouble attracting women, and he didn't expect that to change. As far as he was concerned, any setbacks had been their fault not his. Caro's reaction to that business with Vanessa was a case in point. If she'd been less insecure, she would have understood. Okay, been angry for a few days, but he'd have expected her to come around without too much trouble.

But a niggling doubt was creeping in. Caro had been different to most of his other women. Maybe she meant more to him than he'd realised, and anyway, he wasn't about to let her end it all. No woman had ever done that to him before, and he wasn't going to allow that to change. What's more, the present situation was a bit more serious. It didn't just affect his relationship with Caro, it affected his business life as well, and that was an entirely different matter.

CHAPTER 16

Eleanor looked at Caro where she sat curled up on the floor, the early afternoon sun streaming through the window turning her hair to blue tinged ebony. She was surrounded once more by the contents of the suitcase, totally absorbed in her work.

"Did you and Alex manage to sort everything out last night?" Eleanor ventured tentatively.

"Oh yes. I know exactly what I need to order now. I've got to make a couple more phone calls and arrange to divert a consignment of stuff I've got ordered for some of my jobs at home." She waved her hands expressively. "You know, bring a few things for Alex's house to Guernsey, then re-route the rest to the mainland."

This was frustrating. Although she was interested in how the work on La Cotte was going, what she really wanted to know about was how things were going between Caro and Alex.

The night before Eleanor had been determined to stay awake until they got back but she hadn't managed to do so. At three in the morning she'd woken up, the light still on and her open book on her chest. This morning Alex had popped in on his way to the office. Caro's face had lit up at sight of him and the atmosphere between them positively sang. They'd spent some time talking about colours and fabrics and poring over catalogues, heads close together and voices murmuring, and at lunchtime they'd driven to La Cotte to take various measurements, but Alex hadn't stayed long after bringing Caro back.

I'm still none the wiser, thought Eleanor, and dying of curiosity, damn it. She tried to take herself in hand. Nosey old ladies were not attractive, so self-control would have to be imposed for a little longer. No doubt they'd tell her what was going on in their own good time.

"I've just got to ask the carrier to pick up the chest of drawers from Alphonse," Caro was saying, "and order some material from a supplier I know, and add all that to the consignment, hopefully for shipment on Monday. It'll be a little expensive, but Alex says that doesn't matter just this once."

"Can you change it all so easily?"

"Seems so," said Caro airily. Eleanor got the distinct impression she wasn't being told the whole story, but once again she forced herself not to ask questions.

"It'll mean we can get on much more quickly. Once we have everything we need, I can start organising painters and decorators. And I must find a good curtain-maker. Do you know of anyone?"

"I've got a friend who might be able to help. Shall I ask her?"

"Could you? That would be really useful."

"I'll do it now," Eleanor said, taking her mobile from her pocket.

By three o'clock Caro had the names of two curtain-makers, both of whom had showrooms in St Peter Port.

She borrowed Eleanor's bright red car and visited first one then the other, spent a useful hour talking colours, fabrics and designs, and then began the drive back to Villette House through the snail-slow rush hour traffic.

She was waiting at traffic lights a few hundred yards from the house, when the door on the passenger side opened suddenly. "Hallo, hallo," said Craig. "Fancy meeting you here."

"Craig! What the—"

"I was just coming up to see you," he said, getting into the car. "What a piece of luck. You can save me the walk."

Heart thumping, Caro sat there, rigid for a moment, her hands clutching the steering wheel. He'd taken her completely by surprise, and it wasn't until the driver behind sounded his horn that she came to.

"The lights are green, my sweet," Craig was saying. "Hadn't we better get going?"

Fuming, she let in the clutch, jerked forward and nearly hit the car in front.

"Careful." Craig smiled at her, obviously enjoying himself.

Caro swore under her breath but started off smoothly this time. Her mind racing, she tried to think of some scathing put-down. But how could she? Nothing had changed. She still had to be careful. But she had to get rid of him. The thought of Alex arriving to find Craig still hanging around was too awful to contemplate. And it was all very well for Paul to say she shouldn't be alone with Craig, but he hadn't told her how she could avoid it. She tried to comfort herself with the thought that there was plenty of traffic. He could hardly be a threat on a crowded rush hour road.

"What do you want?" She tried to sound cool and calm.

"Just a little talk. Meeting you like this is a stroke of luck. It'll be much better to talk away from the old bat's place."

"Don't call her that," she snapped.

"Okay, okay. No need to be so touchy."

His self-assurance had always undermined her, and she found it particularly disturbing now. What was he up to?

"It'll be easier to talk away from Eleanor Devereaux's house," Craig said, mocking her with each precisely enunciated word. "You can take me for a drive."

"No, I can't. Eleanor's expecting me back, this is her car." No need for him to know that Eleanor wasn't at home.

"Well, she'll just have to wait. Caro, my sweet, do as I ask," he said, a steely note creeping into his voice. "I have something to tell you and you won't want an audience while I do so."

"Tell me now."

"No. I want your full attention, and we can't have you driving into people."

"I'm sorry, Craig, but—"

They were at a standstill in the stream of traffic. It'd be so easy simply to get out of the car and leave him there, but she couldn't bring herself to do it. He must have read her mind. He gripped her shoulder, so hard that she could feel his nails digging into her flesh.

"I'm not taking no for an answer, Caro. So, if you know what's good for you, you'll drive straight on. Keep to this road and it will, eventually, take you to a beach called Vazon." He must have felt her reaction. "Ah, you recognise the name. Have you been there?" he asked, his tone conversational now.

"Yes." But she didn't tell him she and Eleanor had walked there on Sunday. It'd been such a lovely walk. Telling Craig about it would tarnish the memory.

"But not with me." He was back to smooth mockery now. "Never mind."

Leaning his head back, his eyes half closed, he gave every outward sign of being relaxed, but she could feel the tension in him. If she made any unexpected move, or didn't keep to the route he'd suggested, he'd be alert in no time at all. Seething inside with the familiar mixture of fear, impotence and anger, she went through half a dozen things he might want to tell her. It could be anything that would serve his purpose. There was no point in speculating, she'd just have to wait.

* * *

Fifteen minutes later, as she parked by the sea wall, she wondered how it was circumstances could make a place look so different. Facing the wide expanse of sea, now a shimmering grey blue in the late afternoon light, the whole place looked frightening and unwelcoming. So different from Sunday afternoon when she and Eleanor had watched the bright sails of the wind surfers as they dipped and swooped across the water.

"Ah," said Craig, apparently completely relaxed. "This is nice. Shall we go for a walk?"

"No, thanks. Just tell me what you want."

"Darling, what's the rush?"

"Stop playing games, Craig."

He tried to take her hand, but she snatched it away. "Caro, Caro, relax. Why don't we sit and look at this beautiful view for a bit, enjoy each other's company?"

That was the last straw. She felt a wave of anger so intense that all the warnings she'd been given, and the fear, were swamped. Paul's advice went out of the window, along with his contradictory request to be nice, swiftly followed by her promise to herself that she'd take care.

She leant forward and started the car. "I've had enough of this. Get out!" she spat at him. "Get out now."

The merest flicker of anger shadowed Craig's eyes for a moment. Or was it uncertainty? A moment later he had himself under control again.

He looked straight at her. "Okay, no more games." He was no longer provocative, and Caro clenched her teeth, waiting.

139

"I have something to tell you about your precious hostess."

This was completely unexpected. Caro turned off the engine.

"I think you should listen," Craig went on silkily, "if you care about her at all, which you seem to. If you don't, well" – he shrugged – "no matter."

"What about her?"

"She seems to have something of a reputation."

"What on earth do you mean?"

"In dealing circles."

Still she didn't understand.

Craig turned slightly and looked straight at her, his lips twitching in a satisfied little smile as if he knew he had the upper hand now. Caro felt sick and cold, and desperately anxious not to be in this confined space with him. She got out of the car and went to lean her hands on the sea wall, feeling the cold roughness of the granite under her fingers. She took a deep, shuddering breath of the crisp salty air. Craig came and perched himself on the wall and leant towards her, so close she could smell his familiar aftershave. She tried to step away, but his hand shot out and grasped her wrist.

"Now, my little one, you're going to listen to me. I've got something to tell you about Eleanor Devereaux that might well shock you. On the other hand, you might not care at all. Your elderly friend is something of a collector, and she's not above buying the occasional suspect piece of art. Aha, I thought it would come as a surprise to you." He grinned. "She's a collector, mainly of nineteenth-century oil paintings, English, French, sometimes watercolours, and she sometimes picks up an interesting piece of porcelain. She's not that bothered about their antecedents so long as the price is good. We're talking about a very shrewd woman here."

For a moment he waited, but Caro remained stubbornly silent. Shrugging, he went on, "I'm told she rather enjoys the risk. She did, after all, marry into a family that, way back, were famous privateers. Sounds romantic, doesn't it? That's where they made their money. The wine, and respectability, came much later. Of course, she only married into the tradition, but she was well suited to it. Her own family's history was much the same."

He stopped speaking but, never taking his eyes from her face, he waited for her to react. Caro forced herself to meet his gaze, and the satisfied smirk that curved his lips made her itch to push him off the wall, anything to get rid of him.

"You think I'm going to believe this garbage?" she asked, trying to inject as much contempt into her voice as possible. "And who told you all this?"

Directly she'd asked the question she realised that, in a way, it legitimised what he'd said. But there was no taking it back now.

"My sources are reliable."

"Ha! Ashley no doubt. And you'd believe her, would you, when she has every reason to want to get back at Alex, and Eleanor?"

"Has she now?"

"You know perfectly well—"

He gripped her arm again. "What do I know? That he's ditched her in favour of you, is that it?"

"Don't be stupid. You're just trying to avoid telling me who's been spreading this poisonous gossip."

"My dear Caro, I would have thought you'd know what a small world the antiques business is. What's more, in such a close-knit community, everyone's bound to know everyone else's business." He shrugged, still mocking her. "But you want more tangible proof than that, don't you? Well, I have an associate who acquired some pieces for your elderly friend. I could give you his name and number. You could ask him yourself."

"No, thanks. I still wouldn't believe it," Caro said with as much conviction as she could muster.

"Come back with me to the *Sally Anne*. One short call and you'd know whether or not I'm right."

She could feel his sharp eyes studying her reaction and tried to remain as impassive as possible, but his silky voice was chipping away at her confidence.

"Haven't you noticed the goodies she has in that house of hers?" he asked. "Think about it, Caro."

Caro was thinking about it. She wished she could stop thinking about it. Unable to keep up the facade any longer, she turned her back on him, but this didn't stop the drip, drip of the poison in her mind.

"So, my dear, you're not mixing in such fancy company as you thought. And her precious grandson's probably much of a muchness, in spite of his oh-so-respectable front. What a pair of pals you've acquired! And you, so very law abiding. It's rather amusing, in a sad sort of way."

He stopped speaking and Caro knew he was waiting for what he'd said to do its work. He wanted her to go on arguing, defending Eleanor and Alex, but she didn't. She was damned if she was going to dance to his tune.

At first, she'd dismissed what he'd said, even felt relief at the absurdity of it all. But it hadn't taken long for the canker of doubt to start spreading. One by one trivial incidents and conversations begun to wriggle up to the surface. What had Eleanor said about Paul Le Page? That he was overzealous, too nosey, and she'd made it clear she had no time for his profession, which would be entirely understandable if what Craig said was true. Who'd want the authorities nosing around in a house full of stolen goods? Another memory came worming in, of Eleanor asking Alex to move the painting in the hall, hadn't that been just before Paul arrived? Caro was sure Alex had thought it an odd request at the time. But it went further than that. Alphonse had mentioned William Devereaux, he'd said, 'William was obsessed with his collection… he'd search them out with great passion.' So, William was an avid collector. Perhaps he too had been keen enough not to be scrupulous about where his purchases came from. Maybe that was acceptable to the Devereaux family.

And like icing on some ghastly cake, Caro finally remembered the conversation she'd had with Eleanor on this very spot. 'My kind of excitement?' Eleanor had had a strange smile on her face as she'd gazed out towards the horizon. 'Other sorts of risks. Alex says I'm not really happy unless I'm breaking the rules.' The words echoed in Caro's mind. 'At my age life's too short to be bound by petty little laws laid down by bureaucrats with no imagination.' And when Caro had remarked that she was a very unusual person, Eleanor had taken it as a compliment, as if taking risks and breaking rules was something to be admired.

Craig's voice, full of mockery, dragged her back to the present. "My darling, I expected you to spring to her defence, a positive tour de force of righteous indignation. On the other hand, perhaps you know more about her than I do."

"Of course I don't. You really must be desperate if these are the lengths you'll go to to poison my friendship with the Devereaux. What did you do, Craig? Make all this up thinking I'd throw my hands up in horror?"

Again, there was that flicker of uncertainty in his eyes. It gave her courage. She warmed to her theme. "Did you think I'd run wailing into your arms crying, take me home, take me away from this place? God, you must be desperate."

"Not at all, my dear Caro. I just happen to care about you and would hate to see you" – there was an infinitesimal pause – "hurt, that's all."

"Hah! That comes fine from you." She'd had enough. "It hasn't worked, understand? I don't believe a word."

Taking him completely by surprise, she swung round and opened the car door, slammed it, locked it, and turned the ignition. Waves of relief coursed through her as the engine started first time. He had his hand on the door handle now, but she ignored his protests, backed out of the car park, spraying gravel everywhere, and drove off. In the rear-view mirror she saw Craig running after her, waving and shouting. She laughed, laughter tinged with hysteria, and shouted aloud, "Serves you bloody right! You can find your own way back." But the canker was still spreading. Over and over in her mind went conversation after conversation, and each one seemed to back up what Craig had said. Would Eleanor really break the rules to the extent she'd implied?

As Caro drove through the gates of Villette House she could hardly remember how she'd got there. Glancing at her watch as she walked up the steps, she saw that it was half past five, prayed that Eleanor would still be out. Her plan had been to walk into town to meet up with a friend, and she'd said she might stay on into the evening. Caro hoped desperately that she had. She wasn't at all sure she'd be able to face Eleanor's sharp perceptiveness at the moment.

CHAPTER 17

Caro wandered out into the lengthening shadows of the garden, her hands thrust deep into the pockets of her jacket. In a few minutes Alex would be here to pick her up.

She'd had time to think about what Craig had said and get it into proportion. What more useful to him than to drive a wedge between her and Eleanor and, thereby, between her and Alex? Well, I'm not going to let him do it, she told herself. And now, with Alex about to arrive, there were other problems occupying her mind.

Over the rest of yesterday evening, and through this morning while she and Alex worked at La Cotte, tying up the loose ends of the designs they'd decided on, Caro had been keenly aware that she'd never before experienced such a strong physical attraction to someone. They'd known each other for such a short time, but her life before she'd met Alex seemed to have retreated, become colourless. Only the present was in sharp focus. And yet the warning voice in her mind kept telling her to be careful, don't rush. Haltingly she'd tried to explain some of her feelings to Alex and he'd seemed to understand, had agreed they should take things slowly, get to know each other. But this morning she'd had to be very firm, both with herself and with him.

"Right. Now we've got to make sure that bed of Alphonse's isn't going to overpower your room size wise," she told him briskly as they went up the winding stairway to his bedroom. Once there, he'd closed the door decisively and pulled her towards him, the impish grin on his face making him look more like a badly behaved schoolboy than a grown man. She'd wriggled free of his hold.

"Behave, Alex!"

Slightly breathless, she'd thrust the end of a tape measure into his hand. "Just hold the end of that and do as you're told," she'd insisted, reaching for her notebook and pen. She found it easier to work if she didn't look at him.

And now, in a matter of minutes, he'd be picking her up. Caro had her doubts she'd be able to hold out for long. When he came walking through to the garden in search of her, she was wondering why she should.

"I thought we could drive to the west coast, there should be another fantastic sunset tonight," Alex said as they turned out at the wrought-iron gates. "We'll go just along the coast from where you went with Eleanor on Sunday, a beach called Cobo, near the restaurant we had dinner at."

Caro's stomach jolted and she turned quickly to look out of the window, afraid that her face might give her away. But he was looking straight ahead, concentrating on his driving.

"There's a marvellous view," Alex went on. "Very romantic. Just right for my mood."

With great determination, Caro pushed Craig and his vicious gossip firmly from her mind and began to tell Alex about the arrangements she'd made that afternoon.

"Alphonse is delighted that you want some of his furniture. He's going to have the chest of drawers delivered to the carrier's depot tomorrow, bless him, and he says the bed will be ready in about two weeks."

She didn't tell Alex what else Alphonse had said.

"You're in love with this Alex Devereaux, that is certain."

"What do you mean?"

"Is it not clear, what I said? I hear it in the voice. The voice of my Caro says she's in love with this Alex every time she mentions his name."

"Nonsense, I've only known him for a matter of days." But she couldn't help smiling as she said it.

"*Po, po, po.* What does that matter?" There'd been a throaty chuckle at the end of the line. "This bed, it will be needed soon, I think."

"Alphonse!" Caro had protested, but he'd laughed again, and with a breezy, "*Au revoir*, my darling Caro," he'd ended the call.

No, she definitely didn't repeat any of that to Alex.

"That all sounds great," he was saying. His hand came up to caress the back of her neck and his voice changed. "And after we've watched the sunset, we'll go back to La Cotte, okay?"

His touch said it all. She felt as she used to when playing childhood games in the park, starting at the top of a steep slope of grass and rolling willy-nilly down to the bottom. Breathlessly exciting games, they might have been, but always with an element of fear. That had been half the fun. But she wasn't at all sure that was how she wanted to live her adult life. Falling for Alex had happened so quickly and in such extraordinary circumstances. What if she was wrong about Alex as well? What if there was truth in what Craig had told her? The doubts and the questions gnawed away at her.

"You're very quiet." Alex's voice broke into her thoughts. "Penny for them?"

"Oh, nothing much," Caro said, rooting around quickly for something to say. "I was just thinking about all this business with the smuggling and everything."

"Don't let it worry you, not this evening."

She gave him a smile but didn't respond.

A moment later they'd parked. They got out of the car and went to sit on the sea wall. Below them was an expanse of smooth sand, and here and there people were walking their dogs. The rocks either side of the bay looked very dark now, although Caro knew in the daytime they'd be the warm, apricot colour of the granite in this part of the island. On the horizon, the sun had nearly disappeared, leaving stripes of scarlet and purple behind, and the water reflected the brilliant colours. Two people were standing on paddle boards, moving slowly towards the shore, and there were a few boats moored in the distance. Two looked very like Alex's *Pauillac*.

Alex put his arm round her shoulders and pulled her close. Perhaps in an effort to distract him, she said, "Those boats out there look a bit like yours. Why did you buy an old fishing boat, instead of a yacht or something?"

"Ugh," he made a slightly scornful sound. "They're not for me. My dear old girl suits me much better." He grimaced. "I'm not one for the yachty, gin palace circuit. *Pauillac's* got so much more personality than those sleek modern efforts. I almost feel I can talk to her sometimes." He grinned. "Sounds loony, doesn't it?"

But Caro understood entirely. "Not a bit, and I'm glad."

"About what?"

"That you're not a yachty type. I can't be having with all that. Craig loves it, lots of glossy smart people with loud voices and large bank balances. They always made me feel small and out of place." She gave a little shudder inside, but not entirely at the memory of those uncomfortable gatherings, partly because the conversation had come around to Craig again.

"I've never tried paddle boarding," Alex said as they watched the two wet-suited men drag their boards up the beach. "I used to do a lot of surfing, but now I've got *Pauillac*, I'd rather be out on her when I've got some free time."

"That's something I've never tried, surfing." Caro grimaced. "Too much of a coward."

He grinned. "I wouldn't put you down as a coward."

"No?" She grimaced and turned to look at him. "Just wait till you get to know me better."

She felt Alex's arm tighten around her shoulders. "And are you going to let me do that?"

This was no simple question. It charged the atmosphere all around them, and it begged for an answer. Alex's eyes looked down at her – dark pools in the dusk – and Caro was unable to look away or to pretend any longer. Her lips parted as she tried to think of an answer, but she had no chance to speak. Alex put up a hand to cradle her cheek, bent swiftly and covered her lips with his own. It was a gentle, tentative exploration and when he lifted his head, the question was still in his eyes. Caro put her hands up to his chest, intending to be sensible, give him an answer, any answer. But it didn't work out like that. Instead she found herself sliding her hands up and around his neck, drawing his face down to hers. This time the kissing wasn't as tentative.

For some time all that could be heard was the whisper of the waves up the beach and, occasionally, a laugh or a snatch of conversation from the few people left around, and the distant thrum of music from a pub a little way along the road.

At last Caro stepped back, holding him off now. "I'm sorry," she said.

"Why?"

"I hadn't intended that to happen."

He laughed. "That's not very complimentary."

"Sorry–"

"Stop apologising."

"I mean, I'd meant for us to take things slowly, but it's so difficult."

"What? To keep your hands off me?" This time his laugh was full of amused delight.

"Alex!" But it was true.

Caro shivered and immediately he was serious. "You're cold," he said. "Come on, we can carry on this, um, conversation in comfort back at the house. What you need is a nice hot cup of coffee, maybe with a spot of brandy in it."

In the dusk they drove round the coast and up through the lanes until they came to the one leading to La Cotte. As they got nearer and nearer to their destination, Caro could feel the tension building up. Her imagination conjured up irresistible images. Following Alex up those winding stairs to that low-ceilinged room, making love in his warm bed, then sleeping in his arms all night. Maybe waking to make love again. But no, she couldn't – shouldn't go through with it.

While he made the coffee, she wandered around his kitchen, unable to keep still, picking up a plate here, a mug there, and carefully replacing each piece without really looking at it. When the coffee was ready, he carried the mugs through to his study, swept some books off the ancient sofa so that Caro could sit down, and threw himself into the dilapidated old chair beside the fireplace. He didn't touch her, and she was grateful. When he began to talk about the plans they'd made that morning, she hardly heard a word, and after a while he stopped speaking.

As the silence stretched out the tension rose. Alex was the first to move and, when he did, it was decisive. He put his coffee mug down on the floor with a crack, came and sat down next to her and pulled her firmly into his arms.

"Alex!"

"Don't talk."

"But–"

"Ssh." And he stopped any more argument by kissing her, gentle touches of lips and tongue at first, but soon they changed, became deeper and more urgent. At last Caro responded without reserve. She felt Alex's hands move softly up inside her jumper, warm on her bare skin. She moaned at the waves of sensation his urgent touch produced. Any minute now it would be too late, there'd be no turning back. But that cold voice of caution, completely drowned a moment ago, became louder and louder. She struggled slightly against him and abruptly she was released. Alex slid down to sit on the floor, breathing hard, his head bent down, leaving Caro lying back, dishevelled and bereft on the sofa.

For a moment neither of them spoke, then Caro put out a shaking hand to touch his cheek. Hungrily his lips came around to kiss her fingers. She was close to tears.

"I'm so sorry," she whispered. "It seems I don't know my own mind. I feel so bloody confused. It's like being in a car with no brakes, and I just can't cope with the feeling of being out of control. I've never, ever felt like this about anyone before, Alex, but can we slow down? Just until this bloody business is over. I'm sorry. I'm probably not making any sense at all."

He looked up at her, his eyes dark and frowning. "Yes, you are, making sense I mean. It's just that I want you so much. What you said last night went right out of my head."

"Give me time, Alex. Give us time."

"Okay." The word came out on a sigh. "But I'm not going to wait too long. I feel the same as you, this is a first for me."

She didn't answer but sat up, began to pull her clothes back into some kind of order and pushed her tangled hair back from her forehead. Alex watched her and she gave him a shaky little smile. "I bet you wish you'd never rescued me."

He took her hand quickly and kissed it. "Never, ever think that, Caro. Never."

His intensity frightened her. All of a sudden, she was desperate to be on her own. "Would you take me back now, to Eleanor's? Do you mind?"

For a moment Alex said nothing, then he burst out. "Of course I mind. I want to go upstairs and go on where we left off. I want to wake up with you still there." It was as if he'd read her mind. "I want some way of knowing this isn't some flash in the pan." Then he lifted his hands in a gesture of surrender. "I'm sorry, I'm sorry. I won't say any more, except one thing…"

She held her breath, wondering what was coming next.

"I don't care if it's been less than a week. I don't care if we've got Paul's men swarming all over and half a dozen ex-lovers knocking at the door. I'm not going to change my mind."

Caro put up her hands to cup his face and smiled a sad little smile. She wondered if he'd still be saying the same thing in a few days' time. "I'll try to, Alex. Now take me back to Eleanor's, please."

CHAPTER 18

A large van marked with the logo of a local carrier drove along the main road linking Rennes and St Malo, beside the picturesque banks of the River Rance. But the driver hardly noticed his surroundings, he was in too much of a hurry. He didn't see the bright red ochre and blue sails of the pot-bellied boats on the river, or the billowing white sails of modern yachts. Nor did he see, a little way up the river, the two bridges – one old and traditional, one a graceful sweep of modern concrete. Hands tense on the steering wheel, his foot hard on the accelerator, and with little regard for the speed limit, he kept going until he got to the outskirts of St Malo. Here he slowed down and, ten minutes later, arrived at a shabby, derelict industrial estate, uninhabited by busy workers and other vehicles. It was the perfect venue.

Jean Peron stopped the van once he'd manoeuvred it out of sight of the road. He jumped out, his small ferret-like eyes darting around, checking the surroundings before he opened the back of the van, hauled himself up, then stopped. He knew immediately that something was different. At lunchtime, when the depot had been quiet, he'd done a quick check to plan how to fit the merchandise in and that polished wood chest of drawers had not been there, nor the two paper wrapped tubes that he recognised as bolts of cloth stacked behind it. Ah well, he thought, at least it had been done before this evening and not after.

He glanced at his watch. A quarter past six, fifteen minutes to wait. They'd better not be late. He hadn't much time. The van had to be back at the depot by seven thirty. The driver had said he'd collect it before the weekend, insisting it would make things easier for him on Monday morning.

Twenty minutes later Jean was getting impatient, then he heard the sound of a car. Good. That should be them. A black four-by-four swept around the corner and parked next to the van. Two men got out.

"*Hein*, Marcel! What kept you?" Jean asked irritably as they shook hands.

"The traffic, *mon vieux*, the traffic. Don't panic, there's plenty of time." Nothing ever seemed to worry Marcel. He was a large man with a deceptively benevolent air, who would willingly have sold his sister for a decent profit. He turned to the younger man with him, "This is my son. Come on, you great oaf, get the stuff."

The boy, looking sullen and resentful, his enormous hands dangling by his sides, did as he was told. He leant into the car and brought out a briefcase. Marcel took it from him without thanks, placed it on the floor of the van and opened it. Inside were several small packages.

"You can check them if you wish," he told Jean, his tone implying that it would be offensive for him to do so.

But Jean took no notice. He knew his job. He picked up a package, heavy for its size, and opened it up to reveal carefully folded tissue paper. He unwrapped it to find, nestling inside, a beautiful brooch. It was about the size of the palm of a baby's hand, formed in the shape of an elaborately decorated sea serpent curled in upon itself, and for its eye there was one large and perfect emerald. The two other men bent forward to look and they all stood in silence for a moment, somewhat overawed by the sight of such riches.

"*Mon Dieu!* Some trinket, that," Jean said reverently, but he was the first to recover. "Okay," he said, and replaced the brooch in its wrapping with infinite care. "Let's have a look at the rest."

After a thorough inspection of the contents of the briefcase Jean was satisfied. Snapping it shut he handed over a brown envelope. "That's half the dosh. When this arrives at its destination you get the rest, but not before. The boss says he wants to check everything is okay before he hands over the full amount."

"That was the arrangement," said Marcel, shrugging his enormous shoulders. "Unnecessary, but if that's what he wants. Just so long as I get the rest pronto, otherwise there'll be trouble, understand?"

"When have you known him not to pay up?"

"Not yet, but there's always a first time."

"Don't be a fool, man, he'll pay." Jean jumped up into the van and took the briefcase to the back. "Give me a hand with some of this furniture. I can't get to the hatch."

* * *

At ten past seven Jean drove up to the depot, swung himself out of the cab and opened the tall iron gates, then jumped out and closed the gates behind him. No sign of the driver yet. He passed his hand across his forehead in relief, got back into the cab and drove quickly round to the spot from which he'd taken the van a couple of hours ago. So far so good. But he was only just in time. As he walked across the forecourt to his car, the gates were pushed open and the driver came striding up the driveway.

"*Hein*, Jean, got no home to go to?" he asked with a grin.

"Just off now," said Jean, trying to sound off-hand. "I had some paperwork to finish before the weekend."

"Did you leave the keys like I asked you?"

"Sure. On the hook under the third step up to the office. But this is the last time, the boss would have a fit if he found out we hadn't followed those official procedures he's so fond of."

"Well, he's not going to find out from me." The driver's weathered face split into a grin. "He's paying me time and a half because the route's been changed, so I'm not about to complain. He might change his mind."

Jean had been about to get into his car, but this stopped him in his tracks. "What did you say? What route?" His voice was sharp.

"The route on Monday, it's changed. I've got to take this load to Guernsey, dump some stuff there, then go on to England. Would you believe it? I can tell you, I made sure he knew I wasn't best pleased. Safe enough to make my feelings clear since he couldn't get another driver at such short notice." He grinned, pleased with himself. "So, he's promised me time and a half. Good, eh?"

"When did he change his mind?" Again, Jean's voice was sharp, and the man gave him a curious look.

"This afternoon. What's it to you?"

Jean tried to smile and gave a shrug of his shoulders. "Nothing. Just curious. He's a bloody pain, that man."

"I'm not surprised you think so. Found another job yet?"

"Of course," Jean said. It wasn't entirely untrue.

"Anyway, it's probably the artistic temperament. At least I'm making a bit out of the deal." He hoisted himself up into the cab. "*Au revoir*," he said, with a wave of his hand out of the window.

Jean stood staring at the retreating van. He felt a cold, sinking feeling in his stomach. He was a superstitious man and he'd felt all along there was something bad about this deal. But there was nothing he could do. Except warn them about the change in plans, and the sooner the better. He took out his mobile, but there was no reception. He'd have to try later.

When he finally got through to Craig on the *Sally Anne* the following morning, the reaction was just as bad as he'd expected. Before Jean had time to relay any of his news, Craig was shouting down the line. "Christ almighty! Where the fuck have you been? I've been trying to contact you since Wednesday night. Why don't you ever answer your phone?"

"Bad reception," Jean spat out, wincing as he held his phone an inch from his ear. He'd used beer and wine to help him sleep the night before and the resulting hangover was of giant proportions. "I have to work, me. And I was following your instructions, fixing up the consignment. What else do you think I do?"

Craig ignored this question. "We've got a problem."

"I know. It's for this reason I telephone."

"What do you mean, you know?"

"What I say. The driver told me."

"About the customs?"

"What is this about the bloody *douane*?" There was a note of panic in Jean's voice. "I hate them! Always with the long nose in other people's business. What trouble do we have with them?"

"Big trouble," Craig snapped. "Is that what the driver told you? How did he know? He's not one of us."

It dawned on Jean's befuddled brain that they must be talking at cross purposes. He'd have to find out what the authorities were up to in a minute. Now he must tell Craig about the change of route. Quickly he did so. When he'd finished there was silence at the other end of the line. It dragged on for so long that Jean asked, "Are you still there?"

"Yes, yes. I was thinking." Craig's voice was sharp and hard. "You'll have to get the stuff back before the van leaves."

In exasperation Jean lapsed into his own language. "*Ah, mais ça, c'est pas possible.* No way. That would be absolutely impossible."

"Why?"

"Because the driver, he's already taken the van. He tells me it will be easier if he fetches it yesterday evening, then he can make the early start on Monday. He has to collect some more packages Monday morning, before he goes to the ferry."

"Well, get it back Monday morning."

"How do I do this?"

"Can't you get hold of this driver?"

"And what do I say? Excuse me, my friend, I must remove my stolen jewels from your van. I am so obliged, monsieur, for your help." He gave a scornful snort then winced as his head throbbed. "I think not, *hein*? Anyway, I don't know where he lives."

"Do you mean to tell me you let this man go off, knowing what was in the van, and you don't even know where it bloody is? You, sodding cretin!"

"*Attention!* I'm not having you—"

But Craig wasn't listening. He cut through Jean's protests. "Then I'll have to try from this end. Christ! This is one hell of a mess. You've really cocked up this time. Jones is going to have our hides."

"What is this?" He didn't understand the English idiom.

"Never mind."

It occurred to Craig that it wouldn't be a good idea for Jean Peron to start panicking. He might end up going to the police, dropping everyone else in it to save his own skin. He said, more calmly, "Leave it with me. Just sit tight, and don't disappear off again. Understood?"

"Okay, okay." Jean's voice was sullen but resigned.

Craig ended the call and began to pace backwards and forwards in the confined space of the *Sally Anne's* cabin. He had to act fast, this really was one hell of a setback, but there was no point in rushing into anything. It all had to be planned very carefully. No slip-ups, no loose ends. And the minimum of information to Jones if it was remotely possible. He, at all costs, had to be kept sweet. Craig had seen the results of his displeasure in the past and was far from anxious to experience anything like it again.

Pouring himself a very stiff whisky, he drank most of it in one gulp before sitting down at the table. Drumming his fingers on the wood, he sat very still, his eyes narrowed, and his lips compressed into a cruel line as he thought of Caro. This was all her fault, but she'd pay, oh yes, he'd make sure of that. No-one, but no-one, screwed things up for him and got away with it.

His mind racing, he planned his revenge, going over what he intended to do point by point. He got up and went to the small, tapering cabin in the bows of the boat, searched around under the bunk for a while and finally found the small suitcase he'd pushed right to the back. Unzipping it he rummaged around inside, finally found what he was looking for – a small brown plastic bottle. He checked its contents, gave a nod of satisfaction, and put it in his pocket, then pushed the bag back under the bunk. Satisfied, he went back to the main cabin and poured himself another, slightly smaller, whisky.

* * *

"I wish Alex hadn't had to go to Jersey for the day," Eleanor said, "and on a Saturday too. Why can't these businessmen confine their activities to weekdays, it'd be much nicer for you to be having a romantic little lunch with Alex instead of sitting here with me, eating salad."

"I'm enjoying my salad," said Caro, spearing a bright piece of yellow pepper with her fork as she smiled at Eleanor, "and your company for that matter."

"You're a dear girl to say so, but it's not the same. Never mind, let's have some wine, that'll cheer us up." She got up and took a bottle of white wine from the fridge, twisted off the top and poured them a glass each. "Cheers. Here's to you and Alex."

"Nothing's definite yet–"

"A mere detail," Eleanor said.

Caro smiled at her, a little uncertain. "Are you sure you're happy about, well, us?"

"I'm absolutely delighted, my dear. I've longed for Alex to find someone he cares about, and now he has. I couldn't be more pleased."

"In spite of the fact we've known each other for such a short time?"

"Oh that." Eleanor waved a dismissive hand. "I was saying to Alex a couple of days ago, when I met his grandfather, I knew immediately that he was the one. He proposed after two weeks, but he said he'd waited ten days longer than he'd wanted to, so it'd been the same for him. It must run in the family."

"But Alex and I aren't engaged or anything," Caro protested, once more getting that pressured feeling of events speeding out of control.

"No, I know, but things aren't the same nowadays, are they? You don't have to do the conventional thing like we did," Eleanor said airily, patting Caro's hand and refilling her glass. "You've got plenty of time to get to know each other."

Caro stared out of the kitchen window at the bright forsythia in the garden. Was it possible to do as Eleanor suggested? In the circumstances it didn't seem so, and yet, the temptation just to push everything else aside and concentrate on Alex was hard to resist. Why not grasp every ounce of happiness before it disappeared again? Eleanor was right. Never mind about knowing Alex for one short week. When he got back, she'd tell him there'd be no more barriers.

The afternoon stretched before her. She looked up at the kitchen clock. Only a quarter to two, hours to wait yet. Feeling like a child looking forward to half a dozen Christmases rolled into one, she decided she would have to do something to fill the time.

"I'd better get some more work done on ideas for La Cotte this afternoon, so that I can show Alex when he gets home."

"You do that. I've got to go out, a friend of mine's recovering from a hip replacement and I promised to visit her. But before that, let's finish this bottle of wine. I feel like celebrating."

"Celebrating what?"

"Alex being happy." She smiled a little wistfully. "It's been a long time since I could say that. Quite apart from the fact that I've become very fond of you, my dear, I couldn't but feel grateful to you for that, if nothing else."

Caro returned the smile. "Okay, go on," she said, and held her glass out for a refill.

CHAPTER 19

It was barely ten minutes after Eleanor had left that a text came through from Craig. "It'd be a good idea if you came down to the *Sally Anne*. I've got proof of the Devereaux's dealings."

Caro's light-hearted mood disappeared in a second. She texted back with shaking fingers. "What proof? I don't believe you."

The response was back within seconds. "I'll show you when you get here. If you're not here within the hour I'm going to the press. I mean it."

Caro paced up and down, her mind in turmoil. What could she do? She knew him well enough to realise that, true or not, if he started spreading damaging rumours about Eleanor and Alex it would harm them, however false it was. She couldn't bear that. Within ten minutes she'd made a decision. Within fifteen she'd written a quick note to Eleanor.

"I've gone into town to do a bit of shopping. I'll get the matches you wanted." Eleanor had remarked that she needed a box of matches for the kitchen. "See you later, love Caro." She left it on the kitchen table.

Grabbing her bag, she strode off down the hill, feeling sick with apprehension but determined to do what she could to spike Craig's guns. As a small act of defiance, she did a bit of shopping, including the matches, and then she made her way down to the Albert Pier. A moment later she felt a hand grip her arm. She swung round. It was Craig.

"You ran out on me, Caro. Did you think you could get rid of me that easily?" His hand gripped her arm as he looked down at her, a triumphant glint in his eyes and the cruelty in his thin lips more pronounced than she'd ever seen.

They were getting curious looks from passers-by. "And don't start thinking you can cry for help or some such theatrical idea," he told her. "If you do, I spill the beans about your new friends right now, full volume, in public. I mean what I say. You do realise that, don't you?"

Looking up at his expression, she believed him.

He kept hold of her arm and guided her, none too gently, towards the railing at the edge of the quay. "Come on. Like I said, I've got something really interesting to show you."

Caro remained stubbornly silent. He grinned at her. "Aren't you going to jump to their defence?"

"No, because I know you're lying." But her voice wavered. He picked up on her uncertainty.

"You're not completely sure, though, are you? Otherwise why would you be here."

"Okay," Caro snapped, glaring at him. "Show me. Just let go of my arm. Let's get this over."

At last he did as she asked but, with a hard hand in the small of her back, he pushed her towards the gangway down to the pontoon where the boat was moored. Sick at heart, Caro preceded him and, a moment later, stepped onto the deck. There was no turning back now.

It seemed like a lifetime ago that she'd last been on board. As she stumbled down into the cabin Craig was close behind her. There was nothing to do but sit down and wait for him to produce his proof. Alongside her fear of him, was a growing fear of what he might show her.

But her ordeal was far from over.

"Let's have some coffee," Craig said, sounding ludicrously hospitable. The mugs were ready on the worktop. He reached for the jar of coffee and switched on the kettle.

"I don't want any."

"Come on, be sociable."

"Craig—"

"Listen, humour me. First coffee, then I'll show you the proof."

She gave in. She'd drink his blasted coffee and then make her getaway as soon as she could. Clasping her hands on the table in front of her to keep them from trembling, she waited as Craig moved deftly about the cabin.

"There you are." He put a mug down in front of her. "You've made it quite clear you don't want to be here any longer than necessary, so drink up and I'll fetch what I wanted to show you."

She picked up the mug and gulped down some of the hot liquid. It was very strong, but never mind, the sooner she drank it, the sooner she could get this awful business over. All she wanted to do was get away from Craig and make sure she never, ever saw him again.

He pulled out a drawer in one of the cupboards and took out a sheaf of papers, all the while watching her with those narrowed, pale eyes.

She banged the mug down. "Okay. Satisfied?" She injected as much scorn as she could into her voice, trying to hide the fear that was making her feel sick. "Now where's this so-called proof?"

He sat down opposite her, the little sheaf of papers under his hand. "First of all, I want to explain how I came by these. I know you're no great fan of Ashley Guilbert, but she has been involved with your friend Alex for some time. She's worked for him for over three years, and they've been lovers for at least a year now."

Caro shook her head, not wanting to hear this.

"No good trying to deny it, my dear, it's a fact. So, you see, she knows him very well indeed." He reached out and took her hand. "Just as I know you."

Caro snatched her hand away and clasped it tight on her lap. Strange how such a small movement could make the boat sway so. Craig was still talking, telling her more that she didn't want to know, and she prayed that he'd get to the point, show her this proof. She squinted across the table at him, wondering why his voice seemed to be getting louder, then quieter, then louder again. Closing her eyes for a moment, she tried hard to concentrate, but when she opened them it made her feel dizzy.

She opened her mouth to speak, but no words came out. Screwing up her eyes, she gazed across the table as Craig's face floated about, disembodied, in front of her. Someone was pulling her up. She turned to look, and her head went on turning, turning, as the blackness came to swallow her up.

* * *

Craig couldn't believe his luck. The drug had worked far more quickly than he'd expected. And the man had been right, the taste can't have been noticeable in strong coffee. Once he'd half dragged, half persuaded Caro down to the small cabin in the bows and pushed her onto the bunk, he went swiftly back to the main cabin. It was important there should be no sign of her presence if anyone came looking for her.

And then he froze. The *Sally Anne* had dipped, and that was more than a mere reaction to the swell. This was the inner harbour and the water was mill pond calm. He moved swiftly to the porthole and looked out, but he could see no-one on the pontoon, and only normal late Saturday afternoon activity on the quay. Telling himself to stop overreacting, he went back to the main cabin.

He poured his own untouched coffee down the sink and washed the mugs and spoons, dried them very carefully and sluiced out the sink. Looking round the cabin he saw the sheaf of papers on the table, picked them up and stuffed them back in the drawer. No need for them anymore. Having put everything away in the cupboard above the sink, he wandered about patting the cushions, checking and double-checking.

Glancing at his watch he saw that it was a quarter past four. That meant an hour to high tide when he would be able to move into the outer pool of the harbour, tie up to a holding pontoon and wait for dusk, he wanted to be as unobtrusive as possible when he left the harbour. But before preparing the *Sally Anne* to leave he must deal with Caro.

He went down to the small cabin where her unconscious body lay like a rag doll on the bunk. This cabin was usually used to store cushions and pillows, and various other bits and pieces. Carefully Craig rolled Caro's body nearer the bulkhead and covered it with a couple of blankets, followed this by propping cushions against them. He stood back to check the result. There was now no sign of her hidden behind them. It looked quite natural, as if he kept all the unwanted bedding neatly piled on the spare bunk. Quickly he adjusted two of the cushions then left the cabin.

But there was something he'd forgotten. How could he have missed it? Under the table, pushed into a corner, was her canvas shoulder bag. He picked it up, took Caro's mobile phone out and put it in his pocket, gave a quick look round the room for one last check, and took the bag into the tiny cabin. Carefully he tucked it away behind the blankets and cushions, closed the door and locked it behind him. When she woke, and that wouldn't be for some hours yet, she wouldn't be able to get past the door unless he let her out. He smiled to himself. She'd caused him enough trouble, now it was her turn to suffer.

Ten minutes to go. He started to prepare the *Sally Anne* to move out of the marina. This would be the worst part, not knowing if the port authorities would pay him a visit before his departure. His dues were all paid up, but it was usual to let them know you were leaving and in what direction you were going to travel. So be it, he told himself, striving for calm. His plans had gone well so far, in fact far better than he'd expected. He reached up for the whisky bottle, slopped some into a glass and gulped it down. Not long now and he'd be out of this place. Gripping the glass, he slumped down on the divan to wait.

* * *

Hands trembling, Ashley started her car, feeling a wave of relief as the engine roared into life. She manoeuvred recklessly fast out of the parking space and made her way through the traffic and out of town. Every few seconds she glanced in the rear-view mirror, but no-one was following her. It wasn't until she was well away from the marina that her heart stopped thumping and her breathing returned to normal.

When she'd stepped carefully down onto the *Sally Anne*, she'd intended to appear suddenly at the cabin door, give Craig what she hoped would be a pleasant surprise. Then she'd recognised Caro's voice, but only just, it hadn't sounded right. She'd waited, her mind racing, and then bent down very slowly to look through to the cabin, then straightened immediately, shocked to see Craig half dragging, half carrying Caro's limp body the length of the boat, her arm draped round his shoulders in some travesty of affection. Getting her own back on Alex and his prissy new girlfriend was one thing, but this was quite another. She couldn't wait to make her getaway.

When the two of them had disappeared through the door at the end of the cabin, Ashley had waited, the seconds dragging out into what felt like hours. Then, forcing herself to move, fully aware that any movement of the boat might warn him of her presence, she'd crept along the deck and finally made it to the pontoon, run along it as fast as she could, and dashed to her car.

God Almighty! He'd told her what he planned to do, making up that fairy tale of smuggled artwork and the Devereaux family. But he'd said nothing about this. What had been wrong with the girl? There'd been no sign of violence, no bruises, no blood. Ashley felt a wave of nausea well up into her throat. What the hell had he done to her?

I don't want to know, she told herself vehemently. I do not want to know.

When she was home, safe in her own hallway, she made sure the latch on the front door was down, put the chain on and retreated upstairs. Nothing, she told herself, absolutely nothing is going to persuade me to have anything more to do with that man.

CHAPTER 20

For once Eleanor didn't feel like visitors, particularly not the gossipy, empty-headed kind. But there was no way round it now, she'd arrived back just before Geraldine Lacey, like a battleship dressed overall, had marched up the driveway.

"Eleanor my dear," she boomed. "I'm so pleased to catch up with you. May I have a quick word?"

"By all means, do come in." But the touch of sarcasm was lost on this large, loud woman.

Eleanor led the way into the sitting room and her long habit of hospitality took over. "Can I offer you tea? I was just about to make some."

"That would be delightful." Geraldine's small eyes – like a pig's, Eleanor thought – darted round the room, taking in every detail.

"Is that seascape a Lavalle?" she asked, indicating the painting above the fireplace.

"Yes. One of his earlier ones."

"But I thought his work was impossible to come by."

"Harry bought it, oh, years ago," Eleanor said dismissively, and added, "I'll go and make the tea."

Knowing Geraldine, she made a pot and got out cups and saucers, mugs would not be acceptable. She didn't notice the piece of paper that had blown off the table in a breeze from the open window, as she got out a plate and tipped some biscuits onto it. Picking up the tray, she went through to the sitting room.

"So, what can I do for you?" Eleanor asked, as she placed the tea tray down on a table and began to pour.

"I'm here on behalf of one of my pet charities, the new concert hall? I was sure you'd want the chance to contribute, with your keen interest in the arts. It'll be such an asset to the island. We really need a facility that will cater for the upper end of the art market, don't you think?"

"To tell you the truth, I'm not sure about that." If Geraldine had known Eleanor better, she would have seen the warning signs, but she didn't. "I've never been very keen on anything that only serves a small, privileged section of the community."

"Oh, but Eleanor, think of it." The piggy eyes glowed with enthusiasm. "We do so need a venue for smaller concerts, select gatherings for the more discerning. Art exhibitions could be held there, and the antiques fair desperately needs a home since the Wingham Hotel closed. Surely you can see the merit of it."

"Oh yes, but there are many other calls on one's budget," Eleanor said smoothly. "I appreciate your enthusiasm, but I'm afraid I don't feel able to contribute this time."

"What a pity." Geraldine's voice was noticeably cooler. "We all know how much you love the arts. I thought this would be right up your street."

"I do appreciate good art, but I want everyone to have the chance to access it, not just those who happen to be able to afford it," she said, knowing this would hit home with someone who'd always behaved as if poverty was a fault rather than an unfortunate circumstance. "I'm sure you understand."

"Well, if that's how you feel, so be it." Geraldine was obviously put out. She sipped at her tea and changed the subject abruptly. "Is your young visitor still with you?"

"Caro?" For a second Eleanor wondered how she knew about Caro, then it came back to her. "Oh yes, of course, we met you in town, didn't we?"

"I thought she might still be here after seeing her at Vazon the other day."

"Yes, we went for a walk on the beach last Sunday. Such a lovely day, we couldn't resist."

"Oh no," Geraldine said, "this wasn't Sunday. Now, when was it? Ah yes, last Thursday. I took my young granddaughter for a walk, she does so love to go to the beach, even at this time of year."

"Thursday?" asked Eleanor, more sharply than she'd intended.

"Yes. She was with a tall young man, rather good looking I thought."

Eleanor desperately wanted to find out more, but the last thing she needed was for her visitor to realise how anxious she was to do so. She smiled, trying to seem relaxed and friendly. "Alex, I expect," she said, knowing it wouldn't have been him. "She's doing some work on his house. She's an interior designer, you know."

"Oh no, it wasn't him. I would have recognised your lovely grandson. No, this man was fair-haired, very smart and sleek." Geraldine gave her an arch look. "They seemed to be very friendly, at least they were standing very close, deep in conversation by the sea wall." Geraldine's darkly pencilled eyebrows crept up questioningly. "Perhaps she's found herself a boyfriend."

"Perhaps she has," Eleanor made herself say casually, but her mind was racing. What had she been doing on Thursday afternoon? Ah yes, that was the day she'd gone to visit her cousin and stayed on rather later than she'd intended. Caro had said nothing about meeting Craig – from Geraldine's description that was who Eleanor thought it must have been. Why had they been there? What had they been talking about? Maybe she'd be able to find out more later on. She hoped Caro would stay upstairs. If she didn't, Geraldine would hang around prying and gossiping for ever.

She began to put the cups back on the tray. Persuading visitors to leave without causing offence was easy, if you knew how. With practised ease she got up, saying how pleased she was to have seen her visitor, how sorry she was to have to refuse her request for a donation, and, with many expressions of regret, how she must get on as she was expecting Alex for dinner. Before Geraldine realised what was happening, she was through the hall, out the front door, and Eleanor was waving goodbye from the top of the steps.

More slowly now, Eleanor walked back into the sitting room and, ignoring the tea tray, went upstairs to find Caro.

* * *

Paul Le Page stretched his arms above his head, easing his stiff muscles, and glanced at the clock on the wall. Half past five. Still, he'd better try to get through a bit more; after all, that was why he'd come into the office on a sunny Saturday afternoon. He thought back to his wife, Jane's caustic comments when he'd told her he'd be going to work after lunch. There was no way he could afford to do this too often, she'd have his guts, but this bloody paperwork had to be got rid of or he'd end up buried feet deep in it.

He tried to concentrate, but his mind kept wandering, searching for an excuse to leave. Finally, it came up with one. He'd promised to drop in on the chaps at the Harbour Office watch tower at some point today, just a quick check to see what was going on. He reached for his mobile then changed his mind. Much more pleasant to take a quick walk down there, after all it was only a few hundred yards away.

He grabbed his jacket and shrugged it on. He could always come in early on Monday and tackle the rest of the paperwork.

"Hi, Gary," he said, as he walked into the watch tower, which overlooked the entrance to the harbour. It looked rather like the control tower at a small airport and served much the same purpose.

Gary Blackburn, the assistant harbour master, looked up as Paul came in. "You must be psychic. I was just about to give you a call. You know you said you wanted to know if there was any movement from the *Sally Anne*?"

"Yea." Paul was alert immediately. "Has something happened?"

"It has. Paxton's moved her out to one of the holding pontoons. Looks like he's getting ready to leave."

"Do you know where he's planning to go?"

"He hasn't contacted us, but he'll probably do so before he goes. On the other hand, his dues are paid up so he may just scarper. We're keeping a close eye, just in case." He handed Paul a pair of binoculars.

Standing by the wide window Paul swept the binoculars round. Across the harbour entrance was the Castle Cornet breakwater, its small lighthouse sheltering several fishermen who leapt in size as the binoculars found them. Paul felt a small pang of envy, wondered if they'd caught anything worth having, then travelled on round, searching the boats in the outer harbour. The *Flying Christine* lifeboat, with its orange and navy livery, slid from view, as did several fishing boats and yachts, until he found the *Sally Anne*, dipping as she rode a slight swell. For a minute or two he studied the boat, but there was no sign of Paxton.

"Okay." Paul turned and handed the binoculars back to Gary. "I've got to get going now but let me know what happens. I want to know if this one sneezes, let alone anything else. Understood?"

"Got it. You don't want us to stop him then?"

"No. Definitely not. He's been searched, and he's more use to us left alone but carefully watched. We've had a surveillance team keeping an eye, but I had to haul them off on to something else yesterday. Damn staff cuts, that's why I asked your lot to let me know if anything happened. If there are any developments, you can get me on my mobile."

"Okay, I'll let you know immediately he makes another move."

"Do that. Thanks, Gary."

Paul was frowning as he walked to his car. His gut feeling about this wasn't good. Never mind, there was nothing he could do about it right now, and he was convinced giving Craig a bit of rope was the right thing to do. I wonder if the Bennett girl knows her boyfriend's making a run for it, he thought. It'd be interesting to get her reaction. Slamming the door of his car, he didn't start the engine immediately but reached for his mobile and scrolled down to Eleanor's number.

The receiver was picked up the other end even before he heard the ringing tone. "Hallo? Caro? Is that you?" Eleanor's voice sounded anxious.

"I'm afraid not. It's Paul Le Page here, Eleanor. It was Miss Bennett I wanted to speak to. Is she out?"

"Yes, she is." There was a slight pause then in a rush she said, "In fact I'm a little worried, Paul. Caro must have gone out this afternoon. I thought she was upstairs working, but when I went to look earlier on, there was no sign of her. I've no idea what can have happened. She didn't leave a note and her mobile just goes to voicemail."

"Perhaps she decided to go out for a walk, maybe into town."

"I don't think so. She was due to pick Alex up from the airport at six, but he phoned just now to ask where she was."

"She could have got lost," Paul suggested. "She's not very familiar with the island."

"I suppose so, and the fog is coming down. Alex's plane just made it before the airport closed. I told him to get a taxi and come straight here." There was a pause on the other end of the line and Paul wondered what was coming next. "Alex is going to be so upset not to find her here. And I must admit, I'm rather worried."

"Is Alex – are she and Alex–?" He was talking to a woman in her late seventies, how should he phrase it?

"Fond of each other?" Eleanor said, sounding impatient. "Yes, very."

"I'm sure you'll find there's nothing to worry about." He tried to sound as reassuring as possible, but deep inside he was beginning to wonder. What the hell had Alex been up to? Hadn't he warned him? Bloody Devereaux, always taking risks. His gut feeling was not good on this, not good at all, and although he tried to ignore feelings like that, experience told him his instincts were usually right.

"I'm on my way home now," he told Eleanor. "I promised Jane I wouldn't be too late but I'll call you within the hour to check if Caro has turned up, or you can call me, then we'll decide what to do."

Eleanor thanked him profusely, obviously forgetting that his interest in Caro might be professional. Paul drove home, and as he did so the feeling of foreboding increased.

CHAPTER 21

As Eleanor put the receiver down, she heard a car pull up in the driveway. She got to the front door just as Alex was taking the steps two at a time.

"Have you heard anything? Is she back?" He didn't even bother to greet his grandmother. His face was bleak and closed as he looked at her.

"No, my darling," said Eleanor gently, putting her arm through his and leading him into the kitchen. "Now, sit down, I'll get you a drink."

But he didn't sit down. Instead he paced about the room, his hands thrust deep in his pockets. He scowled at his grandmother. "I suppose I might have known," he said.

"Known what?"

"That she'd leave."

Eleanor had known this would be the way his thoughts would run. Oh God, here we go again, she thought. Poor Alex, when's it all going to end?

Quickly she poured him a glass of wine and handed it to him. He took it without comment.

"Why should she be any different from all the other bloody women?" Alex went on bitterly. "I hardly know her, for God's sake. One week, that's all. There's no way you can really get to know a person in a week. I should have learnt my lesson by now, shouldn't I? Not to worry, at least–"

"Stop it, Alex!" Eleanor's voice was sharp enough to bring Alex's pacing to a halt. "Now listen to me. Caro is not one of those 'bloody women', and she's not left you."

"How do you know?" he snapped at her.

"Trust me, my darling," Eleanor said. Pushing thoughts of Geraldine Lacey and her gossip out of her mind, Eleanor said, "I know people. I am, as I think I've said before, a very good judge of character. Something has happened to delay her, that's all, and I expect we'll find out what it is soon enough. Paul rang, by the way, and he suggested she might have got lost on the way to the airport. She'll probably turn up any minute, and if she doesn't, he's ready to help find her."

For a moment he stared at her, an agonised look in his eyes. A hard lump rose in her throat. This was how he'd looked when Naomi had walked out on him, and it broke her heart to see it return. She put her arms round him, pulled his rigid body against hers, his dark head on her shoulder as she stroked his hair.

"Ssh, my darling." He could have been a toddler with grazed knees. "She'll be back, Alex, she'll be back. I know she will."

But he pushed away from her and began his restless pacing once again. "You can't know that," he exclaimed. "It's absurd. We hardly know her. She could be an accomplished con artist for all I know. And yet" – he came to a halt and, head bent, his voice dropped to a whisper – "I've never felt like this about anyone before, Nella. Not Naomi, not anyone. I don't know what I'd do if I lost her."

Eleanor felt a wave of panic rise up inside her, but she clamped it down. "You're not going to lose her," she stated, with far more conviction than she felt. "Now, let's think. Where could she have gone that we– I haven't thought of? Did she say anything at all that might give you a clue? Something you've forgotten perhaps?"

Round and round they went, trying to think of some simple reason for Caro's absence. But whatever avenue they went down, they came to a dead end. They were still going over and over the possibilities, however unlikely, when the shrill of the telephone interrupted them. Alex grabbed it from its rest, but a moment later his shoulders sagged, and Eleanor knew it wasn't Caro. "Paul," he mouthed at Eleanor.

She stood close beside him and listened to his end of the conversation.

"Yes, I got back about half an hour ago... No, no sign yet. Seems you were right. She isn't to be trusted. Nella and I can't think where she could have gone, unless, of course, she's run back to Paxton." The grating pain in his voice made Eleanor wince.

Paul was speaking. She could hear the rumble of his voice but couldn't make out the words. A while later Alex said, "Sorry. Yes, I'm still here. I'll let you know directly she comes back, if she does."

He put the receiver down but didn't move. "He thinks she might be on the *Sally Anne* with that bastard, and he seems to be on the way to Jersey or France. Great, eh?"

"Does he know which?"

"No, he doesn't. But the *Sally Anne's* left and..." He shrugged. "She's obviously decided she's better off with him."

"Alex!" Eleanor's voice was sharp. "Tell me exactly what Paul said."

"I've told you."

"And the rest. Stop being such a bloody pessimist, for God's sake."

"He told me she might be on the boat, but he doesn't actually know where she is."

"There, you see—"

"–and would we let him know immediately if we hear from her."

"Thank you. Now that's not quite so bad, is it?"

But Alex didn't have a chance to reply. At that moment there was a knock on the front door. Alex got to it in a couple of strides and wrenched it open while Eleanor prayed it would be Caro.

It wasn't. It was Ashley. She gazed up at Alex with a strange look compounded of bravado, satisfaction and something else indefinable in her face. "Hallo, Alex. Can I come in?"

"What do you want?" His tone was uncompromising as he stood there, barring the way.

"Well it's more about what you want, Alex?"

"What do you mean?"

"I'm not going to talk on the doorstep. If you want to hear what I have to say you'll have to let me in." Her eyes were wide and challenging. "It's about your precious Caro."

Alex grabbed her wrist and pulled her into the house.

"Watch it! That hurts."

"Sorry," he said shortly, and let go.

After a quick glance at Eleanor, she said nothing more but, with a defiant swing to her hips, walked ahead of him into the sitting room. Eleanor followed them in, wondering what on earth Ashley was up to, but it was Alex who asked, "So, what's all this about?"

She's gloating, Eleanor thought. Oh God! What is she going to say?

"Like I told you, it's about your new girlfriend. It seems she's walked out on you."

"Do sit down, Ashley," Eleanor cut in quickly before Alex could react. She added, her voice icy, "Now, tell us what you know."

Eleanor nodded to Alex to sit down. She hoped he'd keep quiet. He couldn't be trusted not to lose his temper. She watched, eyes narrowed, as Ashley clasped her hands in her lap, but not before Eleanor noticed they were shaking. Good, she thought, the girl's nervous and that'll make her easier to deal with.

"I'm sure you're longing to tell us exactly why you're here." Eleanor's tone was silky as she watched Ashley sit back and cross her legs, making an effort to look relaxed. She didn't succeed. It was obvious she was tense in every muscle.

Sitting down herself, Eleanor glanced quickly at her grandson. He appeared to have himself in hand, but she must find out as much as possible and as quickly as possible.

"What makes you think Caro's walked out, as you call it?" she asked.

Ashley's mouth curved in an unpleasant smile. "I don't just think it, I know it. I saw her with Craig on the *Sally Anne*, so she's obviously gone off with him."

Eleanor heard Alex give a quick, indrawn breath, but he said nothing. She looked at Ashley, eyes narrowed. "I don't see that there's anything obvious about it. She might have visited him this afternoon, but there's no reason to think she stayed on the boat."

"Oh, but I saw her, she couldn't have got off."

She'd spoken too quickly. There was something she wasn't telling them.

"Why?" Eleanor's voice was sharp, and Ashley flinched.

"Why what?"

"Why do you think she couldn't have got off the boat?"

"I didn't mean that, I meant wouldn't."

Eleanor was certain she was lying, but let her go on, hoping she'd dig her own grave.

"She was happy to be there." Ashley was speaking very quickly, as if she wanted to get this over now. "That's all. Why wouldn't she be? She and Craig have been an item for years, and they'd obviously made up after some row or other."

Eleanor, her sharp eyes narrowed and her gaze relentless, let the silence drag on for a while and when she spoke again her voice was very quiet. "I don't think so, Ashley. I think you're either lying or not telling us everything."

Eleanor got up and went to stand over the younger woman. Ashley cowered back in her chair. As Eleanor stood there, tall and imposing, her back straight as a ramrod, her voice quietly threatening, she knew perfectly well what a frightening figure she presented. Not once did her eyes move from Ashley's face as she went on, "And I think it would be best, for your own sake, if you told us the whole truth. You see, I'm too old to mind what I have to do to make you, so don't you think it's best if you come clean?"

"Alex!" There was panic in Ashley's voice. She tried to get up, but Eleanor was standing too close and she slumped back in the chair. "You must be mad! You can't threaten me! Alex, do something."

All Alex said was, "No. I don't think so." His voice was as chilling as his grandmother's.

The silence stretched out, but at last Ashley gave in. "Alright, alright. I did see her on the *Sally Anne*, with Craig, but maybe it wasn't quite as I implied."

"How was it then?" Eleanor stepped back slightly. She thought they'd get the truth now. "Start at the beginning and tell us exactly what happened. And make sure you don't leave anything out."

Ashley flashed her a venomous look but did as she was told. "I was in town and I thought I'd drop in on Craig, see if he wanted to come out for a drink, but when I got to the boat he didn't seem to be there. The door to the cabin was closed and everything was quiet." She swallowed and licked her lips. "I made my way along the deck, bent to look into the cabin, and I saw Craig and Caro. Through the porthole I could…" The words petered out as her eyes widened, the fear in them obvious now.

"Okay," Alex sat forward. "What were they doing?"

Just for a second Ashley's eyes flickered with that venomous look again, but this time it was Alex who picked up the warning signs.

"The truth, Ashley, or I won't be responsible for what I do."

"Alright," she spat at him. "Caro was, well, it's difficult to describe."

"Try," Alex snapped.

"Maybe she was drunk." She couldn't resist this flash of spite. "Anyway, Craig was, sort of, dragging her through the cabin. She had her arm draped round his neck, but she seemed all sort of floppy. I think her eyes were closed and her mouth was half open." She stopped speaking, maybe realising for the first time the implications of what she'd seen.

"Christ!" Alex burst out as he pushed himself up from his seat, but Eleanor held up an urgent hand to silence him.

"Was there any evidence they'd been drinking? Glasses on the table or anything?"

Ashley bit her lip. "No, I don't think so. I think there might have been coffee mugs. Perhaps he'd been helping her to sober up. Yes, that must have been it." But it was obvious she was clutching at straws.

"What the hell was the matter with her?" It was as if Alex was asking himself the question, but Ashley took it personally.

"How should I know?" she snapped. "I don't know what she gets up to with her boyfriends, do I? You'd know better than me, don't you think?"

Alex turned to look at her and, just for a second, Eleanor thought she would have felt truly afraid of him if she'd been Ashley. But a moment later his face closed again.

The silence hung around them as the seconds ticked by. Then, abruptly, Alex said, "Fine. I'm glad you decided to tell us the truth." He looked down at her, and his expression wasn't totally without compassion. "And Ashley, don't get involved with Craig Paxton. Take it from me, he's not the kind of person you want to be friends with."

Her mouth twisted. "Don't pretend you care about me, Alex. You've made it all too clear that you don't. Anyway, I can look after myself." She rose from her chair, smoothing down her dress and straightening her shoulders defiantly. "I'll be going then."

"I'll see you out," Eleanor said quietly, following her through the hall. She opened the front door, but before Ashley could escape, the older woman gripped her arm.

"Don't disappear, Ashley. We might need you. If anything has happened to Caro, you're going to have to repeat all you've said to the police. Do you understand?"

"Are you threatening me?" Ashley tried to sound defiant.

"Yes, I am. And don't you forget it." Eleanor's eyes were cold as grey winter mist. "Remember, wherever you go we'll come after you, I promise you that. I know almost everyone on this island, and a lot of their secrets too, so you'd best believe what I say."

She stood and watched as Ashley ran down the steps, got into her car and drove away, scattering gravel as she did so. I sounded like some mafiosa, Eleanor thought grimly, but it might work.

CHAPTER 22

Once Alex had called him, it didn't take Paul long to get to Villette House.

"Thanks for coming so quickly," Eleanor said as they went through to join Alex, who was pacing up and down in the sitting room.

"What kept you?" he snapped, without even greeting his friend.

"Alex!" Eleanor exclaimed.

"Sorry," he said. "I didn't mean to be rude. It's just that–"

"I know, don't worry, mate. Now," he was immediately business-like, "there's a whole lot more I need to know. Particularly now the *Sally Anne* has left the harbour. Can you give me a run down on Caro Bennett's activities over the last few days, say since I saw her on Monday?"

"What?" Alex snapped. "Where did you see her?"

"At my office."

"Why?"

"I needed to have a word with her, officially."

"What for?"

"Alex," Paul said, calm but very firm, "that is really between her and me, isn't it? Like I said, it was official business."

Alex glared at him for a moment and Eleanor intervened. "Alex, Paul has to do his job, and Caro would have told you when she could, I'm sure. She's been in a very difficult position, one way and another." And again, what Geraldine had said came back to her mind. She'd have to tell Paul about that, but how could she add to Alex's pain? She'd cross that bridge when she came to it.

Paul was watching Alex, waiting to see if he'd persist, but he didn't. He just shrugged and resumed his pacing.

"Right," Paul said. "Tell me what you've found out."

Since Alex didn't speak, Eleanor took over and told Paul, in minute detail, exactly what Ashley had told them, but when he prompted her to go back a little, run through what had happened earlier in the week, she hesitated. He waited patiently and she could tell his interest was sharpened by her hesitation. Taking a deep breath, she began cautiously.

"I haven't told Alex this yet."

"What haven't you told me?"

"Look, darling, you are not to overreact. It could mean nothing."

Paul intervened. "Why don't you just tell us?"

"Alright."

So, she told them. She played up the fact that Geraldine was an inveterate and imaginative gossip and insisted she could have been mistaken. Maybe it wasn't Caro she'd seen. And, if it was, perhaps she was there to tell Craig she wanted no more to do with him.

"I know she was scared of him," she said. "Perhaps she had no choice."

Alex was impassive now, and it was difficult to work out what he was thinking. Paul was as business-like as ever. "Let's see what we've got?" he said briskly. "Caro, apparently, is seen talking to Paxton on Thursday. Then today, maybe by arrangement, she goes to the *Sally Anne* to visit him." He glanced at Alex's rigid face and added, "Like Eleanor says, she could have had no choice. A bit later Ashley comes along, looks into the cabin and sees Paxton helping – dragging – an apparently drunk–"

"–or unwell," Eleanor said.

"Or unwell," Paul added dutifully, "Caro through the cabin, and Ashley beats a hasty retreat. Of course, that tells us a thing or two, doesn't it?"

"What does it tell us?" Alex asked, frowning at him.

"Well, if she'd thought it was a case of Caro drinking too much, if it was all innocent, then she'd have made her presence known, wouldn't she? The fact that she slunk off says to me that she was pretty sure there was something wrong."

Eleanor knew there was a battle going on inside Alex. If he believed that Caro had gone with Craig willingly, then he could believe she was at least safe. If, on the other hand, he accepted that there'd been something wrong and she wasn't there of her own free will, that had to mean she was in danger. Eleanor herself couldn't decide which was the worst of the two options.

"There's a problem here, Alex, that you have to understand," Paul was saying urgently. "We don't want to rush after them; after all, Caro may be involved in his schemes."

Alex made a gesture of denial, was about to speak, but Paul went on before he could interrupt.

"I want to give Paxton as much rope as possible before reeling him in. On the other hand, if Caro Bennett isn't involved–" He let it hang in the air and the tension mounted. "Well, we'd need to act more quickly."

"Sod reeling him in," Alex muttered. "All I care about is Caro. I don't care what she's done so long as she's alright. For fuck's sake, Paul, you have to do something."

Eleanor sat quietly, waiting for Paul to react. It was up to him now. She felt a wave of relief when he rummaged in his pocket and brought out his mobile. "I'll just go and make a quick call."

He went out to the hall. Eleanor got up and went to stand by the door, unashamedly listening. Alex came to join her in time to hear Paul say, "Sorry to bother you on a Saturday, sir, but we've got movement on the Paxton case

... yes, he's got going without contacting the Harbour Office. According to them he's making way for Jersey or France rather than the UK mainland ... yes, that's what I thought. But, sir, there's a complication." They listened carefully as he outlined what Ashley had seen. "And it sounds as if she might be an unwilling passenger. If so, we could have a kidnapping on our hands."

Eleanor put her arm through Alex's and held it close. Hearing it put into words was like having your worst fears confirmed. Without saying anything she tried to comfort him, rubbing a hand up and down his arm.

Paul had been silent for a few moments, but now he was speaking again. "Okay, sir, I'll leave that with you and get on to the Jersey chaps. As to France, I thought Jacques Hubert in St Malo would be the obvious contact. I'll keep you informed ... Right, sir. Goodbye."

His second call was slightly different. "Jane? Darling, look, I won't be back for a bit ... I know, I know, I'm really sorry, love, but it can't be helped ... Well tell her Daddy'll be home as soon as he can. I hate to do this ... Okay, okay, put her on."

Eleanor and Alex moved away from the door. They had no wish to eavesdrop on Paul's excuses to his five-year-old daughter.

When he came back into the room he was frowning. "I am not the most popular husband and father on this island, I can tell you that."

"I'm so sorry," Eleanor said sympathetically.

"It's not your fault. It's been a bad week." He lifted his hands as if dismissing his personal problems. "But not to worry, I'll make it up to them. Now I'll get back to the office. I have to make contact with Jersey and the blokes in St Malo. I'll keep you posted. And please, I know it's difficult, but try not to worry too much."

Alex grabbed his jacket. "I'm coming with you."

"What?"

"You heard, I'm coming with you." He glared at his friend, defying him to argue. "Unless it's completely against the rules."

"Well," Paul scratched his head, looking decidedly unsure of himself for once, "not completely, but you'll have to do as you're told, understand? I know it doesn't come easy to you." He grinned, his friendship getting the better of his job for once.

"Okay, you're the boss." Alex put his arms round Eleanor and hugged her hard. "Don't sit worrying. I'll let you know exactly what's going on. Will you be alright on your own?"

"Of course, my darling, off you go. I'll be fine. I'll do something useful. Bake a cake for when Caro gets back, whatever." She stood in the front doorway and waved. When they'd gone, she went into the kitchen, but all she did was sit down, fold her arms on the table and stare into space.

* * *

In his office, Paul's voice was smooth and persuasive. "Of course, Ashley, but I'm sure you realise the implications of what you saw could be quite serious … I understand. If you have any information at all about Paxton's plans, I urge you to tell us. Good … Someone will be out to see you and take a statement … Now, if convenient? I realise it's a little late, but … good. The officer's name is Dean Savident. Thank you so much for your co-operation." He cut off the call. "I'd say that's a frightened woman."

"Serves her right." Alex, who was standing leaning against the wall, too tense to sit down, sounded completely unsympathetic. Paul gave him a quizzical look but didn't comment. He turned to his fellow officer sitting upright on a chair, ready for the off.

"Okay, you heard all that? Better get out there and get as much information as you can out of her. Take someone with you, preferably female. I want you back here at" – he glanced at his watch – "eight, or as near as you can get it."

Dean Savident jumped up and quickly left the room. His swift footsteps could be heard receding down the corridor as the phone rang again.

"Paul Le Page."

"Aah. *Bonsoir mon vieux. Comment ça va?*"

"Jacques, you old rogue. I'm well, well. How are you?"

"No complaints. A little flesh around the stomach, a little less hair."

Alex listened to these pleasantries, growing impatience showing in his face. Paul glanced at him as he visualised the rotund Frenchman sitting at his desk in St Malo, his sharp eyes missing nothing, his bald head as smooth and shiny as a billiard ball.

"I received your message," Hubert said. "What can I do to assist?"

"We've got an interesting one on our hands," Paul told him. "Thanks for the prompt response. I think time is of the essence here."

"Tell me."

Quickly, Paul put him in the picture and, at last, Jacques interrupted him. "Hold on one moment. I will make a call on my *portable*. Please wait."

They waited in tense silence while Paul listened to the muffled sound of voices from the St Malo office. They didn't have to wait long.

"Paul. The cabin cruiser *Sally Anne* has not yet arrived, but assuredly she would not have had time to get here, even with a favourable tide. You say she is not in *Jersais?*"

"No. The Jersey chaps say there's no sign of her. She's not moored in St Helier, or any of the other marinas. They've double-checked. I'm pretty certain she's coming your way. Of course, there's a possibility he might anchor in the estuary, but your men would hear about it if he did, wouldn't they?"

"I will put a call out. There's always the possibility he will choose some little bay or inlet far from habitation."

Paul frowned. He had to admit the thought had crossed his mind. "It's possible. But we think all his contacts are in St Malo, that's what makes me think he's more likely to make for your patch. Anyway, any news at all this evening will help. Let me know."

"*Bien sûre, bien sûre.* Immediately I will phone you."

Paul looked up at Alex as he replaced the receiver. "We've done just about all we can for the moment. It's a matter of waiting now. Why don't you go home, Alex? I'll let you know if anything happens."

"No. I'd rather stay here."

"But there's nothing you can do."

Alex ignored this statement. "If they phone to say Paxton's arrived, what then?"

"The chief wants me to fly over."

"But you won't be able to do that until tomorrow," Alex said in exasperation, "and then only if the fog lifts from round the airport?"

"I admit the fog is a problem. We might have to go by boat, not on the ferry, that doesn't leave till midday. I'll have to try and fix something up."

Alex's frown cleared. "Let's take *Pauillac*. There's no fog down here, and anyway, it doesn't matter to her. I've got all the kit, no problem. Come on, Paul, that's the obvious solution, isn't it?" He came over to lean his hands on Paul's desk, willing his friend to agree.

Paul gave him a rueful grin and said, "You're a pain in the arse, my friend." Then he relented. "I suppose if I make it official, commandeer your boat, the chief might wear it. That would, of course, mean you'd have to come with me."

"I was going to anyway."

"Oh, were you?" Paul said, with more than a touch of sarcasm.

"Yes," Alex said, ignoring the undercurrents. "At least now we'll be doing something. I can't stand all this waiting around."

Paul tried to bring Alex's urge to get going under control. "But I hope you realise we're not moving from here until we know where Paxton's gone. There'd be no point."

"I know, I know. It's just so bloody frustrating. Anything could be happening. I almost hope she's gone willingly, at least then she'd be safe."

Paul patted him awkwardly on the back. "I know, mate. Come on." He was brisk now. "What you need is something to eat. It's as good a time as any while we wait for Jacques to come back to us."

"I'm not hungry."

"Tough, I am. And you're going to eat something."

"You sound like Eleanor."

"God forbid!" Paul said, grinning. "Come on. We probably won't hear from Jacques again for at least an hour, and they'll take messages if I'm not here."

Alex followed Paul out of the office, shoulders hunched, feet dragging, but in the end he did eat quite a good meal and Paul could tell that he felt better for having done so.

When they got back to the office there was news. Jacques Hubert had left a message to say that the *Sally Anne* had arrived in St Malo.

"He said to tell you he's got a full surveillance team on the job," the young officer told Paul, "but that there's been no action yet. They're holding back in case he panics, don't want him harming Miss Bennett." The man darted a look at Alex's rigid face, then went on, "Hubert says he's got some of his team researching the background to see if they can find out what contacts Paxton has in France. Apparently, they've already got some information and he's e-mailing it through. He'll contact you if there's anymore."

"Right. Did you tell him I've commandeered a local boat to bring me over?"

"Yes, sir. He said to tell you he won't risk the radio. He'll get through to you on your mobile if necessary."

"Good. There you are," he said to Alex. "He's in St Malo, bold as brass. You give Eleanor a ring while I brief my people here." He grimaced. "And phone my poor Jane as well."

CHAPTER 23

Once they were down at the harbour, casting off and moving quietly through its entrance, Alex felt an overwhelming sense of relief at being occupied. All the pent-up energy and frustration began to dissipate now that he felt he was achieving something. As he stood with the comforting familiarity of the wheel's polished wood under his hands, he braced his feet against the gently heaving deck and felt much more at home. Though *Pauillac* wasn't a large boat, she had a powerful engine and, once they'd left Guernsey's hazardous rocks behind, they made a good twenty-five knots through the dark, glassy water. The lights of the islands, Guernsey, Sark and Herm, where receding swiftly, while in the distance they could make out the glimmer of a few lights on Jersey. There was no sign of the French coast as yet, but it wouldn't be long.

"I think it'll take us about two hours," he told Paul, who was standing beside him, "maybe less with the wind and tide in our favour. It means we should tie-up in St Malo about half eleven. What happens then?"

Paul raised his voice above the sound of the engine and the slap of the waves. "We meet up with Jacques to check on developments, then decide what our next move is."

For a while the only sounds were that of *Pauillac's* engine and the sea as she sped through the water, contentedly riding the waves. Alex felt deeply comforted by the familiarity of his old boat, his eyes narrowed as he gazed ahead into the darkness.

"Why did you go into the family business?" Paul asked suddenly.

"What makes you ask that?"

"It's just that you seem so much more at home here, on *Pauillac*, than in a boardroom. You could have gone into the navy or something of that sort."

It was an effort for Alex to force his mind away from their immediate problems. But after a moment he gave a twisted little grin. "Good Lord, no, that wouldn't have been any good for me, all that obeying orders and keeping to the rule book."

"I had noticed."

"Thought you might have. No, if I'm at sea I much prefer being my own boss."

"But what on earth made you go into Devereaux's?" Paul persisted. "At school you used to swear you never would, remember? I'm going to do something interesting with my life, you said. No getting buried back in Guernsey after uni, you said."

Alex was silent for a while. He'd never had to explain this before, had always avoided talking about the things closest to his heart. But somehow out here, the two of them alone on *Pauillac*, Paul's questions didn't seem so intrusive.

"I suppose," he said at last, "it was because of Nella. I always used to come home for the vac, I wanted to most times, especially in the summer when there was the beach and surfing and all that. Then, the last vac before my finals, Nella was having trouble with my father's two younger brothers who were running the company. She thought they weren't doing a good enough job." He gave a rueful grin. "She was right of course, usually is. Profits were down and we were losing some of our long-standing customers to the opposition, who'd just employed a new marketing manager. Those poor old buffers just couldn't compete. Anyway, the two of them were much more interested in golf and fishing."

Paul snorted. "They should be so lucky."

"I suppose so," Alex said. "Anyway, Nella asked me to sort things out and, since Naomi wanted – then – to live in Guernsey, it seemed appropriate for me to stay."

He fell silent, checked the radar screen and then the time. "Do you think Jacques has found anything?"

"There's no point in speculating, Alex," Paul said firmly. "Tell me more. What happened when you did join Devereaux's?"

Alex forced himself to go on. "I thought it was a bloody awful idea at the time, cocky young business graduate waltzing in to show everyone how to run the show, but they couldn't have been happier. So, here I am, MD of the family firm, and I have to admit, I love it." He glanced at Paul. "Why did you start me off on that?"

"I don't know, curious I suppose, and at least it took your mind off worrying about Caro."

Alex's face closed in again.

"Sorry," Paul said. "I shouldn't have reminded you."

"She wasn't far from my mind."

"How much longer now?" Paul asked, gazing ahead through the salted glass of the wheelhouse, they could see the lights of the French coast.

"About three quarters of an hour. That cluster of lights over there is St Malo." Alex pointed to the South.

"Looks closer than I'd expected," Paul said as he rubbed his hands together to keep out the cold. "Shall I get some coffee?"

"Yea, good idea. There are two tin mugs under here."

Paul unscrewed the top of the flask he'd brought with him and filled the mugs. The night air had a chilling bite to it and the coffee was very welcome.

Alex put down the empty mug. "We've made good time. Do we go straight to Jacques Hubert's office?"

"Yes. You'll like him. He's a good chap. But when we get there, leave the talking to me, okay?"

"Can't I–"

"Alex, for once in your life, don't argue. The last thing we need is for him to get the hump because civilians are poking their noses into official business."

Alex had to admit he could see the sense of this. "Okay. I'll leave it to you," he said, hoping he could keep his promise.

* * *

It was just before midnight when Alex and Paul arrived at Jacques Hubert's office. He greeted Paul like a long-lost brother and expressed delight at making Alex's acquaintance. Much to Alex's annoyance he refused to get down to business until they had yet more coffee, then he enquired after Paul's family, what Alex's background was, and ah, yes, he had heard of the Devereaux family. Only Paul's meaningful looks forced Alex to remain impassively polite. By the time they were finally settled and getting down to business, Alex could have screamed with frustration.

A wave of relief flowed over him as, in answer to a query from Paul, Jacques said, "Ah yes, the *Sally Anne* arrived at 8.30 precisely. The usual checks were done but they found nothing unusual, although they did not do a search. We did not want to alarm him by doing anything, how do you say it, outside the ordinary? I have two of my men down there watching her and, at this moment now, they tell me all has been quiet."

"So, he's had no visitors?" Paul asked.

"None at all," he said. "I checked on this Jean Peron you mentioned, Paul. You were right. He has been suspected of smuggling activities in the past, but nothing was proved. He has managed to keep the clean nose. If he tries to meet up with Monsieur Paxton, we will know immediately."

"Good," Paul pulled at his bottom lip, frowning, "I'd like to be able to have a closer look at the *Sally Anne*."

Alex looked up eagerly. That was exactly what he most wanted them to do.

"Would you like me to organise a reason for a search?" asked the Frenchman, eyebrows raised.

"No, perhaps not. It's bound to put Paxton on his guard."

Alex felt a stab of disappointment as Jacques nodded in agreement. "He told the harbour officials that he is on the holiday and he only plans to stay for a couple of days."

"Holiday!" Alex burst out, unable to contain himself. "That's what he calls it!"

"But what else is he to say?" Jacques asked reasonably, with a shrug of his shoulders.

"True," Alex conceded. "God, I wish we could do something."

"Well, at the moment keeping our heads down and watching is the best plan," Paul said repressively.

"I understand your anxiety, Monsieur Devereaux," Jacques Hubert said, not unsympathetically, "but these things must be handled with great delicacy. Slowly, slowly we will catch this unpleasant Paxton and rescue your girlfriend."

"Slowly! But can't we—"

"Yes, Jacques, I'm sure you're right." Unceremoniously Paul cut through Alex's protest, shooting him a baleful look as Jacques went on.

"These things take time, Monsieur Devereaux. Patience is needed," said Jacques, his voice a little cool, but then he smiled. "What we will do next is take you to your hotel.

My sister, she keeps a small establishment in the Rue de Toulouse, and she awaits you eagerly with food and comfortable beds."

Paul spoke before Alex had the chance to respond. "That's very kind, Jacques. There's nothing else we can do until Paxton makes a move. Food and a few hours shut-eye are the best idea at the moment."

With obvious reluctance Alex agreed, after they had been assured by Jacques that they would be the first to know if anything happened.

"The smallest change, do not worry what it is, I will contact you immediately." He patted Alex on the shoulder in friendly sympathy. "It is a disease, this *amour* business. I feel for you my friend, but worry not, we will rescue your girlfriend, I assure you of that."

Alex wished he had as much confidence, and anyway, was she his girlfriend or Paxton's? God knows, he thought bitterly.

* * *

Craig had checked several times on Caro and, as dawn crept into the sky, he went out on deck to stretch his legs. The first thing he noticed was the dark blue Peugeot. It had been there last night, and it was still there. From the shadow of the cockpit he trained a powerful pair of binoculars on the car. With the help of the light of a nearby street lamp, he could study the two occupants. What was it about policemen that stamped their job so clearly on them? These two were either police or from the French border force, the *douane*. He stood for a moment longer watching them, his mind racing. It didn't take him long to come to a decision.

He went back into the cabin and searched around for his mobile, found it, and quickly scrolled down to Jean Peron's number. Things would just have to get moving earlier than planned.

Jean answered, sullenly disagreeable at being woken so early, but Craig rattled off his instructions, ignoring the other man's bad temper.

"Yes, a dark blue Peugeot. It's the only car anywhere near, you can't miss it. You've got to fix it, and the sooner the better."

"Okay, okay, I will do my best. She won't be pleased. You'll have to pay well."

"Whatever she asks, I'll pay it."

"*Bon*. Leave it with me."

A moment later Craig was back in the darkened cockpit. It was nearly full daylight now. Fifteen minutes went by, twenty. His fingers drummed impatiently on the wheel. Then, at last, things began to move.

The first thing that happened was pure luck. The driver of the Peugeot got out of the car, stretched, and went into a nearby café which had just opened up. Craig held his breath as a minute later a young woman strolled up and leant down to talk to the other man. Good, Jean had followed instructions. At the same time Jean's car drew up on the quay just above the *Sally Anne* and, leaving the engine running, Jean jumped out and came aboard.

With hardly a word they hurried through to the bow's cabin. Between them they supported Caro's still comatose body up to the quay, her feet dragging in a parody of walking, and, shielded from sight by Jean's car, they pushed her onto the back seat. There was a nasty moment when Craig thought he saw the driver come out of the café, but it was someone else who wandered off down the road in the opposite direction. Within less than three minutes Jean was on his way with his unconscious passenger.

Craig returned to the cabin and stripped off, then lay down on the bunk, still warm from Caro's presence. If they came to investigate it would look as if he'd slept there all night. Heart beating fast, he took a few deep breaths, waiting, but gradually he began to relax and, at last, found himself able to sleep. But not for long. The sound of heavy feet jumping down onto the deck and a hammering at the cabin door woke him. He jumped up and flung on a towelling robe as he went to open the door.

"I'm coming, damn it, I'm coming," he shouted as, making deliberately slow progress through the cabin, he glanced round, double-checking that there was no evidence of Caro's recent presence. Finally satisfied, he opened the door.

It was as he'd suspected. Three men stood there on the deck, obviously harbour officials of some kind or another. The one in charge, who was fat and balding, held out identification in a perfunctory fashion, and demanded to search the boat.

"What for?" Craig protested.

"We 'ave a warrant, monsieur," the man said, flapping a piece of paper at him insolently.

"Very well, if you must, you must."

With icy politeness he urged them to search the boat from top to bottom if they so wished. In fact, he insisted they should do so, whilst complaining at great length about the intrusion, and remarking on how different things were nowadays. Could one not have a holiday without disturbance?

They swarmed all over the *Sally Anne*, but finally admitted there was nothing to find. The fat little officer apologised for their intrusion, insisting there must have been a mistake. Their information must have been wrong. Apologising once more, he and his men left the boat.

Craig watched them leave, hoping that he hadn't overdone the protests. Then, as he stood there gathering his wits, a wave of panic rose up in his throat. Had they found Caro's bag? But no, he remembered now, he'd thrown it into Jean's car at the last minute. Thank God for that, he thought.

* * *

Alex could hear Caro calling his name, over and over, but however hard he tried to run, his feet stayed firmly stuck to *Pauillac's* deck. All around him the lights of St Malo harbour glared, they were blinding, or was it St Peter Port? He couldn't tell. She was calling again.

"Alex, Alex! Wake up for God's sake!"

"Wha-at? Paul?" He sat up. He'd not bothered to undress the night before, convinced he wouldn't sleep. But the combination of the strain and worry, and maybe the wine Jacques' sister had pressed on them last night, had combined to knock him out.

"What's happening? Have they found Caro?"

"Sorry mate, no. We've got problems."

"Problems?" There was panic in his voice.

"Calm down," said Paul, "Jacques is downstairs, he'll explain."

"What's the time?"

"Half seven."

"God! That late." Alex went to the basin and slapped cold water on his face, scrubbed at it with a towel, then clattered down the uncarpeted stairs after Paul.

Jacques was pacing up and down the hall, an expression compounded of embarrassment, anger and regret on his face. "*Je suis désolé, désolé*," he said when he saw Alex, his hands spread wide in front of him. "These two men of mine, they are fools. My sincere apologies. Not for anything would I have had this happen."

"What's happened?" Alex cut through his apologies.

Gradually, from the rush of words and the slightly broken English, Alex managed to piece the story together. It appeared that the senior of the two men on surveillance had answered a call of nature. While he was in a nearby café his much less experienced colleague had been distracted by a young woman. When the older man had returned, he was just in time to see a battered old Citroen driving away from the quay by the *Sally Anne's* berth. They had not given chase but radioed in for instructions. When the number of the car was checked, it was found to be registered in the name of Jean Peron.

"Evidently it was time for me to take over," Jacques said with a mixture of exasperation and apology. "I paid a visit to the *Sally Anne* and this Monsieur Paxton was not at all pleased to see me and my men. But behind all the *fracas*, I could tell that he was pleased with himself."

Jacque nodded in satisfaction as he spoke, perhaps trying to reassure himself after the mistakes made by his junior officers. With more elaborate expressions of regret, he told Alex there had been no sign whatever of anyone else on the *Sally Anne*. "We searched from end to end – this Paxton insisted that we should do so. The only thing I noticed was that, in the cabin at the back of the boat, where Monsieur Paxton had obviously been sleeping, there was the smallest scent of a lady's perfume. My nose, it is very sensitive to these things. I am certain it was not the cologne of Mr Paxton."

Paul was about to speak, but Jacques had not finished. "What a debacle! But" – he held up a finger and jabbed at the air – "all is not lost. We have much information on this Jean Peron. I have instructed some of my men to go to his apartment. If he is not there, they will search it." A very Gallic shrug punctuated what he said. "It will not be too difficult for them to enter. They will do a thorough check and very soon we will know where your young lady is."

Alex said nothing. He felt sick with worry about Caro, sick at the thought she might have left him and gone back to Craig. Whatever way he turned there seemed to be no hope. He slumped down on a chair and put his head in his hands, unable to trust himself to say anything at all.

CHAPTER 24

Craig found it impossible to settle to anything. He'd checked the time directly the officers had left. It had been seven o'clock. He'd checked again at ten past, and again at half past. He tried to contact Jean, but there was no response. He would try again in a minute. The sooner Jean was warned about the search the better.

He made himself some coffee, noticed with annoyance that his hands were shaking. Stupid to let things get to him. He was just about to take it up on deck when the door to the cabin was pushed open.

"Christ!" Craig exclaimed as he swung round, fully expecting the French officials to have reappeared. But it wasn't them.

The man who stood there was a stocky figure, with prematurely white hair and very pale grey eyes that had a glassy look, giving no clue to the person inside. He was immaculately and expensively dressed, and his full lips were lifted very slightly in a smile that was totally devoid of humour, like the smile of a snake.

Craig's heart continued to beat rather fast. Give him the border force men any day rather than this.

"Good morning, Jones. You gave me quite a turn there." He hoped he showed only polite surprise. "This is an unexpected pleasure. I wasn't expecting you yet."

"No?" The newcomer's voice was flat and hard. "I don't suppose you were."

"When... when did you get to St Malo?"

"Does it matter?"

Craig could have kicked himself for asking the question. He should have known he'd get no adequate answer. Spencer Jones loved to keep people at a disadvantage, and this was a perfect way to do so. Without being invited he poured himself some coffee and sat down at the table.

"You seem to have made rather a mess of all this, don't you?" he said, his voice devoid of any emotion.

"I hardly think you can blame me," Craig said, hating the fact that he sounded defensive. Wrong footed again, he thought, I must try to keep my cool.

"Oh, but I do, I do." Those cold, blank eyes gazed at him over the rim of the coffee mug.

Craig made an effort to recover himself. "I see no reason why you should. The local *douane* paid me a visit this morning, but I managed to get rid of them, and the girl is stashed with Peron as you instructed, quite safe."

Still those eyes didn't leave his face. That stare was a habit of Jones's that Craig particularly disliked. He found it far more unnerving than he cared to admit. He poured himself a glass of water. Although he wasn't thirsty, his throat was dry. Anyway, it gave him something to do. When he turned back, Jones was still watching his every move.

"I went to see my boy a few days ago."

Not that again, Craig thought, his heart sinking.

"He's in hospital, he tried to commit suicide." This was unexpected. "He's in a coma, not expected to survive."

"I'm sorry to hear that." What else could he say?

"Of course, there's no doubt who's to blame." This was the first time he'd shown any emotion. The hatred that pulsed in his voice was in horrifying contrast to his previous lack of expression. "That poisonous little bitch of yours and her parents. At least they're dead. She should be too."

"I really don't think you can blame Caro—"

"When I want your opinion, I'll ask for it. They were responsible for screwing the Dorset project, and they were responsible for my poor boy, Darren, going to prison. She is still around, and I want her dealt with once and for all. Do I make myself clear?"

"Look, Jones," Craig tried to speak calmly, but there was the chill of sweat on his forehead, "you can hardly blame Caro for something that happened such a long time ago. It was her father, not her."

"I really do wonder, sometimes, why I have to work with dross like you. I might have known this would happen. You've let yourself be distracted by the packaging, haven't you? Didn't stop to think about the poison inside her festering little mind. You just can't think beyond your own rutting instinct, can you? But then, good judgement has never been your strong suit."

"That's hardly fair. What's more, you told me to get involved. You said I should give her that first job, cultivate her, you called it." But Craig might as well have saved his breath.

Jones lashed out. "Don't be more of a fool than is absolutely necessary. I told you to get close to the little bitch, not climb into bed with her."

Craig had had dealings with this man for many years. He knew only too well how ruthless he was, and how cold, only ever showing any emotion when it came to his son. The obsessive gleam in his eyes was frightening. His fanatical hatred of Caro was surely insane.

Craig decided, then and there, that directly this business was wound up he was going to have nothing more to do with him. But this wasn't the time to be thinking how he'd do it. Trying to sound calm, he said, "Look, she means nothing to me anymore, take my word for it."

"You can't be so crass as to think I'd believe you?"

"For fuck's sake, it's the truth. I promise you, I'll deal with her. Leave it to me."

"For your sake, Paxton, you'd better get it right this time. You've got her out of the way while that consignment goes through, as I instructed. Now I want her dealt with once and for all, understood?"

"Okay, I'll do my best."

"No. You'll do better than that." He rose and set the mug down on the table with quiet precision. He had himself under control now. "That house of Peron's."

"It's his sister's."

Jones ignored the interruption. "The river's right on the doorstep. Use it. I want the Bennett family wiped out, once and for all."

He walked to the door of the cabin, prepared to go up the short flight of steps to the deck. Craig felt an overwhelming wave of relief, but it was cut short. Jones turned at the last moment.

"If she's still alive tomorrow, I won't be back. I'll send the boys instead, with very precise, and painful, instructions. Do you understand me, Paxton?"

Craig nodded. He couldn't trust himself to speak.

"Morning to you." Jones gave him a slow, humourless smile then went up the steps. The *Sally Anne* rocked slightly as he stepped up onto the quay and Craig listened to his footsteps disappearing along the pier.

* * *

Raised voices. Shouting. It made her head throb even more as she crawled along the dark, dark tunnel. Crawled? No, she was swimming, up through the thick water to the light. But the light hurt her eyes, and the shouting made her head throb. Very slowly, Caro opened her eyes. Whitewashed walls. Bright light streaming through a skylight in a sloping ceiling. It was difficult to distinguish reality from fantasy. Her lids were weighted. She let them close again.

When next she opened her eyes, she had no idea how much time had passed, but surely the light was different.

There were voices shouting again, but suddenly they stopped. Fear, like ice in her veins, filled her body.

She pushed herself up, but that was a mistake. Her head swam and nausea rose in her throat. Lying back down, she turned her head carefully from side to side. She was lying on a bed in a strange room. She didn't want to move again in case the nausea came back, tried to lick her lips, but her tongue felt twice its normal size.

Footsteps were coming up from below. She had the presence of mind to close her eyes again and turn to face the wall. A key grated in the lock and the door creaked open. She lay, rigid, as someone padded softly across the wooden boards of the floor. Caro could hear their breathing. The person placed something that chinked on the floor and left the room as quietly as they'd entered. Caro heard the key turn in the lock.

At last she pushed herself up onto her elbows, glad that the room stayed in one place this time. She looked down to see what had been left by the bed. It was a bottle containing what looked like water, with a glass upended over the top. At sight of it she realised how dreadfully thirsty she was. In spite of her swimming head, she swung her legs off the bed, slopped some water into the glass and lifted it to her mouth. It felt wonderful as it slid down her throat. After her second glass her head began to clear.

What was the last thing she remembered? Craig's hand in her back, pushing her onto the *Sally Anne?* Yes. He'd given her coffee, talked and talked. And that was all she remembered until she woke up in this horrid room. The voices interrupted her thoughts, a man's and a woman's, they were speaking French, but far too fast for her to understand.

She began to explore her surroundings. An ugly wardrobe stood against the opposite wall and, other than the iron bedstead, the only piece of furniture was an upright chair. Opposite the door the roof sloped down, and in it was a skylight window, firmly closed.

Someone had taken off the trainers she'd been wearing and placed them by the bed. Next to them was her shoulder bag. Stealthily she took her shoes and put them on. For some reason she felt safer once they were firmly laced. She rummaged in her bag. Everything was there, even the matches she'd bought for Eleanor, but no mobile phone. He must have taken it. As quietly as she could she took the chair across and placed it below the skylight, hoisted herself onto it and stretched up to look out. All she could see was blue sky and a few clouds, and, in the far distance, sunlight glinting on water. She could hear the squawking of gulls, so that water could be the sea.

She crept to the door and tried the handle, but she'd known it would be locked. She'd heard the key turn. Back on the edge of the bed, she tried to suppress the fear and think. Whose house was this? Was Craig downstairs? Would he come running up if she started shouting, knock her out again? Carefully she examined the back of her head and her forehead for bruises or lumps. There were none. It must have been that coffee.

"Bastard!" Caro whispered to herself. "Bastard! Bastard!" She felt a wave of warming anger sweep some of the fear aside. But it soon came creeping back. She tried to concentrate on working out where she was. Those people had been speaking French. There was the sea and the gulls. What time was it? She glanced at her watch. Why hadn't she thought to do that before? Ten thirty, but that was Guernsey time. If this was France, what time would it be? In frustration she thumped her hands on the mattress and clamped her teeth hard to stop herself shouting out. But the longer she was awake the better she felt. She desperately wanted to be clear-headed next time whoever it was came back into the room.

* * *

For Alex it was the most frustrating morning of his life. There was very little he could do. He had enough sense to realise interfering while the professionals tried to do their job would be counterproductive. He gave Eleanor a quick call, but played down the situation, not wanting to worry her.

She told him she'd found a note from Caro under the dresser in the kitchen. "It must have blown off the table," she said, "but it's not much help, just says she was going to do some shopping in town." Alex passed this information on to Paul, who just nodded.

Jacques told them that the result of the visit to Jean Peron's flat was inconclusive. "The concierge let my men in. We know of this Peron, but there was no sign of the girl in this apartment, and unfortunately, there was nothing there of any use to us."

"Where the hell is she?" Alex couldn't stop himself demanding.

"This we do not know, as yet." Jacques was matter of fact. "But assuredly it will not be long. I have a team watching his place. We will know immediately if he returns."

And Alex had to be satisfied with that.

At half past eleven there was another development. Jacques had a call about Peron's sister. "It transpires that this sister has a smallholding, somewhere near Châteauneuf on the banks of the Rance. It is possible that he has taken Miss Bennett there. We are checking now the exact location."

But Paul was getting restive, talking about getting back to Guernsey.

"There are things I could be doing from that end, and the chief's going to get stroppy if I hang around here too long." He tried to persuade Alex to come with him. "Leave them to it, they know what they're doing. They'll probably get on much more quickly without you– us hanging around."

"No. I'm not going."

"Alex, I really do think…"

"Paul," Alex turned on him, his face set. "I'm not going back until we've found Caro, understand? You can do what you like. I'm staying here."

Paul shrugged and gave in. "Okay, if you insist." He took out his phone to check on flights from Dinard. "Shouldn't be any problem now the fog's lifted," he said.

Alex was reluctant to leave Jacques' office, afraid that he might miss something, but an idea was niggling at him. Wouldn't he be better off with his own transport? This feeling of being dependent on the French officers was really getting to him. He wasn't quite sure why it seemed so important to be independent, but it did. And he knew St Malo well, there was a car hire firm not a hundred yards from where they were. Making some excuse, he left the office, feeling sure they were relieved to see the back of him.

It took barely half an hour to organise the car, but for Alex the time dragged at snail's pace. On returning to Jacques' office, he found nothing significant had happened in his absence. Shouldn't they be on their way, searching high and low for that bloody farm?

"These things take time, Alex," Paul told him. "You can't rush it." He sounded exasperated. "Jacques is very thorough. Believe me, if anyone can find Caro, he can."

"Okay. Any luck with your flight?"

"Yup. I'm off in a minute. Can I trust you to behave yourself when I'm gone?"

"I'll behave," Alex said.

"Make sure you do," Paul said firmly. "I've had a word with Jacques, and he'll give you as much leeway as he can. Just don't get in his way."

Paul said his goodbyes to the French officers, clapped a hand on Alex's shoulder and said, "I'll pop in on Eleanor and bring her up to date immediately I get home, okay?"

"Thanks, Paul. She'll be worried sick. I haven't spoken to her since first thing this morning."

It was barely five minutes after he'd gone that news came in of the location of the farmhouse. Alex, sitting quietly in a corner, listened intently to the conversation between Jacques and his men.

"It is three kilometres from Châteauneuf, south along the Dinan road, called Le Mouillage," the man told Jacques. "There's a rough track which takes you almost to the house, but the place is a mess. Most of it is falling down, hardly used."

"Is it possible to approach the farmhouse without being seen?"

"Oh yes. It's very overgrown. The last few hundred metres would have to be done on foot."

"It's of no import. Right. We'll send some men to check up."

Alex couldn't contain himself any longer. "You're not going straight in?"

"No," Jacques said briskly. "We do not know for certain that Miss Bennett is there, and we must go carefully, Alex, so that no warning is given."

"I suppose so." But Alex's mind was racing. He'd take his hire car and do some investigating himself. At least he'd be doing something, and wasn't Jacques being overcautious? Alex's desire for action got the better of common sense and he made up his mind. "Do you mind, Jacques, if I go back to the hotel for a bit?"

Jacques gave him a curious look, but he was so busy Alex hoped he wouldn't wonder about his change in behaviour. "By all means. I will contact you there immediately there is any news."

"Thank you," said Alex, feeling a tiny spurt of guilt at deceiving the man, but he had to do something, or he'd go mad.

Once out of Jacques' office Alex ran to where he'd left the car, jumped in and drove as fast as he could through St Malo, using his horn whenever he needed to clear the way. As the car careered along, he hardly noticed the high wall of the old town as he sped past it, or the boats in the marina. In a surprisingly short time he was surrounded by the flowing countryside of Brittany. He sped through Sunday sleepy towns and small villages. Occasionally he glimpsed the estuary of the Rance as it twisted and turned, crept further and further inland, until he slowed down at last. Somewhere near here was the turn off for Châteauneuf. He hit the steering wheel with a triumphant hand when he saw it, turned and began to drive more slowly through the town and out onto the road the other side. Surely the farm track they'd spoken of should be coming up soon. Driving very slowly now, he searched around. It would have to be on the right if the farm was on the banks of the Rance.

When he came to it, he nearly drove straight past. There was a barely visible gap in a field of swaying young maize, and a battered wooden signpost pointed towards it. He could just make out the letters of the farm's name, Le Mouillage. He turned down the track, searching for a building, any building.

CHAPTER 25

Caro wasn't sure how long she'd been sitting on the bed. Although her head had cleared a bit, it was still difficult to think straight. Half a dozen different escape plans jostled about in her mind, but she discarded them all. When she heard footsteps coming up the stairs again, she jumped up and stumbled to the end of the bed, needing some barrier between her and whoever came in. She was shaking, half with fear, half with anger. The key turned in the lock and the door opened.

The man in the doorway was short with a wiry, slightly stooped body. His small, dark eyes flicked over her and, as he did so, he licked his top lip slowly. Caro backed further across the room until she bumped into the wooden chair and nearly overbalanced. Her heart beat high in her throat and the fear took over.

"Who are you?" she croaked, but she made herself go on. "Why are you keeping me here?"

"I 'ave been told to." At least he spoke English. "That is all you need to know." He stood looking and Caro wrapped her arms protectively around her body. "My sister, she wants to know if you wish something to eat."

Relief flowed over her. Surely, he'd not harm her if there was a woman in the house? A mocking little voice in her mind asked, why not?

"Was it your sister who brought me the water?"

"Yes. Do you wish to eat or not?" he snapped.

She didn't want him to go yet. She needed to find out more. "Yes." The word came out in a gasp. "I'm hungry."

"Okay." He began to close the door.

"Wait!" she shouted. "Where is this place? Tell me why I'm here. Please." She despised herself for pleading.

"I cannot do this."

"But please…"

It was no good, he'd closed the door and locked it again.

Caro gave a little sob as she listened to his footsteps receding down the stairs. She kicked the chair, but only succeeded in hurting her foot. Tears sprung to her eyes, but she scrubbed at her face, determined not to give in. "I will not cry," she muttered. "I will not cry."

A little while later she heard softer footsteps and the door opened. This was a female version of her previous visitor, the same thin body, the same small, dark eyes. The woman was dressed in shabby jeans and tee shirt, an apron tied around her waist. She had a cowed air, as if she was used to being bullied. Bending, she placed the tray she was carrying on the floor just inside the door and prepared to leave.

"Don't go. Please!" Caro begged, but the woman shook her head and slid out of the room. The key turned once again.

After a moment Caro walked over to investigate what was on the tray. There was a plate of French bread and some cheese, and a bowl of what looked like hot chocolate. To her amazement she realised she was ravenous. When had she last eaten? Tears threatened again as she remembered sitting in Eleanor's kitchen the day before, looking forward to Alex's return from Jersey. Is he thinking that I've walked out on him? Oh God, what if he thinks I've just upped and left, and doesn't try to find me. Please, please don't let that happen.

Pushing the thought away, she picked up the tray, placed it on the bed and began to eat. She hardly noticed what the bread and cheese tasted like, nor the lukewarm chocolate. She gulped it down and felt revived. She was determined to escape. But even if she did get out of this room, where would she go? I'll cross that bridge when I come to it, she told herself. First of all, she must have a closer look around.

Moving as quietly as she could, she went over to the enormous wardrobe and opened it, the door creaked and for a moment she stood frozen to the spot, but no sound came from downstairs. Peering inside, she studied every gloomy corner. It was completely empty. In the drawers at the bottom were a few musty blankets, nothing else. Getting down on her hands and knees she peered under the bed, nothing. She crawled across the room studying the floor, wondering why she was doing so, but she continued to search. It was something to do.

As she got to the corner furthest from the door, she realised she could hear voices now. In this dark corner there was a sliver of light shining up from the room below. A gap between the floorboards! For some reason she was jubilant, this felt like a great discovery. A moment later she told herself her jubilation wasn't entirely unreasonable. If I can listen to what's going on, she thought, it could help me decide what to do. The encouraging voice inside her mind cheered her, but only for a moment. What was the point of hearing what they said if she couldn't understand their rapid French?

As she crouched there, she heard a blast of La Marseillaise immediately below her. Someone's mobile. The man answered. "*'Allo?*" And a moment later he broke into his stilted English. Caro couldn't believe her luck. She lay flat with her ear to the crack.

"Yes, all is okay … no, of course not, I would have called you." There was a long pause and then he swore angrily in his own language and demanded, "Who does he think he is, this Jones?"

In the room above, Caro's eyes widened at the familiar name. But his next words distracted her. "What do I do with the girl once the consignment has gone? … But this is not possible … my sister, she is already unhappy … No, no, I cannot do this, it is too dangerous. It is you that must take her away. Ah, *mais non*, I will not…" He stopped speaking for some time then said more calmly, "Okay, I will speak to Nanette, but she will not be content, already she is threatening to phone the *gendarmes*." Caro's heart lifted, but not for long. "No. Do not worry, she will not. Nanette is stupid, she threatens but she is too fearful to do anything. Whatever happens, my sister will keep her mouth shut, that is very sure." Again, there was silence in the room below, but Caro forced herself to stay prone on the floor. She was sure he hadn't yet cut off the call. She was right. "*Écoutez-moi.*" He sounded more angry. "With the river and your boat, it would be easy to accomplish … this is your affair, but so long as she is alive, she is a danger to us all … Yes, yes, but can you stop her mouth forever? Assuredly not!"

Caro couldn't bear to listen any longer. Feeling sick with fear, she crept over to the bed and curled up, foetal.

* * *

Caro had no idea how long she lay there, curled up and shaking. *So long as she's alive, so long as she's alive.* She couldn't make the words go away. All that about the river, and a boat. He must have been talking to Craig, he must have. Had Craig suggested she should be – got rid of? She flinched from putting it in plainer language. And there was that name Jones again. The one that Jason had mentioned when she was standing outside the warehouse. It seemed like weeks ago.

Abruptly she uncurled her body, unable to stay still any longer. She crept across the room and came to halt below the skylight window. Surely, she thought, if I prised it open, I could climb out, perhaps there's a drainpipe. Anything would be better than doing nothing. She needed something to prise open the catch. She looked around, saw her shoulder bag lying under the bed. Grabbing it, she began to rummage in its depths. With a gasp of triumph, she found a pair of tweezers and some scissors. She discarded the tweezers, too flimsy, but the scissors might do it. Standing on the chair she reached up and began to whittle away at the catch. For an age she worked at it, and then the two sides of the scissors snapped apart. She could have screamed in frustration. Fighting for self-control, she got down from the chair and went back to her bag. This time she emptied the contents onto the bed and spread them out so that she could see exactly what she had. There was her notebook, she pushed that aside, and Eleanor's matches. An idea came to her. But surely it would be too dangerous. What if they didn't let her out? Yet the idea persisted. She picked up a small can of deodorant that had fallen from her bag, rolled it back and forth. Suddenly her hands were still. That might work.

For some time her mind see-sawed back and forth between fear and the overwhelming desire to escape. What would Alex do if he was here? But she pushed the image of him out. If she allowed herself to think of him, she'd break down completely.

She'd been so preoccupied that she hadn't heard the footsteps. Frantically she scooped everything back into her bag and sat on the edge of the bed, the bag hidden behind her. Only just in time. The door opened and the man stood there, that same unpleasantly speculative look on his face.

"You finished?"

For a moment she couldn't understand what he was asking, then remembered the tray with its empty plate and bowl.

"Yes. Thank you." It annoyed her that she sounded so polite when what she most wanted to do was beat him to a pulp! Some of her thoughts must have communicated themselves, for he came warily across the room, picked up the tray and returned to the doorway, but there he turned.

"Later, my sister she go to fetch food. Perhaps, when she is gone, I will visit you, *hein*? You will be nice to me." His face split in a disgusting leer.

Waves of nausea pushed up from her stomach as she jumped up and backed away from him. She couldn't speak, the words stuck in her throat. With a final look up and down her body, he was gone.

She stood rigid, fighting an urge to throw up. He'd left her no choice. The plan that she'd discarded a moment ago, now seemed like her only chance. She must move quickly, before the woman went out.

She stripped the threadbare spread from the bed. The mattress underneath was an old one. Would it work? It wouldn't take long to find out. She took the matches out of her handbag, tore pages from the notebook and placed them in a pile in the middle of the mattress. Her heart was beating like a hammer as she sprayed some of the deodorant on the little heap of paper. She picked up the matches.

Closing her eyes tight for a moment, she took a deep breath before striking the first match. A piece of paper lit, glowed red round the edge, then it petered out. She tried again, but no luck. Gathering up the spent matches, she placed them on top of the paper, lit the ends of two or three. The paper began to catch and, at last, her little fire built up. For a few seconds she watched, willing it to keep going. It did.

She got up and backed away from the bed towards the door, the can of deodorant in hand. The centre of the mattress, under her heap of paper, was beginning to smoulder. What will I do if they don't hear me shout? What a fool! I should never have started it.

Banging on the door, she began to scream and shout for help.

CHAPTER 26

Alex crawled along and came to a halt at a small lay-by scooped out of the field of maize. He backed the car until it was half hidden by the maize. Best to continue on foot, he thought. All around his vision was obscured by tall green crops, but up ahead there was a bend in the track and beyond that he fervently hoped he'd find what he was looking for.

He began to walk along the grassy verge, keeping as close to the maize as possible, but when he turned the corner there was still no sign of any buildings, just the track snaking on through the field. He looked ahead, then back the way he'd come. Nothing for it but to keep going.

Just around the next bend there was a small copse of trees, and a turn in the river brought it near to where he stood. Through the trees he glimpsed a building. Making his way more cautiously now, keeping to the cover of trees and bushes, he finally came to the edge of a muddy yard littered with rusting farm machinery.

Then all hell broke loose. There was shouting, the sound of running feet as a man appeared and ran across the yard to the house. A woman was screaming. For a heart-stopping moment Alex stood, indecisive, then he began to run, not caring now if he was seen. He pounded across the yard and stood there, hesitating. A moment later, amongst the shouting and screaming, he heard the sound of breaking glass and looked up to see smoke crawling menacingly out of a skylight window. Then his blood ran cold as he recognised the voice screaming for help.

"Let me out! Help! Help!" It was Caro.

Alex slithered on the mud and quickly recovered himself. Reaching a door, he grasped the handle, pulled. It gave with a screech of unoiled hinges. There was more shouting, a man and another woman, footsteps pounding above him. He was in a kitchen. A door stood open opposite. He ran across and found himself in a narrow passageway with a flight of stairs rising to the right. He could hear Caro's voice somewhere above, and a man shouting in French to bring water. Thundering up the stairs, Alex found himself on a landing with shallow steps down to a passageway. There was a door at the end, and from it came smoke and a pandemonium of noise.

If he'd been in less of a panic, he would have been more careful, but all he could think of was to get to Caro. He could hear her screaming, "Get off me! Get off me!"

He never actually saw what was happening in the room. He got to the door, pushed it open, then something hit him on the back of the head. His knees buckled under him and pain exploded in his side. The next moment the door slammed shut with he and Caro on the inside, the other two on the outside. The key snapped in the lock.

* * *

"It seems Monsieur Devereaux has hired a car, sir."

"He's done what?" Jacques shouted at the nervous young officer standing in front of his desk.

She flinched. "He's hired a car, sir," she repeated.

"How do you know this?"

"Your sister phoned, sir. She said the car hire people had sent someone round with Monsieur Devereaux's licence, he left it at their office by mistake. She thought you ought to know, so she brought it round."

Jacques swore, cursing all interfering civilians to hell and damnation. "Do we know what car he has?"

"Yes, sir. I contacted the hire firm. It's a green Fiat Punto." She gave him the registration number. "And I have checked, Monsieur Devereaux is not at his hotel."

Jacques threw up his hands in exasperation, then pushed back his chair. It rocked for a moment then righted itself. "I need only one guess to work out where he has gone. What damage! I have a bad feeling about this. We will have to move sooner than I'd hoped. Please tell Bernard and the others to come in."

Half an hour later Jacques and several other officers poured out of the building and jumped into two cars. They drove, sirens blaring, through St Malo and out onto the motorway. It wasn't until they left Châteauneuf behind that they switched off the sirens.

* * *

"Alex! Are you alright? Alex?"

He managed to uncurl his body, but he still hadn't enough breath to speak.

"Alex, please say something, please." He felt dampness on his cheek, forced his eyelids to lift. Caro's face swam

216

just above him. She was crying. His head was on her lap, and her tears were falling on his face.

"Don't cry," he croaked. "Please don't cry."

"Oh, thank God!"

"Why?"

"You're able to speak."

"Just about."

"I thought you were…" She gulped, swallowed a sob, and smiled at him through her tears. "Bugger it, I don't know what I thought."

"Language, my girl." His voice seemed to be recovering.

She stuck her tongue out at him, so he pulled her head down with a shaking hand and kissed her with surprising force. This seemed to revive him. He pushed himself into a sitting position. His head was clearer, but the pain in his side concentrated the mind somewhat.

"I'm so sorry, my darling," he said. "I really cocked up the heroic rescue bit."

"I don't care," she said. She wrapped her arms round him, but when he gave a gasp of pain she sprang back. "Sorry. Did I hurt you?"

"It's my side."

"That bastard kicked you." With extreme care Caro put her arms round him again. "I'm so, so glad you're here."

"But it hasn't exactly helped much, has it?" Alex said bitterly, as he stroked her hair. "I've screwed up a treat, bloody idiot."

"You mean you're on your own?"

"Yes, 'fraid so."

"Oh Alex!" She couldn't keep the disappointment out of her voice.

"I'm sorry. But they were dragging their feet so. I just couldn't bear it any longer. I had to do something."

"Who's they?"

"Jacques Hubert – he's Paul's counterpart in St Malo – and the rest of them. Paul's gone back to Guernsey. He tried to persuade me to go with him, but I wanted to stay. He's–"

"Stop! Stop!"

"What's the matter?" Alex shifted his position and looked at her, wondering what had happened.

"I don't even understand how you come to be here, let alone who you're with. How did you know I was in France in the first place?"

It dawned on Alex that Caro would have no idea how he and Paul had found out she was on the *Sally Anne*, let alone across the Channel. Carefully he pushed himself upright, took her hand and led her to the bed. "Sit down, I'll explain it all."

"No," Caro pulled him back.

"Why not?"

"The bed, it's soaked."

Alex took in the charred, soaked mattress. So that was the source of the fire. He looked at Caro. "How on earth did it happen, the fire?"

"I started it. I thought they'd have to let me out if there was a fire, and that way it'd be easier to get away. And I thought, just maybe, it might attract attention from neighbours or something." Her shoulders sagged. "I was desperate. He said he'd come back, when his sister was out," she whispered. "He said I should be nice to him."

Alex took a deep breath and pulled her into his arms, ignoring the pain in his side, desperate to chase away the lurking terror in her eyes.

"Oh, my poor darling. Don't think about it. I'm here now, okay?"

For a long moment they stood there, wrapped around each other, drawing strength and comfort from each other's bodies, then Caro muttered into his shoulder, "It was a stupid thing to do." She looked up at him. "I should have known it wouldn't work. Him and the woman, they both rushed in. He grabbed me, shouted at her to get water and she came back with two buckets. It didn't take long for her to put it out. Then you arrived and she hit you over the head with one of the buckets!"

Alex's mouth twisted in a grim smile. "A bucket, eh? How undignified."

A burst of hysterical laughter spluttered from Caro's lips, but she quickly suppressed it by pressing her face into his jumper. "Then that shitty little man pushed me over and, before I could recover, he kicked you. I could kill him for that!"

Alex kissed her. "Thank you."

"After that they slammed out and locked us in." Caro shivered. "What do you think they're going to do?"

"I don't know. I wish I did."

"Over in that corner there's a crack in the floorboards, you can hear what's going on in the kitchen." She crept over and Alex followed her, watched as she crouched down with her ear to the floor. After a moment she looked up. "Nothing. They must have gone outside or something. That's the most unnerving thing, not knowing what's going on outside this room."

"I know, love, but there isn't much we can do about it. If I was on my own it'd be different, but I don't want you getting hurt."

"Ha! It's you that's got the injuries, Superman!"

Alex grinned. "And I don't want to get any more." He put his arm around her shoulders and led her to the side of the room facing the door. "Let's settle ourselves here against the wall."

They sank down and sat very close together. "From here," Alex said, "even if we don't hear any footsteps, we'll be able to see the second anyone touches the door handle." He took her hand and held it warmly clasped between both of his. "Now, let me bring you up to date on what's been happening."

Alex wondered where to begin. He could hardly tell Caro he'd suspected her of going off with Craig of her own free will. So far Craig hadn't been mentioned, so he still didn't know what had happened between them. But now he told her how disappointed he'd been when she didn't turn up at the airport.

"I'd spent all day looking forward to seeing you, and when you weren't there, I just couldn't understand why."

"I'm so sorry."

"What exactly happened?" It was impossible to keep a shade of accusation out of his voice.

"You tell me your story first," she said, "and I'll fill in my bits after."

"Okay," Alex said reluctantly. "When I got back to the house Eleanor was none the wiser, and she was desperately worried, she'd thought you were upstairs working."

"But I left her a note," Caro said.

"I know, it had blown off the table, she didn't find it until later. We contacted Paul, but he didn't know anything either. It wasn't until Ashley pitched up that things became clearer."

"What had she got to do with it?"

He was quiet for a moment. The silence stretched out, then Alex said, "Caro, I need to get some things straight in my mind. Bear with me, will you?"

She frowned at him. "Okay."

"Nella had a visit from a ghastly woman called Geraldine Lacey. It seems like ages ago, but it was only yesterday afternoon." He took a deep breath. "She's the most awful gossip, always poking her nose into other people's business. What she said really bothered Nella." Alex wondered if that was entirely true. It was he that had been bothered by what Geraldine had said rather than his grandmother. "She was one of the people Nella introduced you to when the two of you went shopping."

Caro nodded, remembering.

"She said she'd seen you on Thursday evening, with a man," Alex said. "From the description it sounded like Craig."

The atmosphere was now thick with doubt and unanswered questions. "I was going to tell you about that when you got back from Jersey," Caro said.

"You mean it was you she saw?"

"Yes," she said carefully. "It was."

"Why?" He couldn't keep the accusation out of his voice.

"You don't think I wanted to be there, do you?"

"No, but–"

"What do you mean, but?" she demanded.

"Well. You may have – oh, I don't know what I thought. I just hated the idea that you'd been with him at all."

With deliberation she detached her hand from his, then ran her fingers through her curls, making them stand on end. She gave an exasperated sigh, and Alex wished he'd kept his mouth shut. He tried to recapture her hand, but she pulled away.

"I'm sorry," he said. "Forget I said it. Just tell me what happened."

There was no reply.

"Please, Caro."

So, she did, everything, and when she'd finished Alex actually laughed. "And he managed to convince you Eleanor and I are quite happy to buy stolen goods?"

"No – yes – well, not really. But I thought that kind of gossip might do damage, and you must admit she does like to disobey the rules, your grandmother."

Alex was still laughing.

"Stop making so much noise," Caro hissed, "you'll attract their attention. And it's all very well for you to laugh. For all I knew that kind of thing was, well, sort of accepted in Guernsey, because of the history of privateering and all that. Anyway, there were little incidents that made me think, just possibly, that it was plausible."

"What incidents, for goodness' sake?"

When she told him, Alex laughed even more and buried his face in her shoulder to muffle the sound, and then he was kissing her neck, kisses which travelled up to her mouth.

"Am I forgiven?" he said against her lips.

"I don't know." Caro leant back so that she could look into his eyes. "Yes, I suppose so," she said. But when he tried to kiss her again, she pushed him away. "No, stop it. We've got to concentrate on the door."

"I suppose." He leant back against the wall. "What a story. You can take it from me, my darling, all that nonsense Craig fed you was complete fabrication, not a word of truth in it."

He wasn't sure, from the look on her face, that she believed him, but she nodded and said, "No need to sound so patronising about it," then added, "so what happened next? What about Ashley?"

Alex began to tell Caro what Ashley had said, but it wasn't long before she interrupted him.

"And you actually believed her when she said I was happy to be there?"

"Well, at first."

"What?" She pushed herself away from him and got up from the floor. "Thanks a bunch, Alex."

"Well, how was I to know…?"

She looked down at him, really angry now. "You don't trust me at all, do you? Even after all you've said, and I've said, you still don't trust me. First you think I go off to meet Craig on the beach, and now you tell me you believed Ashley's version of events rather than mine. Bloody men! All you ever do is judge everyone by your own standards."

"Calm down," he said frantically, as her voice rose higher, and then wished immediately that he hadn't. It just added fuel to the flames.

"Calm down?" she said in a furious whisper. "Listen to me while I explain exactly why I was on the *Sally Anne*."

"Caro!"

"Shut up and listen."

Alex pushed himself painfully up from the floor. He leant against the wall and watched her as she paced up and down.

"Craig sent me a text and said he'd got proof of what he'd told me. He said if I didn't go and see him, he'd give this proof to the press. Now listen carefully here. That's the only reason I went to see him. I was so worried. I thought I might be able to do something – God knows what, but something."

"You don't have to go on."

"Oh yes I do." She glared at him. "He must have drugged my coffee, and at lunchtime Eleanor and I had had some wine, which probably didn't help. I don't remember much after getting onto the boat, just the coffee. Next thing I knew, I woke up here. Are you satisfied now?"

Alex opened his mouth to reply, but the words were never spoken. Both of them heard the footsteps at the same time, not inside the house but in the yard. The firm, decisive footsteps of someone who wasn't afraid to be heard.

CHAPTER 27

Alex lifted an urgent finger to his lips, but Caro didn't speak. Quickly she fetched the rickety chair and carried it over to the broken window.

"What are you doing?" Alex whispered.

"I'm going to see what's going on."

"Wait a minute."

But she was already climbing onto the chair. She stretched up as far as she could, but it wasn't long before she climbed down again. "No good. I can't see any more than I could before," she whispered. "You're taller. You try." For the moment her anger had been set aside.

Alex hefted himself up, grunting as the pain in his side gripped him. He peered out. "I can only see a small corner of the yard, where the track comes into it. No sign of anyone." And then he nearly fell off the chair as they heard a loud knock on the kitchen door below. A man's voice called in French, "Hallo? Anyone home?"

"Where the hell are they?" Caro whispered.

"God knows."

"Should we shout for help?"

"Definitely not. We've no way of knowing who this newcomer is."

"You stay there," she told him, and leaving him standing on the chair, straining to see out, Caro crept across to the corner by the wardrobe and crouched down. She put her ear to the crack. Very faintly she could hear voices below.

Jabbing a finger at the floorboards, she mouthed, "They're down there, whispering."

Alex crept over to her and crouched down too.

"Hallo?" the voice called again from beyond the kitchen door, sounding incredibly loud in the tense silence. A second later they heard the screeching hinges of the kitchen door and the woman asked, "Yes? What do you want?"

They listened intently, then Caro whispered, "What are they saying?"

"He says he's lost his way," Alex told her. "He's on a fishing trip and thought the track would lead him to a good spot on the river."

The woman answered, sounding dismissive. They heard the door creak, but he must have stopped it closing, for his voice went on, asking for directions, that much Caro could understand.

They were both so intent on listening to what was going on that, for a moment, they'd forgotten to wonder where Jean Peron might have gone. But then they heard soft footsteps on the stairs, followed by the chink of metal outside the door of the room. Moving incredibly quickly considering his bruises, Alex jumped up and crept to the door, taking the chair with him. He pressed himself against the wall beside it and indicated, with frantic gestures, that Caro should get behind him. She dashed soundlessly across the room and they stood there, hardly daring to breath.

For what seemed like an age nothing happened, then the woman shouted, "Jean, Jean!" from down below.

A voice sounded from just outside the door. "*Hein?* What is it you want?" There was bravado in it, but fear as well. They heard the footsteps, loud now, retreating down the stairs. It looked as if Jean had decided to brazen it out, which turned out to be a mistake. There was the sound of a scuffle, a stream of invective, several voices raised, all shouting at once, and then the woman began to scream.

A moment later another voice sounded, adding to the noise. "Alex? Mademoiselle Bennett?" It was Jacques Hubert.

"Jacques!" Alex shouted. "Up here, the room at the end of the landing." He banged on the door. Beside him Caro gave a strangled sob of relief. She grabbed her bag from the floor and within seconds the key turned in the lock and the door was flung open.

"*Hah, voila,*" said Jacques, grinning. "You, my friend, are a pain in the posterior. Come. A car is waiting." He led them down the stairs and out of the house. "I will send one of my men to collect your hire car, Alex. We passed it on our way."

It turned out that while Nanette had been occupied by the supposed fisherman at the door, who was one of

Jacques' men, her brother had been creeping upstairs. Two more of Jacques' men had entered the house by a back window and made their way through to the narrow passageway. When Jean had decided to go down and give his sister a hand, he'd walked straight into them and been overpowered.

As they drove back to St Malo, Jacques said nothing further about Alex's escapade, but Alex was sure Paul wouldn't be so tactful when he heard about it.

* * *

Caro felt like a rag doll as she sat slumped in a chair in Jacques' office while the events of this age-long day dragged on around her. The late afternoon light slanted through the windows and she longed to be able to give in and sleep. With half an ear she listened as Alex spoke to Eleanor on the phone, reassuring her. She noticed him glancing at her as he put the receiver down, but she refused to meet his eye. All that could be said between them had been said, too much in fact. There was no point in making bad worse.

There was the sound of raised voices in the outer office, then the door was pushed open. Jacques Hubert, who had left them to make the call to Eleanor in privacy, stood in the doorway, but a second later he was elbowed out of the way by a large, white bearded bear of a man who precipitated himself into the room.

"Caro, *ma petite*! Are you alright? What have they done to you?"

Caro jumped up. "Alphonse!" she cried.

Ignoring everyone else, he strode across the room and gathered her into his arms, studying her face with anxious eyes, and touching it gently with his sensitive craftsman's hands, as if he was checking for injuries. "Are you alright? Madame Devereaux and I, we were so very worried. I came immediately, my little one. What a time you have had."

Caro's eyes filled with tears. "I'm fine, Alphonse, but oh it's so good to see you." She hugged him again, and cried a little on his shoulder, noticing that he smelt of his usual mixture of sawdust, varnish and the particular aftershave she associated only with him.

Lifting her face to scrub at her tears with a sleeve, she watched as Alphonse turned to look at Alex, his eyes alight with curiosity. "And is this your new young man?" he asked Caro.

She could feel the hot colour flooding into her cheeks. "Yes, well, this is Alex Devereaux."

"I knew your Uncle William. He knew his wines, that one." He was glancing from one to the other of them as he shook Alex's hand, with such enthusiastic force that Caro saw Alex wince.

"Careful, Alphonse. Alex was injured."

"Ah, enacting the dramatic rescue?"

"No," Alex grimaced. "I'm afraid I made a complete hash of that. It was Jacques and his men who did all the rescuing."

"*N'importe.*" Alphonse's eyes twinkled at him. "So long as there is a happy ending, *hein*?"

Caro was relieved there was an interruption at that moment. Yet another commotion had erupted in the outer office. They went to the door to find out what was happening. A young gendarme was reeling off a rapid stream of information as Jacques and everyone else listened intently.

"What's he saying?" Caro asked Alphonse. And then her heart gave a lurch. Surely, he'd mentioned the name Paxton?

She heard Alex swear under his breath. "What is it?" Caro asked him urgently.

"It's Craig, he seems to have legged it."

"What?"

"He says," added Alphonse, frowning, "that Craig has left the harbour. But that is not all. It appears that they let him slip the net purposely. What nonsense is this?"

All three of them started to ask questions at once and Jacques, having dismissed the young gendarme, turned to them with his hands held up. "Please, be seated. I will explain." He waited while they all subsided. Alphonse stood beside Caro, his hand on her shoulder. Alex stood a little way off, glancing at them occasionally but coming no closer.

"It is like this," Jacques said. "We need Monsieur Paxton to lead us to his friends. If we arrest him now, we could lose all his associates, this Jones who is the boss, and another, Jason Logan – I am told you know of this man, Mademoiselle Bennett?"

Caro nodded and Jacques went on, "So, if Paxton goes back to Guernsey, and Paul and I feel sure he will because of the imminent arrival of this consignment on Tuesday morning, we might be able to make a clean – how you say – sweep of it? If we are most careful, we could perhaps arrest the whole gang."

"But some of them aren't in Guernsey, they're in London." Caro still found it hard to understand. Her exhausted mind couldn't grasp the complexities of it all.

"No, it is apparently not. Jean Peron–"

"Jean Peron!" exclaimed Alphonse. "This name I know."

"Monsieur?" queried Jacques.

"He worked for me up until a few weeks ago. I had to let him go. He was not a good worker."

"That could be another link in the smuggling chain," said Alex.

"It could, indeed," said Jacques. "This Peron has told us that Jones was planning to send two of his men to Guernsey. He has also told us that Jones was in St Malo yesterday, which we suspected. We think he is probably on his way to Guernsey and we are watching, very carefully, the airports, the harbour, so that we can trace his path. This Jones, he will not escape us." He looked at Caro and smiled kindly. "So, you need not worry, mademoiselle, all is under control."

But Caro wasn't listening anymore. Cold as ice, the thought that had nudged at her when she'd listened to Jean on the phone in the kitchen just below her prison, rose up into the light of day. That was it!

She put up a hand to her mouth. "Oh my God!" she said, her eyes gazing up at Alphonse. "Oh my God! I know who he is."

"Who, *ma p'tite?*"

Alex and Jacques had both turned to look at her, worry at her tone in Alex's eyes, sharp curiosity in Jacques'.

"Monsieur Hubert, what does Jones look like?"

Without hesitation, Jacques told her. "A man of medium height, not fat, muscular, very powerful across the shoulders, white hair and most unpleasantly pale grey eyes."

"That's him." Her voice shook and she gripped Alphonse's hand till his fingers cracked.

He crouched down before her where she sat, his voice very quiet. "Now, Caro, calm yourself." He patted her knee. "That is better, now tell us what is troubling you."

"Some time ago, last week. God, was it really only last week? Craig asked me to go to London to pick up some stuff from Jason."

"Jason Logan, his associate?" Jacques asked.

"Yes, and I overheard this conversation, between Jason and another man who mentioned the name Jones. It rang a bell at the time, but I couldn't place it. Then his name kept popping up, Craig mentioned him, and Paul asked me about him, and when I was shut in that room at the farm, I overheard Jean Peron mention him again. It gave me such a jolt. I must have nearly made the connection then."

"What connection?" Alex's voice was urgent.

Caro looked up at him, her eyes bleak. "Do you remember when I told you about my father, how he was framed by that shit, Darren Durward? I'm so stupid! Why didn't I realise? The name of the property dealer who lost out when the site was discovered was Jones. He was the one who was probably behind all the threats, the e-mails, the phone calls, although nothing was proved."

"This man, he threatened your father?" Jacques was obviously confused.

Alphonse, in their own language, quickly put him in the picture, told him about the archaeological dig, the planners' change of heart, and all that came after it. Jacques' soft Gallic heart was touched.

"What a terrible thing. I am really desolated to hear of your misfortune, mademoiselle."

"Thank you," Caro said, but there was something else that was gnawing at her. "But there's something else. Just before Dad died, it must have been about the time that Darren Durward started his prison sentence, my parents received a letter. I was opening all their mail at the time. My mother wasn't interested, all she cared about was Dad. I never showed them the letter, it was too awful."

"What do you mean?" asked Alex.

"It was from somebody called Jones. He said he'd get his revenge on Dad, and his whole family, for what had happened to his son. I burnt it, tried to push it out of my mind. And I never made the connection before, Darren must be his son. Maybe he made Craig do what he did, to get at me."

"Surely not," Alex burst out before Alphonse's raised hand could stop him.

"Why is it nonsense?" Caro could hear the hysteria in her voice but didn't care. "How would you know? You never read it. I don't think it was Craig's idea to get me away from Guernsey."

"How can you say that after all he's done to you?" Alex exclaimed.

"He's weak, but he's not evil. I think he was acting on orders."

"Oh, come on—"

"Enough," Alphonse said firmly and Alex subsided. "We will think about this problem at another time, not now."

But Caro wasn't listening. She was staring straight ahead of her, fear in her eyes and her voice shaking. "He won't give up. I know it. That's what he's like. He won't give up."

"But we are all here to look after you, *ma p'tite*," Alphonse said firmly and patted her hand. "Come. You must rest. Both of you," he added, glancing at Alex. "What flight are you on back to Guernsey?"

For a moment neither Alex nor Caro answered, staring blankly at him. Alex was the first to collect his wits. "The last flight from Dinard."

"Good. That will be the eight o'clock. Some good strong coffee, with a little cognac, perhaps." He turned to Jacques. "Could this be arranged, Monsieur Hubert?"

"Certainly." Jacques seemed relieved to be able to do something and, calling in a young officer, sent him off to the café next door.

Alphonse looked from Alex to Caro and back again.

"I have one other favour to ask of you," he said to Jacques in his own language. "Could I perhaps use your telephone?"

"I beg of you," Jacques said, indicating the instrument on his desk.

Alphonse flipped through the directory while the others watched him in silence, ran a finger down the page, said, "Ah, *voilà*," and dialled a number. In a very short time, he had booked a seat on the same flight as Caro and Alex, ignoring Caro's perfunctory protests, and then turned back to the two of them. "Now, *mes enfants*, this has been a very big strain for you both. So, no more talk, because it seems to me that you just quarrel if you talk."

Caro didn't dare look at Alex.

"We will drink our coffee that Monsieur Hubert has so obligingly ordered," Alphonse went on imperturbably, "and then we will take this hire car of yours, Alex, and make our way to the airport. I brought a small *valise* with me, so there will be no delay." He turned to Jacques. "I hope these arrangements are in order."

Jacques threw up his hands. "If there is anything I need from these two young people, I am sure they will be able to pass it through Paul Le Page in Guernsey."

And that was that. Caro slumped back in her chair, feeling completely drained.

CHAPTER 28

Late on Tuesday morning the phone on Paul Le Page's desk gave one single ring. He picked up the receiver.

"Yes, Muriel? … Who?" he asked, then listened for a while, frowning. "Right. I'll come out."

Muriel was sitting at her desk. She glanced at Paul as he came in, seeming rather nervous. He wondered why, then turned to the man who sat waiting. "Mr Paxton. Would you like to come through?"

Craig got up and followed him through to his office.

"Have a seat," Paul said as he went to sit behind his desk.

He looked across at his visitor. There was a change in him. The strutting confidence was gone, and he'd lost the slick look. Unless I'm much mistaken, Paul thought, this is a frightened man. The *Sally Anne* had been spotted on the radar the night before, sailing into Havelet Bay at the southern end of St Peter Port. In order not to make

Paxton suspicious, the port authority had been sent round to check it out and collect the mooring fees first thing, but nothing else had been done. Paul had set up his surveillance team and they'd called in when Paxton left the boat to walk into town, but Paul had not expected him to end up here.

Paul leant forward. "What can I do for you?" he asked.

Craig sat back, crossed his legs and gave Paul a smile that didn't quite come off. "This is rather difficult." He laced his fingers together so tightly the knuckles went white, then looked across at Paul and what he said took Paul completely by surprise.

"I… er… I want your help," Craig said, and cleared his throat, "well, your protection if you will."

"My protection?" Paul asked, unable to keep the scorn out of his voice.

Paxton cleared his throat again. "I'm being threatened by someone that you might be interested in and I thought, if I helped you, you could, well overlook…" He took a deep breath, then said in a rush, "The man's a maniac. He's gone completely off the rails."

"Wait a minute, Mr Paxton," Paul said. "Who are you talking about?"

"Spencer Jones. He's threatening me and I want your protection."

"I'm afraid you're going to have to give me a good deal more information, not just his name. Who is he? Why is he threatening you?"

"I'm going to tell you."

"Good. But why did you come to me rather than the police?"

"Well, I know you, and you probably have some of the information already." Paxton gave him a resentful look. "After all, you've been on my case ever since I got to this bloody island."

"And you thought giving me information on this Jones would get me off your back?"

"Yes – no – it's more serious than that. I'm not the only one he's threatening."

Paul held up a hand. "Before you go on, I'll get one of my colleagues in. We'll need to record what you have to say." Ignoring the mutterings of protest, he picked up his phone and punched in a couple of numbers. "Dean? I need you in my office… now, please."

Dean Savident came in and, at sight of Paxton, his eyes widened. "Sir?" he said, glancing from his boss to the man sitting slouched in a chair before him.

"Set up the recording equipment, Dean, Mr Paxton has something to tell us."

* * *

On Monday Eleanor had hustled Caro and Alex off to see the doctor, who had pronounced Caro physically well, but prescribed rest and no more excitement, and Alex, she said, had bruising but no broken bones and she prescribed the same for him. Eleanor had insisted Alex stay at Villette House until he was better, and he'd put up little resistance. Alphonse too had been gathered into the Villette household, his insistence that he'd find a hotel had been firmly vetoed by Eleanor. It had taken two days of diplomatic manoeuvring from Eleanor and Alphonse before Caro and Alex finally made up their differences. They'd spent some time alone in the garden on Tuesday afternoon, while Eleanor had taken Alphonse for a drive to see something of the island. When they got back it was obvious all was well.

"You're friends again, then?" Eleanor said, ever direct.

"Er, yes," Alex said, with a slightly uncertain glance at Caro. "I think we are."

"We definitely are," Caro said decisively, and stretched up to kiss him.

"Bravo!" Alphonse exclaimed. "*L'amour,* that is all that is important."

They both grinned at him, a little sheepishly, and Eleanor whispered to Alex, "You'd better move your things into Caro's room, don't you think?"

"Nella!"

"What did she say?" asked Caro.

"Never you mind," Alex said. "She's a wicked old woman."

"Less of the old," said Eleanor, grinning.

But on Tuesday evening the atmosphere changed. The four of them were enjoying a glass of wine after dinner and discussing what they would do on the Liberation Day bank holiday, which was two days away. Caro had gradually relaxed, although she tensed up every time the phone rang, sure that it would be bad news of some kind. But, in spite of this, she insisted she was keen for them to go into town and see the sights, particularly the fireworks in the evening, before Alphonse went home the day after.

"I feel as if I want to do something that's pure enjoyment," Caro said defiantly. "Sod it, I'm not going to let Craig and Jones get to me."

Eleanor smiled at her defiance. "Good for you, my darling. So, it's agreed, Alex, we all go down to see the fireworks."

He nodded, smiled, but there was strain in the smile. Eleanor was about to remark on his lack of enthusiasm when he gave a slight shake of the head. She wondered what was up but didn't ask until Caro had gone early to bed, still exhausted after her ordeal.

"Right, Alex, what's going on?" Eleanor asked immediately she heard the door of Caro's bedroom close.

Alphonse looked from one to the other of them but said nothing.

"It'll take some explaining, Nella," Alex said wearily.

"Well, start at the beginning and go on to the end, always the best way. Is it something to do with that call you had before dinner?"

"Yes. That was Paul." Alex told them about the visit Craig had made to Paul's office asking for protection. "Craig's being threatened by Jones because he didn't finish the job, is how Paul put it. Jones's son, Darren, died on Sunday, in prison, and he phoned Craig and told him. Apparently, he believes it's all Caro and her family's fault, he's absolutely obsessed with the idea. During that phone call he said, 'That girl is going to pay. A life for a life.'"

Eleanor gasped and put a hand up to her mouth, while Alphonse swore quietly to himself.

"And now, apparently," Alex went on, "Jones has dropped off the radar, but Craig is positive he's planning to come to Guernsey, either that or he's going to send some of his thugs to do the job. He says Jones is after both of them. Craig's in a blue funk about his own safety, but Paul did get the impression he doesn't want Caro harmed."

"Why should he care now?" Eleanor asked angrily. "He didn't care before."

"Maybe he's realised what he's lost, I don't know. Or, maybe he thinks he'll get more help from Paul if he gives the impression that he cares about her. He wants to make a deal, give Paul a pile of information about his and Jones's dealings in return for protection and a lighter sentence, should he end up in court. Paul said he actually asked to be arrested, he's that scared of being around when Jones turns up. But Paul refused, he wants him out there, under surveillance, in case Jones makes a move on him."

"We must keep Caro in the house, not let her go out," Eleanor said firmly.

"Yes," said Alphonse decisively, "we must certainly do that."

Eleanor glanced at her grandson and her eyes narrowed. "There's more, isn't there?"

"Yes, Nella, there is. He's let Craig loose, but he suggested that it'd be useful to have Caro out there as well."

"No!" Eleanor said, aghast.

"Mais c'est pas possible, ça!" Alphonse exclaimed angrily. "No, no, not possible."

"That's what I said." No longer able to keep still, Alex got up and began to pace about the room. "Paul pointed out that if this bastard isn't caught, Caro is going to spend the rest of her life waiting for him to pounce. Paul is positive Craig is right, that he will, somehow, come to Guernsey. He might be here already. But it's too much of a risk. I think I persuaded him it just can't be done."

"Bon," said Alphonse. "He will just have to catch this Jones some other way."

"I agree, Alphonse," Eleanor said. "Paul has got his priorities wrong. We can't have him using Caro as bait, it just wouldn't be the right thing to do."

Once Alphonse had gone up to bed, Eleanor turned to her grandson. "And talking of doing the right thing, go to her now."

"What do you mean?"

"My darling, why wait any longer? Don't waste any more time."

* * *

All day on Wednesday the conversation Caro had overheard the evening before played on her mind. When she'd gone up to bed, she'd realised she'd left her handbag in the kitchen and slipped back downstairs to fetch it. It was as she was walking softly back across the hall that she heard Alex tell the others what Paul wanted her to do. She'd stood silent while they discussed it, feeling cold and alone again, excluded. Everyone else seemed to be making decisions for her. Why hadn't they asked her what she felt about it?

The very idea of acting as bait to catch that awful man terrified her, but even worse was the thought of never being free of his shadow, continually watching over her shoulder for his threatening presence. Anger rose in her at the memory of what he'd done to her father and mother.

Anger, too, at the fact that his luxury development had nearly destroyed a national treasure, which had become, in her mind, a memorial to her father.

When she'd heard Alphonse saying his goodnights, she'd run silently back up the stairs and leapt into bed, lain there shivering, her mind racing. When Alex had knocked on her door and come to her, she'd welcomed his warmth and then, as they'd made love for the first time, thoughts of what she'd overheard had receded. But the following morning, once Alex had gone off to work, it all came rushing back to her.

Since Caro had said she wanted to concentrate on the designs for La Cotte, partly as an excuse to be on her own, Eleanor had taken Alphonse to see some of Guernsey's historic sites. Alphonse had said he'd buy Eleanor lunch, and they planned to be home later that afternoon.

Caro had several texts from Alex during the day, but she put him off coming home for lunch, told him she had to visit the curtain-maker. Halfway through the afternoon, she finally came to a decision and, picking up her mobile, she scrolled down to Paul Le Page's number.

By the time the three of them got home, it was all arranged. But it wasn't until after dinner that she decided to tell them what she'd done. As they sat finishing the last of their wine, she looked from Eleanor to Alex, and then at Alphonse.

"I spoke to Paul today," she told them. Eleanor looked at her, eyes wide. Alex and Alphonse both frowned. Caro went on before any of them could speak. "He told me that they think Spencer Jones is in Guernsey and that he's going to come after me."

Alex made a sound of protest, but Caro reached out her hand and grasped his. "Hang on, Alex, listen to me. I've been thinking and thinking about it all day, and I've made up my mind. I know you all want to protect me from that awful man, I heard what you were talking about last night. I know you all mean well, but I think it has to be my decision whether or not I do as Paul wants."

"But Caro, darling…" Eleanor protested.

Alex's fingers tightened on Caro's. "No, you can't. I won't let you."

But Alphonse was watching her with dawning understanding. He held up a hand. "*Attendez*, Alex," he said, then turned to Caro. "Tell us, *ma p'tite*, exactly what Paul said and the result of all this thinking."

"Paul says they can track me through my iPhone, so they'll know where I am at all times. You three will be with me, and they'll be tracking you as well, and there'll be a heavy police presence in the crowd, plain clothes as well as uniformed, and several of Paul's men too. Then there's the CCTV already set up around town. He's rather proud of how many high-quality cameras they've got." She gave a rueful smile. "I've always been a bit anti CCTV, but all of a sudden I rather like the idea. Anyway, I know it's a risk, but it's better than spending the rest of my life waiting for that bastard to pounce. So that's it, I've made up my mind." She tried to make her voice as firm as possible and looked from one to the other of them, her eyes defiant.

Eleanor and Alex tried to persuade her not to go ahead, but she held out and, in the end, reluctantly they gave in. Eleanor put an arm round Caro. "You're a very brave girl," she said.

"*Ça, c'est vrais*," said Alphonse, and blew Caro a kiss across the table.

Alex said nothing, just held her hand tightly in his.

* * *

The whole of the esplanade in St Peter Port, from Prince Albert's statue, past the Crown pier, to the roundabout with its tall mast, had been closed to traffic. It was a fantastic sight. All afternoon buskers and street performers had entertained, bands and dancers had paraded up and down, countless children had had their faces painted, adults had spent a fortune on hot dogs, ice cream, fizzy drinks and beer. Craft stalls had been set up in one area, a traditional country market in another. And halfway through the afternoon the roar of aeroplanes flying low over the harbour heralded a visit from the Red Arrows making their amazing patterns in the sky. Soon it would be time for the finale, the firework display over Castle Cornet which always marked the end of Liberation Day.

Caro had woken that morning with Alex asleep beside her. She felt much calmer now and having Alex with her had pushed bad dreams to the back of her mind. But throughout the day the tension had risen.

Now, as dusk fell, the four of them were walking down into town. As they got to the esplanade, Alex put a protective arm round her as they joined the crowds. Eleanor and Alphonse walked with them, and Caro felt the tension in each of them. Of all of them she felt that she was the calmest. How strange, she thought. But she was determined that this evening, in spite of everything, she was going to enjoy her newfound happiness. Nothing was going to stop her.

Every few minutes they were stopped by friends or acquaintances of Alex's or Eleanor's, and each time Alex introduced her as 'my girlfriend', which made her, somehow, feel safer. But the crowds began to get to her as they made their way to the edge of the esplanade. There was a cool breeze blowing and, standing looking out across the marina, crowded with boats, Caro shivered, not entirely from the cold. Alex looked down at her, pulled her closer, and asked, "Are you alright?"

"Yes," she said, "I'm–"

Several things happened at once. Caro felt a violent tug at her arm. She swung round, felt Alex pulled away from her. The crowds milled around separating her from her companions. She heard Alphonse call out, then Eleanor's voice. For a second, she thought she saw Craig, then there was a glimpse of a heavy-set man with white hair. Frantically she searched around, shouting for Alex, but he was a few feet away and seemed to be struggling with someone. Then there was a sharp push at her back and she nearly overbalanced into the cold water. At the last moment she was pulled back and looked up into Paul's face. A second later there was a shout, a splash, and a man screamed, then the scream was cut short.

Eleanor was beside her, and Alphonse, and Alex was gathering her into his arms and rocking her back and forth. All around them people were shouting and there seemed to be police everywhere. Some uniformed officers gathered round in a protective group and shepherded the four of them through the crowd and up steep steps to the High Street. As they were ushered into two police cars, there was a crack and a flash of bright light as the first of the fireworks rose into the night sky.

CHAPTER 29

It was just before midnight when Paul arrived at Villette House. He had made a short call to Alex a couple of hours before. "Jones is dead," he'd told him. "I'll explain later."

When he walked in, the four of them were in the sitting room, Caro wrapped in a fleecy warm dressing gown of Eleanor's.

"I think it's time for brandy," said Eleanor, and smiled at Paul. "You too, my boy. You look absolutely knackered."

He gave her a weary smile and sat back in his chair. "I won't say no." He glanced across at Caro who was curled up in the crook of Alex's arm. She looked so small, he thought. God, we took an awful risk there.

Once Eleanor was sitting down again, he began to speak. "First of all, I want to apologise for putting you through that, Caro."

Caro shook her head. "It was my decision, Paul. You asked me to, you didn't tell me to. That makes all the difference."

Paul gave a nod of understanding. "Let me go back a couple of days, to when Craig Paxton came to my office to ask for protection."

Caro's eyes widened but she didn't comment and Paul went on, "We kept a close eye on the harbour and the airport, but there was no sign of Jones. We found out why tonight after going through the airport CCTV again. He was wearing a dark wig, stained jeans and a fleece. He flew in, under a false name, on the first flight yesterday, and he had three of his opos with him, all of whom have been taken into custody, by the way. One of them is beginning to talk so we're hoping that will encourage the others to do so too. I think the fact that their boss is dead has put the wind up them all."

"How did he die?" asked Caro, her voice cracking with tiredness.

"I was close behind you four," said Paul, "along with two plain clothes police officers. Unfortunately, a group of drunken youngsters got between us. We were pushing our way back to you—"

"I remember feeling someone grab my arm," Caro interrupted.

"I think that was Craig Paxton. He says he was trying to get you away from Jones and his men, who were all close by."

Alex gave a snort of derision, but Paul shook his head. "I think he's telling the truth. The man's a rotten fraudster, but I don't think he's a killer." Paul looked at Caro "He admitted to having feelings for you and he says he regrets everything he's done."

"I find that hard to believe," Eleanor said, and Alphonse muttered a few choice words in French.

Paul shrugged. "He may be protecting his own back. He may be telling the truth. I don't think we'll ever know."

"I do think he cared for me, a bit, in his own way," Caro said quietly. "At least, I like to think so."

Alex dropped a kiss on the top of her head. "You're too nice for your own good, that's your problem."

"Anyway," Paul went on, "several things happened at once. We were pushing forward to get to you, the crowd was milling around, and then I realised the man immediately next to you was Jones. He'd discarded his wig. I think he wanted you to recognise him. He was reaching out towards you when, well Eleanor, do you want to tell her what happened next?"

Eleanor gave Paul a straight look as Alex, Caro and Alphonse glanced from one to the other of them, mystified.

"I'm not sure I know what you're talking about, Paul."

He smiled at her. "It can't be proved, but I don't think my eyes deceived me."

Eleanor took a sip at her brandy, placed the glass carefully on a small table beside her chair, and leant back. "It was the only thing I could think of to do," she said, her voice calm. "I– er… pushed him, hard, in the back, to get him away from Caro. I'm not sure exactly what happened next, but I think he tripped on the land tie."

"What's that?" asked Caro.

"It's like a railway sleeper on the edge of the quay, people tie their boats to it," Eleanor told her, then looked back at Paul. "He overbalanced and fell into the water."

"Between the quay and a moored boat," Paul said. "By the time we got to him and dragged him out, he was dead. There'll be a post-mortem which will show the exact cause of death, a blow to the head, a heart attack, we don't know yet. And obviously there'll be an inquest, all of you may be called, but I don't think there'll be any repercussions. With what Paxton has told us, and Jean Peron, and the information we hope to get from the men who came with Jones, I think it'll be concluded that the world's a better place without Spencer Jones."

"*Absolument*," said Alphonse with conviction.

"That's about it. There'll be someone round to take statements from all of you tomorrow." Paul gave Eleanor a very direct look. "I'm sure you'll know what to say." He got up. "And now I must go and get some shut-eye, there'll be an awful lot of clearing up to do tomorrow."

* * *

Half an hour later as Caro lay in the dark, her head on Alex's shoulder, his hand softly stroking her neck, she said, "If Eleanor obeyed the rules, I probably wouldn't be here."

"I know. She's a one-off, is Nella." He lifted himself on one elbow and leant down to kiss her. She slid a hand down his back, and he groaned. "Please, before we go any further, Caro, there's something I need to ask you."

"What?"

"Will you marry me?"

"Was that Nella's idea too?"

"No, aah, stop it." He gasped, as her hands continued their exploration. "Will you?"

"Of course, I will," she said, and pulled him down into her arms.

Acknowledgements

A few thank-yous: to my Guernseyman husband, Niall, for his checking and double checking that I've got my local references right, and for never grumbling when he has to do all the cooking; to Gary for his nautical knowledge; and to all my writing friends and gurus who helped and advised.

And yes, my Guernsey friends, I do realise there are no longer any flights from Dinard to Guernsey, but there were then, and one can but dream.

If you enjoyed this book, please let others know by leaving a quick review on Amazon. Also, if you spot anything untoward in the paperback, get in touch. We strive for the best quality and appreciate reader feedback.

editor@thebookfolks.com

www.thebookfolks.com

Lambert stop her, or realize the value of his former boss to the floundering inquiry?

When an overbearing patriarch and much begrudged ex-army officer is found dead in his home, there is no shortage of suspects. DCI Matt Lambert investigates, but struggles with a lack of evidence. He'll have to rely on his former boss, ex-detective Fabia Havard, to help him. But will their fractious relationship get in the way of solving the case?

Almost ten years after he went missing, a student's body is found. Forensics show that he was murdered and a cold case is reopened. But when detectives begin to investigate his background, many people he knew are found to be keeping a secret of sorts. Faced with subterfuge and deceit, rooting out the true killer will take all their detective skills.

Hopes for a town pantomime are dashed when a
participant is found murdered. The victim was the town
gossip and there is no shortage of people who had a
grudge to bear against him. Detective Matt Lambert leads
the investigation but draws on the help of his girlfriend,
ex-police officer Fabia Havard. Can they solve the crime
together?

When an important film director returns to his native
Wales for retirement it arouses the interest of the locals,
not least Fabia Havard who discovers a family connection
to him. So when he is later found dead, defenestrated,
she'll stop at nothing to find his killer. With too many
suspects, she and Matt Lambert will have to suss out the
motive.

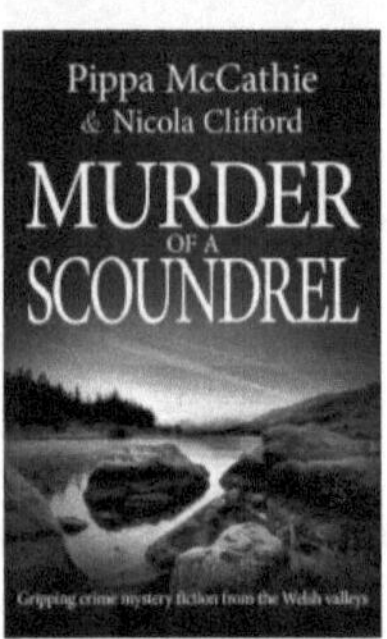

DCI Matt Lambert was hoping for some home-time with Fabia and their newborn baby when a man is found dead in a disused railway tunnel. And more sleepless nights are heading his way when another body is found in nearby wasteland. Clearly foul play, the rural community is up in arms. Can he root out the killer without Fabia, whose mind is on other things?

www.thebookfolks.com